Susan Delle Cave lives in South West London with her husband and has five daughters, all of whom live close by. She speaks three languages and has taught various subjects in a range of schools.

Her many interests include the opera and theatre, genealogy, Sudoku for relaxation and spending time with a growing number of grandchildren.
She would have liked to become an archaeologist.

I dedicate this novel equally to five wonderful women, Maria Grazia, Sofia, Francesca, Rosanna and Lucia, who remain at the heart of this novel-writing adventure and for the inspiration they continue to provide.

Also posthumously, to my dear father, William Thomas Ernest Vince.

Susan Delle Cave

THE UNSTEADY WHEEL

AUSTIN MACAULEY PUBLISHERS™
LONDON · CAMBRIDGE · NEW YORK · SHARJAH

Copyright © Susan Delle Cave 2023

The right of Susan Delle Cave to be identified as author of this work has been asserted by the author in accordance with sections 77 and 78 of the Copyright, Designs and Patents Act 1988.

All rights reserved. No part of this publication may be reproduced, stored in a retrieval system, or transmitted in any form or by any means, electronic, mechanical, photocopying, recording, or otherwise, without the prior permission of the publishers.

Any person who commits any unauthorised act in relation to this publication may be liable to criminal prosecution and civil claims for damages.

This is a work of fiction. Names, characters, businesses, places, events, locales, and incidents are either the products of the author's imagination or used in a fictitious manner. Any resemblance to actual persons, living or dead, or actual events is purely coincidental.

A CIP catalogue record for this title is available from the British Library.

ISBN 9781398479906 (Paperback)
ISBN 9781398479913 (ePub e-book)

www.austinmacauley.com

First Published 2023
Austin Macauley Publishers Ltd®
1 Canada Square
Canary Wharf
London
E14 5AA

A special thank you to Francesca and Isabella for all the IT assistance. I would be lost without them.

The novel title is in reference to a quote by Ovid, who in a letter, refers to Fortuna as… "the goddess who admits by her UNSTEADY WHEEL her own fickleness…"

Table of Contents

Prologue	13
Part One	15
Chapter 1: Inertia	17
Chapter 2: The Sun Beats Down	22
Chapter 3: Nino and His Legacy	27
Chapter 4: Il Convento Di San Rocco	32
Chapter 5: The Wait	37
Chapter 6: The Start of Pasquale's Formation	42
Chapter 7: The Arrival of Padre Floro	47
Chapter 8: Goodbye	52
Chapter 9: Brigida Amato	58
Chapter 10: An Unexpected Visit	63
Chapter 11: Gathering Clouds	67
Chapter 12: Biting the Bullet	73
Chapter 13: Marital, Filial…and Brotherly Love	78
Chapter 14: Heat and Joy	84
Chapter 15: Fun and Games	89
Chapter 16: Two City Slickers	94
Chapter 17: Carmelina	99
Chapter 18: The Gift of Observation	105

Chapter 19: A Layer of Summer Snow	110
Chapter 20: Obliterated	115
Chapter 21: Unfinished Business	120
Chapter 22: Mountain Air	125
Chapter 23: A Different Kind of Woman	130
Chapter 24: After Pasquale	135
Chapter 25: For Sale, an Old Palazzo with Sea Views	139
Chapter 26: That Simple Pleasure of Talking Deep into the Night	142
Chapter 27: The Winds of Change	147
Chapter 28: Looking for Iolanda and Beyond	153
Part Two	159
Chapter 29: Floating in Darkness	161
Chapter 30: Dreamscape	166
Chapter 31: Away	171
Chapter 32: Homeward Bound	176
Chapter 33: Introspective	181
Chapter 34: Out and About	186
Chapter 35: Picking Up the Threads	191
Chapter 36: Future and Present	196
Chapter 37: The Gardener and His Niece	201
Chapter 38: Blood Ties	206
Chapter 39: Another Brief yet Portentous Interlude	211
Chapter 40: Giulia Goes Up a Mountain	216
Chapter 41: On Top of the World	221
Chapter 42: The Unthinkable	227
Chapter 43: Ten Years Later	230
Déjà Vu	*230*

Chapter 44: Sorted	234
Epilogue	236

Prologue

Long before man had begun to record human events or register natural phenomena, a young girl under cover of darkness, placed a newly delivered baby on the rocky outcrop of a mountain, as custom there once dictated. No one had bothered to name her; she was one of an ongoing multitude. A life not considered worthy of human investment. However, within a clutch of desperate hours, something unimaginable happened; her cruel fate had been overturned. With an act of brave generosity on the part of an elderly local…together with a constitution, which had allowed her to survive the suffocating waves of hunger, falling temperatures and cravings for maternal love, a rescue took place; she had been plucked from the rest, sifted out, selected.

As the foundling grew strong in heart, mind and body, on the precarious journey towards adulthood, people began to refer to her as Fortuna…

It appeared she wanted others also to benefit from her own life-giving chances.

Aeons later, we might also ask ourselves how ready we would be, should Fortuna make that rare appearance in our own lives. There are of course well publicised examples of those who get to win the lottery or a universal beauty pageant, achieve Olympic gold, or even go on to become Nobel Prize winners (not to be underestimated even here the shower of Fortuna's good luck). The results of such bounty need no explaining.

We could even argue that Fortuna works in a complex, subtle or seemingly playful manner. Do the selected few really deserve her attentions, and for how long, if good luck does come their way? On the other hand, is it that she merely scatters, carelessly, her life-changing gifts? Does she ever look to see if she has distributed equally the clusters of good luck?

Seemingly not…

By re-examining the history of the prestigious Kennedy family (those proud twentieth-century Americans of humble Irish beginnings) as a signpost to the possible mechanisms of Fortuna's practices, we are soon struck by the high number of untimely Kennedy deaths, fatal accidents, assassinations, suicides, addictions and illness (both mental and physical), which have plagued them across the generations.

Could this then be the price the Kennedys (and other such illustrious families or individuals) are obliged to pay for their fabulous rise to power and continued wealth, fame and notoriety? It would appear then that Fortuna does keep such accounts. She really does keep her eyes open and a steady hand on her mythical wheel…

What about the rest of us then, we ordinary folk?

How does she 'feel' about her dealings with us? Does she ever bother to track the outcomes? Does she in effect, as tradition teaches us, still wear a blindfold as she pilots her awe-inspiring ship around the oceans, her ancient space capsule around planet Earth?

What we do know is that she has the power to steer part of our own story…when she does turn up…if we allow her.

Part One

Chapter 1
Inertia

Pasquale had been restless all morning. The shimmering rage that burned holes in the pit of his stomach was once again about to spill over. What to do with it, who or what to take it out on?

He looked across at the makeshift bed his horizontal mother occupied each day, at her murky glass beaker, the tarnished spoons and at the collection of sticky medicine bottles, which permanently littered the tiny table. She now appeared to be in a state of semi-sleep, stone silent, wholly detached from him and the world. Their neighbour, a kind of relative by marriage, and godmother to one of his older brothers, had already popped round with a pan of knobbly green soup, she would feed his mother later. Having had already tidied up a few things on and around the bed, leaving him with the usual burst of "Guagliò, nu ti priuccupà" (now don't you worry lad!). He called her 'Commare', but as was the way of their dialect, the name, when uttered, rarely reached its final syllable…

She was just one of a gaggle of women, some young, but mostly of early middle age, permanently dressed in black, who helped them out in various ways, women from the village. He felt neither annoyance nor gratitude for their continued presence in and out of his home. Merely part of his limited landscape and narrow horizons.

His eyes, carbon black, now wandered slowly around the room, as they had already done many times beforehand. His gaze inevitably revisiting the shabby unpainted walls, permanent home to a nailed collection of battered pots and pans. There were the hanging twists of onion and plaited garlic; the cheap and dusty religious paraphernalia, several austere and posed for family photos (one being an earlier version of his mother, when she was still young and hopeful), multifarious keys held together by string. He looked up at the bunch of bright red 'corni' for good luck, which up to now had hung redundant, finally settling his eyes on a smoky mirror, which also adorned the room, lopsided, a mirror no one bothered to look in any more. What was the point?

How well he (albeit subconsciously) knew each piece. How long he had blindly stared out at them, over the months and years. At those worthless objects, which were never cleaned nor replaced (unless cooked and eaten), which he too would one day leave behind. The sole evidence he had lived at all; he, the youngest child left to his own devices whose brothers were living dangerous lives far from home; he, being the last of a doomed generation…his tiny world, claustrophobic, anachronistic, stuck and permanently excluded from a wider world of untold possibility…far beyond his grasp, far beyond his godforsaken village.

Even worse, he had once taken a brief glimpse into that forbidden world's glittering ball, partly through the exaggerated tales of a brother who had run away to serve a group of local outlaws, but more specifically, because a friend's uncle had one day made a flying visit from a foreign land. As a (cruel?) treat for the two boys, he had driven them by car (an elegant Fiat 520) to the hitherto unknown city. Motor cars of any kind had not often found their way to his village…and for a young adolescent boy to ride around in such a vehicle driven by an equally glamorous individual…was the stuff of dreams. But this experience had also been Pasquale's mental ruin, the city now no longer a made-up word in a newspaper article or fairy story. He had seen with his coal black eyes what it could offer and he drank in everything, starting with the sight of beautiful women, accompanied by elegantly clothed men with perfectly styled hair and smiles to match. He had seen rows of awe-inspiring buildings located either side of a vast central thoroughfare. He had glimpsed gated gardens with ornate, cascading fountains. He had crossed huge piazzas with churches the size of cathedrals and seemingly everywhere, carefree people sipping espressos and smoking elegantly held cigarettes, as they lingered casually at pavement cafes.

There had never been a sign that any of his peers felt as he did; they, like their parents and grandparents before them, made up an inert community, each villager resigned to his or her established fate.

On that one extraordinary day, he had listened into what he considered to be, a beautifully refined rendition of his language, which sounded almost magical, royal even; like a foreign language, but one he could also comprehend. He thus hankered to join this new race of people…a breed he now knew existed beyond the pages of a book. He had seen, for the first time, the world splashed with technicolour.

His mother had been sick for as long as he could remember. She had folded herself away from the world around her, the only change being that she was now getting visibly worse, steadily weaker. Pasquale being the youngest stayed at home with her. No one bothered to speak to her anymore…as it all seemed pointless…other than when they gave out absurd little instructions, when lifting her, persuading her to eat just a little more or while rearranging her bedclothes. She had not given birth to daughters. Daughters did all that then, many still do. Having daughters would have meant constant care and companionship, the cooking of regular meals and the undertaking of proper housework, even after they got married and had families of their own to take care of.

This however wasn't expected from Pasquale, the youngest male child. No one expected anything from him or for him.

The village women therefore rallied round as best they could, most having some kind of family or religious connection with them. By now, they (absurdly) enjoyed the regular coming together, even if it meant an increase of their own daily workload!

Distinguishable words of course no longer slipped off his mother's receding lips but for those courageous enough to look, her green-blue eyes, when open, still spoke an ocean as to how she felt. Her husband never returning from the War, her elder sons having fled to join anarchists (or anti-Christs), as an unusually witty Don Beppe had once referred to them.

It also meant that any lingering secrets of her own could now die with her…

When the women, usually in threes or fours, came of an evening to tend to the house and put his mother to bed for the night, Pasquale would often retreat to a little outside spot just under the open shutters. There he had positioned a pile of old straw-filled pillows to sit on, and would spend this time…the dregs of yet another futile day…throwing or kicking about the odd stone or would just sit and brood, after seeing to the chickens and sweeping the yard. He could hear the constant drone of the women's chatter, sometimes punctuated by shrieks of laughter, but which of course for the most part was of little interest to him. They would make comments about the children of women not present, often exchanging bits of their own precious wisdom and advice, stating for example, that wayward girls in particular could be easily 'dealt with' by tying them by their long plaits to a chair leg under the table, so with no possibility of escape.

They also released their habitual venom on those women in the village, whose lives didn't measure up to the godliness of their own, and more recently had taken to exchanging derogatory remarks about the new priest who had replaced the familiar, tried and tested ways of Don Beppe. He came from somewhere in the north apparently; not a good sign, he may as well have come from another age or another continent!

Instead of returning to their own homes on completion of the chores, the women would sometimes linger, (especially during the long summer months) seated in a semi-circle formation, to continue their verbal exchanges along with their crochet work and embroidery, which grew steadily in length and colour upon each dark lap.

Yet sometimes the steady drone did transform itself into meaningful strings of language, becoming something precious for Pasquale to grasp. They never appeared to check where he might be, provided he was back in the house before they made their very short journeys home. Pasquale had developed a sixth sense, or at least had grown a talent for picking out a certain trigger word, which allowed him to absorb such bits of their conversation he might find useful. In this manner, he had learned about a legendary, local doctor who when called to the home of an ailing villager, would rarely accept payment for his services (or for the medication) on learning of the family's dire economic circumstances, which characterised many of their lives. Each seemed to have a ready anecdote or two about how in days gone by, he had visited a member of their own family and how this extraordinary individual was surely now on the road to sainthood.

Where did such goodness come from? Did it grow out of privilege or study? He sometimes felt inclined to ponder such questions.

His ears also once picked up on an amusing little story of a local brother and sister, who had set up a fortune-telling racket in their home, which involved the weekly services of a visiting medium (in effect their widowed uncle from another village). The team proved to be highly successful in reuniting mourner and deceased relative. Until people found out, that the brother would lodge himself in the partially open wardrobe of an adjoining room…and from there carry out the required number of knocks and taps in answer to each of the questions the guest medium would ask on behalf of the foolish client!

The locals, so hard headed and cynical in business and in protecting any land they owned; so gullible when it came to matters of life and death. The users and the used. The abusers and abused. The result of longstanding economic hardship, prodding man, woman and child to exploit even their fellow parishioners…a circular game.

Another such story also sprang into his mind from time to time. The story of a village family who had saved up just enough money to pay for what they thought would be a one-way passage to New York (or Nuova York, as they called it then). A chance to start again. His people, however, were illiterate and uneducated, referred to, especially by northerners, as 'terroni' or 'analfabeti'! The family in question had unknowingly paid a group of fraudsters to take them in a small boat, which followed the rocky coastline south for the best part of a day, eventually disembarking…not under the gaze of the goddess Liberty…but merely in another part of Italy. They had lost all their money, all their worldly goods…and in a state of despair and humiliation, had been obliged to return to the village of their birth, with even less than they had before…would his people never learn? He concluded that they deserved their misfortune.

Pasquale, however, had been fortunate enough to attend school for a few years; he had learned to read and write to an acceptable level, although never admitting to himself (let alone to anyone else) that a secret part of him had actually enjoyed the experience. It was something he could carry out with relative ease and the rewards, those rare little bursts of praise by teacher or peers, left a warm, gratifying feeling deep within. It had also removed him, if only temporarily, from his daily misery.

Not enough for him to further pursue his studies though. He had not since picked up any kind of book… No one around to suggest that he might. No one he knew who chose to read.

Chapter 2
The Sun Beats Down

One day Pasquale woke up with a mad plan. An outlet for his rage. He would take himself off on a mission! He would head for the village beyond, acting upon information he had gleaned, while eavesdropping from his semi-hidden evening perch outside the kitchen window. He had not prepared his lines…the meeting would take care of itself! Deep emotions and survival instincts would see him through! The journey was to take him across multiple scorched fields and a good few kilometres into unfamiliar territory, even beyond his grandfather's little farm, which when still a young boy, had seemed to mark the edge of the universe. It was surely a bad time to act but nothing could stop him now; the sweltering heat of the early afternoon, the dry and exposed landscape, the beating down of a summer sun at its deadliest. The brooding mountain peaks and ridges looking inwards at one another from high up.

Just how would the man in question react to the arrival of an impetuous young stranger to his country home, and on having to drag himself out of bed at the start of his habitual siesta?

Pasquale travelled light, not expecting the encounter to take very long…he would be back well in time for the visiting women to perform their evening rituals. His young body taut with determination, a brain harbouring one single thought. Stiff, resolute, ignoring the arrowhead formations of black migrating birds, and the cicadas pouring out their senseless caterwaul, as he trudged barefoot ever forward, through high weeds and rough stalks. It was of little consequence that this furnace world appeared vast and noisy that day, as it lay deep under the sky's cobalt blue shroud, the heat only just bearable…or perhaps not at all. On that particular afternoon, Pasquale believed that he possessed more than enough power to keep nature, climate and human vulnerability at bay.

Eventually the image of the house began to drift in and out of focus, in the form of a shimmering stain of connected, flickering shapes.

A good couple of hours later…Pasquale made out a figure, possibly walking towards him. Accompanied by a trail of unintelligible words, which echoed in the scorching air.

"Pasqualì, Pasqualì, (sounding like Pashqwalee) what on God's earth?"

At his grandfather's farmhouse, the scrawny young man merely flopped down, exhausted and feverish, not yet able to give any kind of intelligible reply. Slumped on the cool stone of the kitchen floor, mouth Sahara-dry, the rims of his eyes red with dust. He had propped himself up against Angelo's armchair and was soon sipping something thick and dark his grandfather had just poured for him, with Angelo in the meantime dragging inside the huge and heavy assortment of bags, baskets and packages Pasquale had mysteriously brought along with him. He checked once again on his ailing grandson, who appeared slightly more energised now, well enough at least to tell Angelo that he needed to go and lie down; that he would explain everything later. Nonno Angelo (known locally as Giulillo) then took it upon himself to hide all the stuff under a pile of what looked like other sacks and crates (of his own), away from the curiosity of any visiting eyes.

About two hours had passed and twilight was performing its daily dance across the vast skies of the valley. Angelo, looking up and out at that very scene, his hands forming a finger pyramid on his lap. He would wait as long as necessary, in order to get a clear picture of what his grandson had been up to…and although well-earned wisdom had taught him not to jump to conclusions…it wasn't looking good…it all smelled like trouble. Trouble in their part of the world often meant treading that fine line between life and death.

All of a sudden, Pasquale appeared at the door, looking all the worse for wear, dark circles around bloodshot eyes and his swollen, cracked lips a vicious red. The blistered rawness of the soles of his feet causing him to limp across the room. He said he was now ready to spill out his story.

"Santo cielo, nipotino mio, what in the name of heaven is this all about?" indicating the booty he was pulling out from under the mound of crates and dusty sackcloth.

"And just look at the state of you!"

Pasquale promised he would tell his grandfather everything, provided he could count on his unwavering support.

It was a story that Pasquale could barely believe himself…it was, he stated, as if he had been caught up in somebody else's dream (or nightmare), only to discover that he had been its protagonist all along. In just a few hours, he felt he was now five, no ten, years older; an abrupt and unexpected reaching of manhood and he was now at last ready to listen to Nonno Giulillo's wise counsel, whatever form that was to take. They had always shared a tight bond, never spoken about or acted upon…but intuitively felt by both. Now, because of what had just happened, Pasquale decided, they were…almost…equals.

"Okay, yes, I stole it. The guy was dead. It was like a dream. The side door was open, so I just walked in… he…the body…was in the chair near the worktop…sitting, but dead. He was still warm but nothing moved. There was no blood, well none I could see. It looked as though he'd just gone to pour himself a drink of water…I don't know, maybe he just had a massive heart attack…"

"Whoa there, hang on a minute. It's important I hear this from the very beginning. What were you doing there in the first place? What was your business with that man? You do know who he is…was…don't you?"

"Well, yes, sort of. I've listened in to the women. You know Etta and that other one, Brunella, talk about him sometimes, saying he was some kind of moneylender. I was desperate, Nonno, I can't take any more of this life. You know, what with my mother and everything. I've seen real people NOT living this way…it doesn't have to be like this! There was no one there…I checked. Nobody saw me. And the funny thing was those hidey holes Mamma showed me all those years ago at home, you know where she kept a bit of money and her treasures, so she called them, only to be used in an emergency, were exactly the same places as where I found all this stuff in his own house. Stuffed in and under the mattress; stuffed in the rafters; under the obviously loose floorboard in the cellar. The same hiding places. It made me laugh. I just couldn't believe my luck. It was all in bundles and I worked hard ramming it all into any bags and baskets I could see lying there. Anything I could lay my hands on as I knew I didn't have long. Anyone could have turned up at any moment. I didn't want to leave a mess either. I had to be sure I was able to carry all this back as well. Only then, as I made my way outside, I realised the effect the sun had had on me. I knew the signs…I've had heatstroke before. I hadn't had anything to drink in hours; I'd left home without a hat. Out in all that heat and sun. Stupid I know. What with the shock of finding him dead and my brain on overload. I just knew I had to act and act fast. This was destiny. I just needed to work fast…no other thought came into my head. I had to take as much as I could and then get out of there…"

Angelo didn't speak straightaway…but Pasquale was already reading his thoughts.

"You don't think, you don't think I killed him, do you? That is ridiculous. I promise, Nonno, you just have to believe me…the thought never entered my head…I just wanted to speak to him, ask him…look, look at my hands, my clothes. I'm all dirty, yes, but there's no trace of blood…I have no weapon on me…look, come and check. You do believe me, don't you?"

The newly emerging grown man was beginning to sound like the little boy again.

His grandfather had heard as much as he needed for the time being. Towards the end of his 'confession', Pasquale had seemed feverish again and was starting to rave. The rest could wait until morning. Angelo managed to drag him back upstairs and help him into bed after making him drink…all in one go…what must have been half a litre of water and then told him to close his eyes. Tomorrow the two of them would work on a plan. Pasquale's last thought however before falling into a much needed, deep sleep, was that he hoped the plan wouldn't involve having to take back the money…no, he couldn't go back, there was no going back now.

Pasquale slept until about midday the following day and felt all the better for it. He could hear Nonno Giulillo pottering about outside; his grandfather had no doubt been up for hours. There was a bright red sauce gently bubbling, singing almost, in a dented old pan and the whole house had already captured its familiar Sunday aromas. After having a bit of a wash in cold water and passing a well-used metal comb, left on the window ledge in the privy, carefully through his hair, he went to find his grandfather, to see if he could help in any way. Far too late was the brusque reply.

The two did eventually sit down to eat, Angelo with an old cloth stuffed into the top of a holey vest, which served as a bib. Pasquale had now done all he could to help, lay the table, check on the progress of the 'penne' as they softened in the boiling water and a few minutes later grate some cheese over the two bowls of 'pasta asciutta', from a hard slab his grandfather kept in a handy drawer.

The meal proceeded in silence…apart from some occasional slurping or gulping…the two men, one old, one very young, both heads bent low over their bowls, each holding his fork in exactly the same way. They finished eating at more or less the same time, after mopping up the last traces of the red sauce with pieces of bread, cut roughly from a loaf that would last a few more days. They referred to this as 'scarpette'. Angelo then deftly peeled a few small pears and 'percocche' (a kind of peach), which came from the little orchard, for the two to enjoy. Pasquale was instantly reminded of the sausage thickness of his grandfather's fingers…and how they didn't seem to belong to the rest of him at all, he being quite lean and wiry, and his hands in themselves not otherwise large. Had his own father inherited them too? It was a question he, shamefully, was unable to answer. Pasquale had quite clearly got his mother's long slim fingers, quite unusual in their village his people always commented.

His grandfather got up to fetch a bottle of wine from the cellar…they had only drunk water up until then…and although still no conversation took place, as was customary among the 'contadini' at mealtimes, each of them knew there would be a lot of talk to follow the afternoon siesta.

Time being of the essence.

Chapter 3
Nino and His Legacy

A few years before this somewhat alarming interlude, Pasquale had crossed paths with a boy called Nino.

Pasquale hadn't liked him at first; there was something about him…possibly the way he, the new boy, had nonchalantly strolled into his new classroom, eyes pointing straight ahead…that bothered him, but he couldn't quite make out why that was. Neither had Nino paid him any attention. The boy had come from another village, about 20 kilometres away. His mother, Adelina, had inherited the house and a bit of land from a distant uncle and it being bigger, meant that they had decided to leave the home where their children had been born. This had been seen as an unconventional step…some villagers even believing that it was sacrilege, to abandon the place of your children's birth. But Nino's mother, who ruled the home with an iron fist (and very quickly her new village piazza), defended their decision in terms of practicalities…she, her husband and their eight children needed more space…and that it was a property which had belonged to family in any case, not the house of a mere stranger.

She put any lingering criticism down to envy, very rarely bending to the antagonistic will of others.

She was a harridan, who passionately loved each of her children, but with a ferocity, society could only condemn today. A galvanised ferocity, which soon manifested itself throughout the village, in the wild and colourful language she regularly employed. Insults, threats and curses aimed at whichever of her offspring happened to rile her at the time. Her children loved her back unconditionally, in spite of all of this…even more proof of her raw, but always authentic, primitive love for them. Each of them deeply conscious of it. Heaven help anyone outside of the family who had a bad word for them; that was her right alone…she would have fought to the death to restore their good name, regardless of an obvious lack of formal education on her part. With the exception of teachers. If Adelina ever heard that any of her children had got into trouble at school (and as a village school such news always got out, and got out very quickly), there would sure enough be another punishment waiting for them at home, which would have more than matched any shaming or permitted corporal punishment in the classroom.

Her husband, and their father, was a quiet man, who kept a low profile in all such matters.

Whether he realised it or not, Pasquale, in spite of his shrouded dislike, harboured a fascination for the new boy and his colourful entourage, made up of such a large and vibrant family. He couldn't make out just why Nino had appeared to command, in an instant, everyone's respect at school, at least amongst their peers. It all seemed so quick and effortless. Admittedly, he was tall for his age (unusual in itself in that part of the world) and had an athletic build. Yet, the attractive appearance being counter balanced by the troubled look he frequently wore. Giving him an air of gravitas in one so young. He never appeared to work hard or with any enthusiasm in class. Never a positive role model, concluded Pasquale. At the same time, Nino always giving the impression that if he had applied himself to his schoolwork, even just a little, he would have produced brilliant results. He never failed a test; he always just got by. He rarely spoke without purpose. He always seemed to know when to stay quiet and never needed to resort to underhand or bullying tactics.

Alongside this precocious maturity however, was the fact that Nino's classmates often caught him sucking his thumb, as he pretended to pour over his books especially towards late morning. This unexpected activity he partially managed to disguise by turning his head to face the wall. Not even the shock of dark brown hair falling over his eyes enough to hide the spectacle. Everyone knew but stayed quiet on the matter. Any other child they would have teased mercilessly, like those whose ears stuck out or others who were cross-eyed or had to wear glasses with thick lenses, or those who stammered. Like anywhere in the world, such students would have found themselves hounded for such attributes or babyish behaviour…but not Nino.

The two boys, Pasquale and Nino, did however begin to spend a little time together after school. It all started when Nino had to wait for one of his brothers to finish his lessons, and Pasquale, with nothing much to rush home for, would wait with him and the pair would kick around the 'cortile' a rag ball, that one of the village women had once hand sewn for the unfortunate orphan. They would also see each other at mass on a Sunday morning, where the priest, Don Beppe, had recently encouraged them to join a club he was setting up, an 'oratorio', which would take place on Tuesday evenings. Here the boys could come and pray and afterwards play football (with a proper ball this time), and with the view to creating a proper team.

There was also the time when Pasquale had taken Nino back to his home, already having mumbled something to him about his mother's condition, in order to prepare him. It was Pasquale, however, who had remained shocked. By the way, Nino had subsequently behaved, how his new friend had swiftly and quietly drawn up a chair by Maria Rosaria's side, had taken her hand in his and started to speak to her in kindly tones, yet so low that the invalid's son was unable to make out what exactly he was telling her. What did the boy Nino have to say to this stranger, this pathetically ailing woman, one who no longer communicated with anyone, a vegetable-like person who simply lay there? Day after day.

In later years, he would also remember the shafts of laser sunbeams, which had flooded part of the room. In this way, an uncomfortable image of Christian love seared onto his heart, as Nino gently bent over her. A short bittersweet scene that seemed none the less endless. Pasquale, excluded from the picture, had once again felt the penetrating bullet of corrosive shame. He, her son, having given up on her long beforehand. She having become yet another object taking up space in the room, like the dusty crucifix, the hanging garlic and the keys. He had even given up on the previous greetings he used to utter on seeing her in the morning and before her being put to bed every evening, words which were taught to him when still a tiny child, 'buongiorno, la mia dolce Mammina; buonanotte…e sogni d'oro' (and sweet dreams).

The two boys became practically inseparable after that encounter…though neither of them ever happened to refer to it. For reasons of their own.

The deep shame, he had felt that afternoon, hadn't, however, nudged Pasquale into changing his ways; his feelings and behaviour towards his mother. The situation was already beyond salvaging. To kiss her now on the forehead or touch her hand would have been a travesty…he would have felt diminished in some way, a mere actor, playing the part of a baddie, an unscrupulous character, feigning kindness for glory or for gain. Pretending to look good to those around him. He could not and would not do this! He was angry at the world but by the world, he really meant his village; angry with his family; angry with his mother in particular for abandoning him in such a way. He was also full of ugly pride! To him Nino's harridan of a mother was a thousand times more preferable. She had breathed life into each of her children and continued to do so. She fought for them. She was ever on their side.

Loud and larger than life itself, she would never have chosen to fold herself away from them.

The two boys gradually disassociated themselves from the other members of their class. It was nothing to do with gangs or arguments; they just realised they didn't seem to want or need anyone else and this state of affairs was (surprisingly) also accepted by the others. The rest appeared to back, and therefore, further legitimise the current situation. It had all happened softly and fluidly and without words or rancour.

The pair did fall out however, quite often in fact. They argued about the best way to climb the cherry, apple and pear trees, which littered Nino's new orchard; about which of them could produce the loudest or the smelliest farts in an enclosed area (such as in the classroom cupboard…at the end of the school day). They competed in hundreds of sprints and races, each accusing the other of cheating should the other one win.

"You pushed me!"

"You tripped me up on purpose!"

"You started running before I had shouted VIA!"

They also made wild accusations at one another during Don Beppe's overambitious football sessions.

"Why didn't you just head the ball, you cretin?"

"Oh, just fuck off! What's it to you, you dickhead?"

And so on…the friendship was not an easy or comfy ride but it was an equal one, each boy having to work hard to outdo the other, each boy happily rising to the challenge, each boy needing the closeness of the other in order to reach his own set of personal, if uncalculated, goals.

After school, they would tear off the starched 'grembiuli', which were supposed to protect their clothes and head off to consort with nature. On hot days, in particular, they would also kick off sandals and remove woollen vests (useful for soaking up summer sweat), leaving only their strange looking 'pantaloni alla zuava', a kind of knickerbocker-shaped garment popular at that time and place, as a nod to civilisation.

Their most relaxing moment of the day being when they would stand side by side at the edge of their little river and deliver two parallel pee arches into the water, after having searched for frogs and grabbed sunbathing lizards by their tails, which sometimes fell off in the process.

Within eighteen months, Nino was dead.

Chapter 4
Il Convento Di San Rocco

Many hundreds of years beforehand, there lived a man called Rocco, who in Pasquale's part of the world, went on to become a popular saint. When still very young, Rocco decided to follow in the footsteps of St Francis of Assisi, likewise discarding all worldly trappings and distributing his considerable wealth among the poor. He also happened, centuries later, to bequeath his name to the 'Convento' (or monastery) which stood on the outskirts of Pasquale's village. He is the saint we most associate with those who are falsely accused or as in medieval times, with victims of the Black Death, a bubonic plague, which had once been the scourge of Irpinia, as it also spread over great swathes of Europe.

The Convento di San Rocco's first stone was laid down in the late 1600s, created out of a pressing, practical need…the closest Franciscan monastery of the province no longer deemed ample enough to cope with the swelling numbers of would-be religious and seminarians. It housed Franciscan Friars of the Minor Order.

The church and cloisters occupied most of the ground floor, and upstairs were the monks' cells on one side and offices on the other, uniformly laid out at the top of a vast staircase. There was a large courtyard at the front of the building, where a statue of St Rocco himself (complete with buboes on leg and dog at his side) dominated. Behind the Convento's elongated structure, dipped slightly sloping meadows, where the friars kept bees, and where many years before that sheep had grazed, whose fleeces had provided those early friars with their characteristic 'habits'. To complete the overall scene, vast tubs of stout, gnarled and ancient olive trees framed each entrance. A scattering of willow trees and dark umbrella pines at the far end of the site had also chosen at some point to anchor down their roots deep into the by now hallowed ground.

Sturdy drystone walls, about two metres high, surrounded the building, and cobblestones paved the way underfoot.

Visitors, so it is said, often felt humbled by the series of Baroque frescoes, lining each of the cloister's four walls, whenever they looked up to examine the faces of each painted protagonist…eloquent faces, which spoke of love, pain and humanity. Key scenes from the lives of both St Francis and St Rocco.

Pasquale's grandfather, Nonno Angelo, had always loved the place and felt far more at home here than in the village church. Many an hour had he spent over the years, in these tranquil cloisters, seated on a side bench, deep in thought, looking towards the central space, which housed a deep, rain-filled 'pozzo'.

He was a good friend of the Padre Guardiano, Bernardo and the two men tried to meet up as frequently as possible.

This time of course Angelo had an especially important reason for turning up, not made easier by the fact that his friend was not in residence, having to attend a meeting with the 'Provinciale', over 20 kilometres away. He told the housekeeper that he would wait for Bernardo, no matter how long it took his friend to return. He was therefore a bit later led upstairs by the elderly 'perpetua', Mafalda, into a room, in the opposite direction from the friars' cells, and just off the Guardiano's huge study. There he installed himself in an armchair, just as he had done at home a few weeks beforehand, when waiting for Pasquale's account of the stolen money. Upper body poker straight with face to match, somehow unable…on this occasion…to appreciate the vast and dramatic views spread out before him from the windows opposite. Once again, he had to sit this one out.

Hours later an out of breath Bernardo poked his head around the door, apologising for his delayed return and begging Angelo to wait just another few minutes, whilst he went to 'tidy himself up'. He came across as a jovial sort, in spite of what had turned out to be a very long day, the kind of holy man we would expect to see in such a setting. Complete with tonsured head, wide and corded girth…and the dark brown habit, which showed up all those little signs of age and neglect…stains, discoloration and fraying. He appeared to be genuinely touched by his friend's unexpected visit and very long wait.

Knowing that Angelo was not a time-waster, of his own time or that of other people, he quickly discerned that his presence there spelled seriousness.

The friar even managed to persuade his friend to stay and share a light supper…visitors were always made welcome there…succeeding only after a great deal of protest on the older man's part. The refectory was a long, rectangular room, just off the kitchens and the monks ate together whenever possible at its long, rectangular table. Angelo, after the meal and a few glasses of wine, even agreed to spend the night there, as their conversation ebbed and flowed, drifting precariously into the early hours of the following day.

Playing down any anxiety he might have been feeling, he was definitely not on a mission to pour out his heart, or confess his own part in the moneylender incident. He knew friendship was a precious thing, but family silence was an even more sacred, when seeking advice or a favour. Never say more than is necessary. In spite of this golden rule, his character still required that he go back to the beginning of his 'semi-fictitious' account, Bernardo already being in possession of much of what he now heard. It was the only way Giulillo knew how to explain any given set of circumstances and his discourse was not without the well-anticipated contorted ramblings and unfinished phrases.

It also meant having to lie to the friar, Angelo telling him that for many years he had been saving, unbeknown to anyone, an amount of money for when he would no longer be part of the earthly world, in order to support his beloved Pasqualino.

He told the truth however when speaking of the love he felt for this grandson…how he was the baby Angelo had held up to the sun in joyful thanksgiving on the day of his birth, over 16 years ago. Confessing how for some unknown reason he had never managed to build a rapport with his two older grandsons who had all but disappeared from the village, and so it was Pasquale upon whom he focussed his attention and pinned hope for the future. Much of this his friend already knew, of course. However, he let him continue without interruption. The old man's afflicted daughter-in-law Maria Rosaria was seemingly nearing the end of her own earthly days, and as for his own son, who had never returned from the Great War…and then Angelo himself…he had never needed much, living off the land, off what he reared and sewed, grew and harvested, self-sufficient in mind and body….He couldn't ask the same for his grandson, not being a life-style that suited many in these swiftly changing times. He realised long ago, that the restless Pasqualino wasn't ever going to hanker after the harsh life of a simple farmer…that is, after a life, which mirrored his own.

Eventually he got to the point. What Angelo had come to ask for was EDUCATION…learning, books, culture, etiquette, knowledge… no, not for himself, but for Pasquale. He was ready to donate a substantial sum of money into the monks' communal pot...provided that, they might take the young man under their wing. Pasquale was ready at last, he was certain of that, and the money was there. Who knows, by spending time with the 'frati' (or friars), he might even get a taste for spirituality, a vocation perhaps...who wouldn't benefit from a second chance? Yes, his awkward grandson had been lazy, foolish, dismissive of the sacraments, unwilling to listen to reason; sullen, rude on occasion...but there again, look how life had treated him...all the things he hadn't brought on himself; his father in the war, the condition of his mother, his brothers' disappearance...the death of his friend...the terrible loneliness.

Bernardo assured his guest that he would try to help Pasquale in whatever way he could. He would discuss the matter, as soon as possible, with the rest of the fraternity and very much looked forward to seeing the young man in person. It had been a long time...yes, it was vital he spoke to Giulillo's grandson face to face and hear directly from him, what he himself wanted to achieve, and the money, although of secondary importance, would of course be deployed wisely for the ever-growing needs of the poor.

A subsequent meeting was proposed.

Nonno Angelo had of course spoken about all of this with his wayward grandson the day after Pasquale had unexpectedly turned up at the farmhouse. He found himself speaking strictly and purposefully with him. Yes, he would support him, but at a price. It was as though God (or Destiny) had deliberately arranged the series of events leading up to the robbery. It felt both personal and highly deserved. After all, there had been no murder; there had been no intention to kill or even to steal. Who would have otherwise benefitted from the surly moneylender's dubiously obtained wealth? A distant or hitherto unheard-of nephew or cousin perhaps? As far as Giulillo was aware, the man had never married or had children...he would of course want to check, though. There was no one, he was certain, who deserved the opportunity more.

In this way, he was able to distance himself...and his conscience...from the gravity of the actual circumstances. As far as he was concerned his story had been convincing; Father Bernardo having drunk in all the details about his made-up savings and the true plans he had for his grandson's future. He needed to be certain now that Pasquale would play his part to benefit from the opportunity that he, Giulillo, and the Padre Guardiano were providing for him.

It would mean the young man could rise to a higher social status.

In this way, he could one day leave the village and transfer to the city. Something Pasquale had always dreamed of…not as a factory worker or rich person's servant…but as an equal, become a cultured man who could discuss religion and politics; art, science and literature…a man who might even enter the political arena, a man who could choose a profession. A world far from where and how he was living now.

For some unexplained reason, it was important for both Nonno and grandson that Pasquale could properly carry off the role, not merely become a 'cafone arricchito', who in a sophisticated city environment would be ridiculed for uncouth manners, broad local accent and unworldly ignorance. Forever open to mockery. Giulillo wanted nothing for himself…he had lived his life in the best way available to him…as a maverick, a man who kept himself to himself! Nothing could give him more joy and peace of mind at this late stage of his long journey, than to know his beloved Pasqualino might soon be ready to climb not just one, but a good few rungs of the proverbial ladder, to gain respectability…without falling into the net of local 'camorristi' vultures. The only alternative escape route. One that perhaps his grandson had already been considering. Just how long it would all take he didn't know. Two years? Three maximum?

He said his final prayers that morning, before taking leave of the Convento and his old friend Padre Bernardo, one prayer asking for forgiveness…and a second requesting that he might live long enough to see the fruits of his labours. The image of Pasquale in a suit and tie, perfectly groomed, manicured hands…set against a city backdrop…rarely leaving his mind's eye.

Chapter 5
The Wait

Nonno Angelo, with his 'contadino' way of seeing the world, was probably not the best-placed person to give professional sounding advice to Pasquale, as regards his grandson's subsequent meeting with Padre Bernardo. He was, however, all there was available.

What the old man did have to draw on though was a vast store of wisdom he had accumulated over many, many years. This was bedded in the still frequently spouted sayings and proverbs passed down from the ancients, who had themselves lived alongside the regular threat of nature's ravages. Floods, landslides, earthquakes, fires, drought, pestilence, famine…poverty; these had all contributed to the present day and his people's endless struggle for survival. An education he had also gleaned from the weather patterns of the changing seasons, from the soil and the sky, the position of the sun and the workings of the moon.

He also possessed that rare ability to read into people's hearts and minds; an insight into human nature and behaviour. Together with that special mix of being self-sufficient but at the same time knowing when to join forces with others, for the good of all. Knowing how to work alongside your fellow man and alongside nature.

All this he had in abundance. In short, he possessed a strong and independent character, which allowed him to work things out for himself, not simply pass on or add to the rumours and gossip that so often swept through the village, like pestilence itself. Some commented that his brain worked a bit too slowly to consider him a truly intelligent man, that he was just a bit too quiet; an introvert, but it could also be argued that it was precisely these 'shortcomings', that stopped him from making rash and foolish decisions. A tried and tested patience working in tandem with his albeit sometimes slow-moving thought processes.

He didn't have any formal learning, barely knowing how to sign his name.

In the weeks and months following the death of the moneylender, Angelo simply watched and waited, never allowing himself to show more than a modicum of interest in the latest village gossip...in other words, to stay in character. He was nevertheless all ears...and it seemed to be going his way. Some 'neighbours' had found the body of a certain Signor Vestrini, after a couple of days, in his kitchen with no hint of suspicious circumstances (even in a cynical community such as theirs). His heart had obviously just stopped beating. With a reputation as a private man and a shrewd one, always playing his cards close to his chest, Vestrini had died unexpectedly. Yes, it happens. How old was he? Around 50 was the consensus. No wife or children. A nephew and niece apparently...neither of whom having judged him old enough (or sick enough) to start visiting...any future inheritance too way off to concern them.

A small group of 'carabinieri' had searched the property, surprisingly finding nothing of interest. Perhaps he had kept it all elsewhere. Maybe village gossip had exaggerated his presumed wealth.

The day of his funeral came and went. The nephew and niece present among the mourners looking deliberately tearful and downcast. Needless to say, at the shock of the loss of a beloved uncle, whom they had...unfortunately...not been able to see as often as they would have liked...and here followed a litany of excuses... covering up the fact that not a single visit had taken place in the last ten years. To go and spend time with this somewhat cantankerous old man would never have crossed their minds. They outwardly glossed over any presumed disappointment, however, that their blood relative didn't appear to have been quite as cash wealthy as rumoured.

Yet it looked as though there were at least a couple of properties coming their way!

There were also a good few people present, who were very happy indeed that Vestrini had died so unexpectedly, as they would never have to pay back outstanding loans to him. Thanks to sacredly exchanged agreements, an absence of paperwork and therefore an absence of proof any loan ever existed.

Nonno Angelo continued to listen and observe. They were safe then as long as no suspicions were aroused. He certainly went on living in the way he always had, likewise his grandson. He knew his people were busy people; they had their own concerns and problems to grapple with. There would be other local events or trivial scandals, which would soon replace this story. He now needed to make sure that Pasquale…no longer his little Pasqualino…was fully prepared for what this serendipitous opportunity meant; a secured future, higher social status, education…a way out of his misery. However, the boy would also have to be patient and play his part. Living with a great deal of money but with no plan for investment was of little significance. He would not allow Pasquale to fritter it away. Was his grandson old enough, mature enough, to see this and stick to his Nonno's rules? Would his patience hold out? Life with a community of religious wouldn't always be…pleasurable…for the needs and desires of an irascible young man, for someone like Pasquale.

"Yes, of course I see that. Of course, I was tempted to just look for it and run away with it, leave this place once and for all, but you kept coming to find me, to talk to me, saying that I first had to have a plan. It kept me awake at night…and in the end I just realised you were right, as always. You've risked your life…and good name, just for me. Of course, there is still my mother…"

"I'm really trying to come round to your way of thinking about being taught by the friars…yeh, they are a bit odd with their delicate white hands, their funny, long nails and weirdo hairstyles, but on the whole they're not a bad bunch I don't think, less two-faced than the 'parroco' (parish priest), in any case. I have to admit that even though I've got all this money now, Nonno, those guys at the Convento have also got something to give me. I can see that now…you know that 'cafone arricchito' thing you always bang on about…and it's only going to be for a couple of years, isn't it? Okay, three at the most…I promise I'll study hard. You know how curious I am about the world. I don't have to pretend to be religious, though, do I? Yeh, I believe in God and Jesus and Mary and the saints and all that, but I don't want to keep praying and going to mass all the time. I hope they won't think I'm there to become one of them. You have made that clear, haven't you?"

This was the kind of conversation (or at least Pasquale's contribution to it) that took place over the following weeks and months, between grandfather and grandson. Nothing was to be rushed; every new step carefully planned; Angelo needing to be sure that Pasquale understood what he was undertaking. Was Pasquale being fully truthful to his Nonno…or even to himself? He probably didn't know. He was at an age of shifting sands, of repeated trial and error, when one believes wholeheartedly in something on a particular day and yet may feel the opposite upon waking. He was at an age when you believe that the happy-endings of fairy tales of Hollywood movies go on forever. Let's face it, though, life owed him this. Everything up to now had been awful. Unjust. But Nonno Angelo knew his grandson's character was also a little suspect. Hard, antagonistic, impatient, bitter, unforgiving. The old man could not protect him from this as well. The best therefore Angelo could expect was provide him with a structure only available from within the Convento, and his own unswerving support…from the other side of its sturdy ancient walls.

He had also taken the wise decision to deny Pasquale direct access to the money, so that in spite of all the pleasing words the young man was now spouting, he would not be tempted to flee with it. This state of affairs was heavily problematic. Angelo had no one to confide in; certainly couldn't bring himself to confide in Padre Bernardo. The money also had to remain well hidden, as in a bout of adolescent madness, Pasquale could feel compelled to search for it.

Like most of us, young or old, Nonno Angelo simply had no idea when his own last day would arrive.

They made a pact that for the time being at least, or more specifically, until Pasquale could show his Nonno that he was abiding by all the rules of the Convento. That he was applying himself seriously to his studies, and so there would come a time when it would feel right to reveal to his grandson where he had stashed it away.

Pasquale, before going to sleep each night, permitted himself the luxury of dreaming monumental dreams about what his wealth would one day buy him. The exotic food he'd only heard spoken of, the fine wines he would drink from his own vineyards. A magnificent villa overlooking the bay, the respect he would command…and all those aspects of a 'dolce vita' that were bandied about by people who probably had very little concept as to what it all really meant or felt like.

He would sometimes lie on his back, arms deliciously folded behind his head, in the silky darkness of his room, savouring every moment of the hour and its soft intimacy. He lay there beneath a single sheet and although it was late September, the nights were still mild…and it wasn't long before he would remember the cards he had wedged under his bed, which fed other profane dreams. These were slightly bigger than playing cards but contained treasures far more precious than cups or coins, this batch being the latest passed, surreptitiously, around the local male community. He would be their custodian for just a couple of days, before having to pass them on. A series of nubile young women in various stages of déshabillé…one in particular, with wavy blond hair and dark lips who seemed to be beckoning him…and only him…from the dark reaches of the studio she used for her poses.

None of the village girls possessed such glamour or promise and the desperate couplings he had recently shared on more than one occasion with the local 'puttana', all the groping and wild moaning, paid for with money he had earned during the annual 'vendemmia' (or wine harvest)…he now, almost surprisingly, found vile, ugly and demeaning.

He continued to eavesdrop, with greater urgency than before, from outside the kitchen window, to listen in on the women's chatter, against the sound of the wind's intermittent rattling of the shutters. What were Brunella and the others saying about Vestrini's death? When would their curiosity move to a newer, more sensational source of interest? Up to now, all that had concerned him was that one of the others had commented that he, Pasquale, seemed to be showing a bit more of a spring in his step these days. This couldn't have been down to any improvements his mother was showing…so wasn't it a bit odd? Fortunately, none of the others had felt the need to add to her observations. It prompted him, however, to be more aware of his movements, of his behaviour in general, whenever he was around them. For the following week or so, he made sure he was back to his old ways, eyes downcast, characteristic scowl, slumped shoulders. Not for much longer, though. Not for much longer. He knew Padre Bernardo was already putting plans into place for him at the Convento. He tried to be patient as he contemplated the weeks and months ahead. He didn't want to let down his beloved Nonno Giulillo…or for that matter let go of his wild dreams.

Chapter 6
The Start of Pasquale's Formation

Pasquale dragged himself to mass every Sunday morning and had done for as long as he could remember. In this particular instance, he found it was much easier to follow the others rather than stay away and deal with the unending backlash of village scorn. It wasn't as though he was being taken away from anything more stimulating. It would all be over well within the hour.

A set of loyally washed and pressed clothes, the by now less baggy suit, a second-hand version of 'Sunday best', was left out for him every Saturday evening, ready for him to step into upon waking. There was nothing like competition to achieve the best results. These clothes would be scrutinised each Sunday, by the woman whose turn it would be next to see to them. It was the same for the little troupe of villagers responsible for the cleaning of the church and arranging the flowers.

At least, a couple of the women would rap on the door about ten minutes before the antiphon rang out into the piazza, and he would half walk half run after them, as they continued, arm in arm, ahead. In the direction of their little seventeenth-century parish church, the centrepiece of the village square. On its proud wooden doors was engraved, in images, the story of its protector saint and inside the building was housed a painting of the Holy Family bequeathed by a celebrated local artist of a bygone era. Only the rare outsider or 'straniero' would bother to make sense of the story or study the artwork.

The locals were proud of it nevertheless. Created by one of their own.

Mass was conducted there (and around the world) in Latin, and the priest instead of facing his congregation, as is the case today, presided with his back turned away from the faithful. It was a very stiff and stern affair. Don Beppe, and now his successor, delivered up meandering homilies, dispensed in harsh tones that also provided a wealth of opportunity for fiery crescendo. These sermons focussed more on (the villagers') sinfulness than spreading the word of God's love and His power for forgiveness. If God had made us this way, surely, He couldn't be too surprised that we found it impossible to behave differently! This antagonistic thought (and many others) often whirling around Pasquale's brain, manifesting an ever-prosaic way of perceiving the world, as the priest continued his weekly Sunday rant. However, he would, occasionally (between musings and daydreams), turn his mind to the content of both the Old and New Testament readings, interpreted with fervour in their own language, not Latin now, in words they could all understand. And thus, after many years of somewhat sloppy an erratic attention to the mass, he had ended up with a sketchy knowledge of the Church's immovable Sacraments, of Christ's message…for us to love one another…contained within the four Gospels…absorbed as if by osmosis. He had managed, under duress, to learn his Catechism by heart.

His favourite time of year being Easter; for its depth and drama, its treachery, the Romans, Peter's disloyalty, the bloody murder of an innocent…the mysterious removal of the stone, the presence of angels and the miraculous Reincarnation itself.

Its links with his own name!

Pasquale had been baptised within just a few days of first greeting the world and had made his First Holy Communion at about the age of eight. A few black and white photographs of these milestone events in his young life remained for posterity in the one and only family album, which considering its age, still looked remarkably new. These could be found a couple of pages on from some hazy images of his father dressed from head to toe in military garb and of course those of his parents' wedding, in which Pasquale found both his mother and father looking particularly sour; joyless. How many times he had explored their sepia faces for any trace, no matter how tiny, of secret signs of love or complicity or even anticipation…but nothing! His mother had once explained to him that in those days it never dawned on people posing for photographs to wear a smile…nor was it ever asked of them. The concept of personal fulfilment or happiness equally alien.

The Hollywood age of 'happy endings', or even that of Cinecittà glamour, was yet to penetrate the old ways of living and thinking in these parts.

Pasquale's ongoing thought trail found him wondering. Whether anyone in the days when his parents had been young, had harboured feelings of disappointment regarding the end of personal dreams or desires (which he just wouldn't accept didn't exist), after the rapid realisation that life was not turning out as planned, not up to expectation. When everything was set in hard village stone. There again, past generations must have known from the outset that there was little point in entertaining such whimsical nonsense. There was no possibility for change of any kind, no moments of freedom or satisfaction. Holy Scripture kept you on an even keel as you made your way along the straight and narrow path. Characters in myths and fairy tales were to blame of course…they gave false hope (as well as temporary respite) to the wistful, providing a misplaced cushion against the harshness of the real world. Nothing good would come of it, however. All they needed to do was follow their set path. Simple. Straightforward.

There lay the paradox. Assuming the role already assigned for us, as if in a play written for the stage.

As Pasquale too had already discovered, hankering after higher things such as freedom and love and truth and beauty only made the heart heavy, the soul thirstier and more restless…but then, as far as he was concerned, Fortuna had stepped in to change all that! Meaning he was now beyond such dilemmas. He had unquestionably seized the opportunity she had carelessly tossed his way.

The Convento di San Rocco educated seminarians from about the age of 18, taught by the friars themselves. Though occasionally they brought in a lay teacher for subjects such as music or art, or wherever (home grown) convent expertise was lacking. The friars offered these impressionable young men a rigorous curriculum, which included the study of Latin, Ancient Greek and philosophy, in preparation for those who were going on to read theology at university in Rome, the study of Old Testament Hebrew, and Aramaic, the spoken language of Christ.

Many of the young men from poorer backgrounds would have already attended a Franciscan seminary elsewhere in the province from about the age of ten, which resulted in their having to live away from home. It became particularly hard if a boy's family then decided to emigrate (nearly always for economic reasons)…the son understandably feeling abandoned, once again having to remain behind. However, in time, with the help of the community members, each of the boys appeared to accept his fate, and in the hearts and minds of his parents, it was a beautiful and sacred sacrifice they were making. Their son one day (possibly) taking Holy Orders, a route out of financial hardship, in receipt of an education, something precious and something for which they could be forever proud, gaining admiration and respect from their compatriots, both at home and wherever migration trail had taken them.

In their previous seminaries, the boys would have occupied separate areas of the building; the elegant rooms given over for the education of the sons of wealthy families, the poor boys getting the more basic facilities. There was no such segregation now they had graduated to the Convento di San Rocco, but many of the young men from poorer backgrounds would continue to pay homage to those well to do individuals, often known to them by name only, their sponsors, or 'benefattori'. These were religious patrons, who promoted the continuity of the Faith and the ongoing creation of new friars, monks and priests, who might follow in the shoes (or sandals?) of the likes of Saints Francis (Francesco) and Rocco…and of Jesus of Nazareth. In reality, it was yet another case of the rich paying for the education of the poor. Without their investment (and that of the wealthy in their own sons' futures), there wouldn't have been opportunities for their poorer counterparts. Not all of course went on to experience a calling, a God-given vocation, and it was true to say there were far fewer vocations amongst those from a more privileged background. Likewise, not all those who became friars here went on to receive ordination to the priesthood.

The sometimes irreverent and ever restless Pasquale therefore found himself slotted into this highly structured and deeply spiritual way of life. In a place created for men, young and not so young, to mirror the humility and simplicity of the saints. He tended to stay at the Convento during the week, making himself helpful in both kitchen and garden and took up his place in some of the seminarians' lessons. There were however huge gaps in his knowledge, and so he received individual tuition from some of the teaching friars, when available. He studied a variety of subjects, which ranged from history and geography, English and Latin, music, maths and some science. He kept a healthy distance from the seminarians outside of lessons, even though they had made him welcome and encouraged him to join the community for meals and prayer at any time of day (or night). There was no animosity on either side but he wanted to guard against becoming drawn any further than necessary into their, as he saw it, bizarre, anachronistic world.

It was here that he became aware of an inner unease, a knot of guilt, tight, hard, and therefore unravelled. Not for his actions at the house of the moneylender…he felt no guilt at all for that…but something to do with ongoing feelings towards his ailing mother, Maria Rosaria. The ubiquitous image of the Virgin Mary in statues, paintings and prayers haunted him continuously. As his everyday life criss-crossed that of the fraternity. They with their quietly bowed, tonsured heads, dark brown habits and sandals, their gaze never far from the three reminders, dangling from their ropey belts. Symbolising their daily-renewed vows of poverty, chastity and obedience. Quite different from that inner knot Pasquale now carried everywhere.

Together with his dreams of escape, of power and Mammon.

Father Gerardo, the friar who had been tutoring him most, called him into his office one day telling him that unfortunately (but fortunately for him) the time had come for him to leave for Brazil, where the Franciscan Order was building a mission. It had been a longstanding wish for Gerardo to join it, believing he had a special calling for missionary work in that part of the world. Seeing the somewhat crestfallen expression taking shape over Pasquale's face, he quickly began to reassure his protégé that there was no cause for alarm, that a new Franciscan, recently ordained, would soon be joining them at San Rocco. He seemed highly qualified for the task and had already said that he was happy to teach him.

This meeting also doubled as an opportunity for the older man to compliment his student for the commitment he had shown thus far towards his studies, manifested further by the kinds of questions he would regularly ask, and the rapid progress he was making in each of his subjects. He was showing strength of character by never giving up. Everyone had noticed.

This news came as a shock for Pasquale. He didn't quite know why. He had always respected Gerardo. They had shared a sound relationship over the past three or four months in spite of the clear line drawn between tutor and tutee, religious and lay. So why did it feel as though something precious was being wrenched from him? He had not been tossed aside, it wasn't personal. A new teacher waiting in the wings to replace him.

It did show Pasquale however that no matter how it might affect the sanguine image he had of himself, that the pursuit of knowledge had become an important feature of his life, not merely a means to an end! There was so much more to discover. He certainly wasn't ready to relinquish all that…yet!

Chapter 7
The Arrival of Padre Floro

Pasquale never forgot the moment when substitute teacher, Padre Floro, entered…or rather floated into…the little study, ready to give him his first lesson; it was a crisp winter's evening. The lesson was on nineteenth-century literature. Poetry.

> E come il vento
> Odo stormier tra queste piante, io quello
> infinito silenzio a questa voce
> vo comparando: e mi sovvien l'eterno,
> e le morte stagioni, e la presente
> è viva, e il suon di lei. Così tra questa
> Immensità s'annega il pensier mio:
> E il naufragar m' è dolce in questo mare.

There have surely been times in your own life, or perhaps only the once, or perhaps it hasn't happened yet, where for some unfathomable reason, there arrives out of nowhere an ear-splitting spark of personal enlightenment, and everything is opened up and transformed in a tiny second. No one else sees it or even senses it. It can't be explained because the science or the words don't yet exist. It can't be repeated and yet it stays with you forever. No fading into the mists of time. No going back.

The new arrival seemed so unlike the other friars and seminarians. Each of course slightly different, one from the other, but broadly falling into one of two groups, of those from simple backgrounds, coarser in their physical features, still often speaking in the local dialect when amongst themselves…and then those from more refined and cultured families, slightly taller, slightly more effeminate in tone of voice, appearance and body language. Floro fitted into neither. A fine young male specimen, exuding total confidence yet seemingly free of any signs of arrogance. Pasquale's first conscious reaction to his presence in the room being one of instant shame for his own humble origins, for his hitherto masked awkwardness now laid bare, for his profound lack of knowledge...and the newcomer still to open his mouth.

It marked for him, Giulillo's grandson, the beginning of an unconscious detachment from the local dialect; the words in his head already starting to shape themselves into the silent sounds of a more refined Italian.

He felt, in a split second, he had discerned a way out of village life for good.

Over the rapidly passing weeks, Pasquale dutifully continued to meet with his Nonno, usually at the Convento itself. Giulillo would fill him in with the latest local concerns...and of course would tell him if there had been any developments in the Vestrini case. Nothing so far. Neither was it becoming a regular topic of village gossip... 'grazie a Dio'!

Their latest encounter had included a jokey interlude about a few of the locals, both men and women (those with a little time to spare), who were currently making the 30-minute pilgrimage each day to the nearest town. All in the quest to be present at a trial taking place at the 'tribunale'. It was the kind of case, which in addition to its complexities, offered up to the devout 'pilgrims' a gripping tale, set against a backcloth of family squabbles, sexual innuendo and vendetta politics.

The matter in question, Giulillo explained in his slow, somewhat meandering manner, centred (or teetered) on allegedly forged documents and unwitnessed verbal agreements, as to the rightful owners of certain fields (and other strips of land) which were dotted around the local area.

No one appeared to be in possession of the exact measurements of any of it. Instead, land was referred to in vague terms, such as occupying the space between two particular plum or peach trees, or the number of steps it would take a man to walk around, and so on. There were accusations made against owners of adjacent properties (whose land was likewise free of visible boundary markers) who had knowingly dug into their neighbours' land. This, they had claimed in time, to be their own, after having stealthily annexed it piecemeal. Whenever witnesses needed to refer to short measurements, they would demonstrate spontaneously by placing their right index finger somewhere along their outstretched left arm...which also included the length of its hand's pointing index finger. A metre would have required them to place their right finger on their nose. The distance between nose and straightened left arm, including extra centimetres indicated by the all-important left finger.

All the protagonists came from people who would have fought tooth and nail, in order not only to preserve their good name, but also to possess even the smallest scrap of property, which they felt rightfully belonged to them, over which they could claim ownership. Notwithstanding the fact that they could erect no more than a shed like structure upon it. Name and land. Name and land. Everyone seemed to have a stake in this case, if only emotional.

Witnesses had arrived from diverse parts of the province, in order to give testimony or support to those from all sides of the dispute. Tangible evidence was in short supply…hardly any available land documentation. Whose version would be the most credible? Which of the warring factions would ultimately win out? What would happen to the losers? Such cases were relatively common in those parts…this was just the latest and most intriguing for quite some time. Unsurprisingly many of the local (and visiting) witnesses proved to be highly comical figures (much of the satire however lost on those in the public gallery,) as each held centre stage and spelled out their own version of events.

This allowed for great entertainment value for the swelling numbers that made up the daily audience, who took as much or as little as they could cope with…something therefore for everyone. There was the witness who suffered convenient memory loss, those that could only communicate in dialect, much to the magistrates' frustration. Those who repeatedly mixed up their lines or mispronounced legal jargon (such diction outside of their normal daily needs) and those who tried to sound far more important than their position in society had hitherto permitted. This case offered them their big opportunity, a starring role. For them to stand up in public, to be listened to, to hold court…literally and metaphorically! There were those who contradicted themselves. Those who exaggerated their own roles as peacemakers in the affair. Those who pointed out the discrepancies, lies and weaknesses of others…and yet never stopped to reflect upon their own! Those who overdressed (or underdressed) for such an important occasion.

Sheer comic theatre, often sinking into farce or pantomime. Something for all tastes. In an age preceding the massive cult of television, the public arena of the courtroom could often provide unrivalled, free and scandalous entertainment both for those taking part and for those fortunate enough to attend…and then all to be reported back to those, who unfortunately, couldn't be there.

Later into their conversation, and on a far more serious note, Nonno Angelo was keen to hear from Pasquale as to how things had been proceeding at the Convento…surely a world away from the base human activity currently playing out at the 'Tribunale'. It struck him that his grandson seemed to be growing in stature, perhaps even physically taller now, or perhaps just holding himself more confidently as he entered and exited. He couldn't be certain but Pasquale appeared to be speaking in a different tone, using new ways of expressing himself. Could it also be that this young and determined young man was already growing away from him? If so, this was surely a good thing.

Giulillo knew from the beginning that this was going to be the price he would to have to pay in the process. For Pasquale, the necessary formation for entry into a much bigger world. All part of the old man's original plan…and it appeared to be working, working much better…and faster…than he could have expected. To rationalise, however, was not an antidote to pain. No going back, of course not. It was already clear the young man's life was never going to be a replica of that of his own. It had already gone up a notch or two. One day soon he would be ready to leave behind their simple village, as had his own son and other grandchildren had done many years beforehand. But this time, thanks to Giulillo and Pasquale's cool quick-witted actions in the face of a huge and unanticipated stroke of luck, the circumstances would be completely different. A reason to rejoice. An honourable departure.

Not a soldier's presumed death on a frozen battlefield; not the selling of one's soul to a band of outlaws. Pasquale would become a great man…ennobled by education. Angelo could die happy.

Not knowing why, or maybe not wanting to analyse possible causes, Pasquale didn't say much to his Nonno about the recently arrived young priest who was now tutoring him in a variety of subjects. Limiting replies to Giulillo's question; yes or no, it's fine, he's okay. While diverting his gaze, the young man once again looked across at his grandfather's gnarled hands, the decades' old dirt of his fingers and fingernails, by now wholly ingrained; the deeply etched parallel and crisscross lines, which covered the loose flesh of his face. The smell of stale garlic on his breath, apparent as if for the first time to Pasquale, when the pair embraced. The signs of old age he already knew, of course. Why dwell on it now?

He also felt an uneasy distance growing between them.

He could have spoken volumes though about Floro. What was really going on? Pasquale himself had little idea…and he didn't want to utter words whose meanings didn't yet make sense to him. His present situation not seeming to fit into any kind of known model or pattern. He therefore stayed silent. A beautiful silence which only added to the delight of the moment; each moment spent in Floro's company; each intervening moment as he waited in anticipation of the next encounter, their next lesson.

Waiting for the time when he would hear once again that beautiful voice.

Pasquale continued to push himself very hard, pouring over his books, reading, learning, delving and questioning.

Chapter 8
Goodbye

About three months on from that encounter, the news came out that Arcangelo Sebastiani, Pasquale's Nonno Giulillo, had died and had died, mercifully, in his sleep and in his own bed. He had achieved, in the latter months of his life, all he had set out to achieve. We can't ask for a better end than this, for him…or for ourselves. He was 82 years old. Very old by village standards.

As was customary (and because he had no surviving children), a few of the village women took it upon themselves to wash and then dress the old man's body, easing it into a clean white shirt and a dark suit that long ago would have been wrapped and then carefully stored precisely in the event of his death. Clothes he would have worn before, on merely a handful of occasions, the day of his marriage, for family baptisms and funerals.

His laying out. The two arms crossing his heart. His narrow coffin home.

The previous night Pasquale and others had stayed with the corpse, sitting (and sometimes standing) around the no longer creaking bed, as they recited the rosary in Latin, this holy lament gradually evolving into a mesmerising chant, a muted yet unending stream of ancient and angelic sounds, which appeared, seamlessly, to transcend human language. Produced in unison, linking their lives to Mother Mary's…and likewise to his.

The time for exchanging anecdotes involving Angelo and a new batch of hand-made theories as to the meaning of life would no doubt follow on over the forthcoming days and nights…in homes, bars and the village square. As the group consisted of men, there was little in the way of sobs and tears during the customary and oft-practised vigil.

By the following morning, the air in the room was just beginning to cloy with the first odours of death but Pasquale couldn't be certain whether it was by now there all the time…still only bordering on the sickly sweet, or whether the smell came and went in waves. He stood transfixed by the face's yellowish skin, stretched liked fine paper, over the high cheekbones of the man he had once loved.

Not the first time, that he had seen a dead body.

There again, there was his mother, long inhabiting the murky world of the living dead, that vaguely grey halfway home, a no man's land connecting the two polarised states of breathing and no longer being.

It was however the first time that he had remained hour after hour alongside the spectacle, even taking an active role in it.

At various moments during the night, his mind had appeared to play tricks on him. In fact, a few hours into the bedside vigil he imagined, repeatedly, that he had caught sight of his grandfather breathing once again, the body gently rise and fall, rise and fall…and later that he'd even changed position slightly…was it all a joke? Would Nonno suddenly jump up out of his bed and go boo?

Giulillo had never been a joker though…

Questions, questions, doubts and questions. Did the body sense that they were all there reciting these magically ridiculous prayers? Was the ritual playing out in effect for him or for them? Did he wonder if anyone present had ever afforded him such reverence and attention in life? Did he know now where he was heading? No, of course, not how we know things. No longer able to communicate back with his estranged, once fellow travellers.

Father Floro, upon Pasquale's request, had administered the Last Rites and from then on had rarely left the room, taking responsibility for the uptake, continuity and rhythm of the ancient prayers and litany of saints…'San Francesco, prega per noi (Saint Francis, pray for us)', 'San Rocco, prega per noi' and so on.

Later that morning Pasquale could be seen, carrying his Nonno's coffin into the little church, together with seven other pallbearers, each boasting a claim on Giulillo's life during his final presence among them. Father Bernardo from the Convento di San Rocco came too, having arranged for a small choir of young seminarians from the province, to add their pure and prepubescent voices to the hymns and prayers. They were all dressed in a variety of starched white albs, some gowns relatively short, and others, which almost trailed underfoot. In most cases, the boys' hair neatly combed, slicked down and perfectly parted for the occasion.

Rows of lighted candles in tiered racks brightened up the internal space of an otherwise gloomy and slightly damp smelling church with its collection of dark oil paintings. Each candle while burning, continuing to offer up a requested prayer, for Giulillo's soul to be admitted into Paradise as quickly as possible from its current position in the waiting room of Purgatory. The freshly arrived yellow and gold chrysanthemums, providing colour comfort, positioned either side of the altar, and the terracotta potted aspidistra plants, with their long, dark spear-shaped leaves pointing heavenward, adding an air of gravitas. The overwhelming and ever-increasing effects of dense smoky incense tumbling out of the thurible, as the priest shook it back and forth around the coffin.

A raised wooden coffin facing the altar, providing the central focus.

Pasquale never tried to remember the words, encounters or actions of that day. He played his part perfectly to the outside world but once done it was all lost on him. Something to be borne but then left untouched, no return visit. He decided there and then that his thoughts…his cares…were only to occupy future time and space.

Meanwhile he continued to receive tuition from Father Floro and sometimes from some of the other friars. His studies were going well. He had even taken to reading for pleasure, or sometimes simply out of curiosity, whenever staying overnight at the Convento. No shortage of books there. Nothing from the intriguing forbidden list, however, the Church's Index Librorum Prohibitorum, which he had only recently heard of…and had sparked a new curiosity.

He was experiencing however an element of inner turmoil, unusual for him, in spite of all the promise his future held. All those dreams, which had continued to sustain him, especially during the first awkward days and weeks of his presence within the Franciscan community. He needed to concentrate on his future but he felt stuck in limbo, in a confused present. Something else was troubling him, gnawing away at his soul. He had inherited Giulillo's little farmhouse (where he now spent most weekends), and now had full access to the vast amount of money he had stolen a few years before. Another donation to Father Bernardo having been made shortly before his Nonno's passing. Yet he felt trapped somewhere in the old life…perhaps also because his beloved Nonno was no longer there to give guidance, to prod him on his way.

There was of course another 'situation' needing clarification but he never allowed himself to think too much about that, preferring to take in and savour each moment as it came.

For Pasquale, Father Floro, the young friar-priest, had remained at the centre of gravity. The natural elegance of voice and movement, his calm and even kindness, his immeasurable patience and impeccable manners, his ability to break down complex concepts into much simpler entities, his own continued love of learning...all running alongside and around a Catholic vocation. Pasquale tried to imagine what he would look like without the medievally imposed tonsure, and so with a full head of hair, that silky black hair quite similar to his own...and how he might look wearing normal everyday clothes. Of course, Floro always appearing to Pasquale in the characteristic Franciscan habit, keeping intact yet another monastic rule.

All former clothing cast aside, given to the poor. Sandals only, for summer and winter alike, not even the comfort of socks.

He found himself comparing the young friar's hands with his own...they were in effect the same slim fingers, the skin just a little paler, a little smoother perhaps.

He wondered if he himself might ever become refined and cultured, calm and knowledgeable...universally respected. Humility of course was of little interest.

Yet nothing other than teaching, knowledge and courtesy passed between them...nothing of an even slightly intimate or personal nature, no allusive or effusive words or gestures. His gaze revealing nothing more than detached kindness, but was it the same kindness he showed each member of the community? Unlike the restless Pasquale, Floro appeared at ease with the world, comfortably travelling the starkness of his chosen path. Comfortable with life at the Convento, from where he took up the many opportunities to preach, say mass, and hear confessions in the churches and chapels of nearby villages. At the same time so different from the rest...they with their head bowed humility, he with his quiet self-assuredness.

The promises symbolised by the three reminder knots therefore remaining forever intact.

Floro had also found the time in his busy schedule to go and visit Maria Rosaria, Pasquale's mother, having heard about her condition, both through gossip and directly from her son. Sometimes he accompanied Pasquale and sometimes went alone. The first time they had gone together and with great turmoil, Pasquale remembered those times Nino had been there. He, like before, would always linger in the background, noting that Floro's words and actions, his gentle attitude seemed to mirror those of his one-time friend. The natural intimacy, the whispery tenderness…where did that originate? That patient acceptance…none of which he himself could muster especially as far as his mother was concerned.

Then shock set in…something Pasquale had never anticipated. Unready, alone.

One of the friars turned up in the study one afternoon and handed him a letter, which he proceeded to open immediately, its bearer having quickly departed. His dark eyes quickly scanned the page of hurriedly written lines, before he was willing to take a deep breath and read it more closely. A sense of foreboding having already taken root as he ripped open the envelope.

And so for this reason, I am unable to say goodbye in person. It's been particularly rewarding for me, a privilege in fact, tutoring you and getting to know you, your grandfather…may he rest in peace…and of course your dear mother. Your progress has been considerable…and in such a short time. I hope I was able to help realise, even if only in a small way (due to my short stay here), some of your grandfather's hopes for you. I wish you well for the future. Who knows what it holds for you now? Place your faith in God's love and He will guide you every step of the way, just as He continues to do for me.

I will of course keep you in my prayers and might ask you to do the same for me…I will definitely need them. A new language to learn, a new culture to embrace, a new country to explore.

All signed off with that universal Franciscan salute,

Pace e bene,

Floro

Yet another moment of no return for Pasquale, a moment of pure, distilled pain.

How dare Floro walk out on him! How dare he leave him with only a few scrawled lines of empty platitudes? Delivered by a stranger. The man to whom he had recently devoted all his waking hours. No, it wasn't just for the loss of the lessons.

More a profound sense of hopelessness, coupled with silent rage, the unthinkable knowledge he would never see him again. Following in Father Gerardo's footsteps; the mission in Brasilia, on the other side of the world. He had never said a word, never once hinted he might not always be there. Most of the other monks having been there for years! His (now fallen) idol must have known about this a long time beforehand. Okay so he had taken the Vow of Obedience…but Father Bernardo wasn't the kind of man to send someone away on a dangerous mission in a faraway place, if it had been against their wishes.

As far as Pasquale was concerned, Floro was now dead. Felled in an instant. No, even worse, he had never existed, a mere fake and a fraud, now fully exposed. He froze him out of his life just the same way as if he had stabbed him through the heart.

Chapter 9
Brigida Amato

Brigida Amato had had her eye on Pasquale Sebastiani for as long as she could remember. One of a typically large family, she had heard mention of his name long before their first encounter. She had learned…and remembered…that his father, who was called Giulio, had probably died in the Great War, at least had never returned from it, but that no one seemed to know much else about him; his short time on earth uncelebrated by shared memories; no name gloriously recorded on memorial stone. Like so many of us…with lives that just don't appear to count much, that daily battle for survival unmarked and unrewarded in life and beyond death.

Notwithstanding heroes then, only for men and women imbued with an unshakable religious faith, might there be the remote prospect of a life that continues.

He had produced three sons however; Arcangelo, Romano and of course the youngest, Pasquale. His wife Maria Rosaria had become, since his departure, very ill with a mysterious wasting condition, which also permanently affected her mental state. Within a short period of time, she had stopped speaking and listening, and could no longer walk or keep house. No longer able to engage in the simple rituals of daily life, becoming wholly dependent on the care of others. Predictably, there were a myriad of possible causes, put forward and bandied around by the locals, as regards her condition. Reference to past misdemeanours (real, exaggerated and imagined), God's wrath, an unlucky star, victim of the 'malocchio' (evil eye), a defective bloodline. Doctors summoned for a diagnosis or possible cure were likewise baffled. Prayers raised heavenwards seemed to remain unanswered.

Eventually Brigida did get to see the unfortunate orphan around the village and then, more regularly, when she started school. She was about a year younger.

In that strange way, life works, when we don't know why something draws us, slowly or suddenly, towards another person…sometimes happening, as in her case, at a very young age.

In a village like theirs, where romance was never encouraged, but where common sense was, especially when it came to matchmaking! Not how pretty the face, but how likely the couple would make a good marriage, for the production of healthy children and the wellbeing of the whole community…the ability to work hard, the joint belief in being frugal, rejecting all that was frivolous…and continuing the old, and therefore the only way of doing things.

Brigida was a sturdily built, fresh faced young girl with thick brown hair, good teeth and a cheery smile. Labelled as 'una brava ragazza', 'una ragazza seria', therefore one of those destined to make a good wife. As the oldest of the Amato children, she had grown up fast and from an early age had begun to help her mother in all sorts of ways. With the housework, the washing of clothes on their self-appropriated stone, made ever smoother by her mother's constant use of it, at the nearby stream. The cleaning out of the henhouse, the piggery and other farm buildings. The cooking, the mending of clothes and the care of her younger brothers and sisters. It soon became clear she could turn her hand to almost anything…and, unlike her younger siblings, very rarely moaning about her lot, just getting on with each task as it presented itself. If anyone was critical of her handiwork, it had to do with the fact that she had little notion of finesse, lacking the desire to perfect her skills, never taking just a little more time for a more pleasing result…it being enough that the job was done! Fast and sorted.

Although she had 'bagged' Pasquale as her husband to be, this did not mean she was love struck in the way we might think of it today or that she harboured romantic dreams about him. She just knew that they belonged together and that fate would one day step in to tie up loose ends. She didn't even wonder whether her parents (or brothers and sisters) had guessed her plans, but she certainly hadn't discussed the matter with anyone, in or outside of the family. There was never discussion about anything anyway. Her father set the rules, the rules of his father before him, and his ancient wisdom cascaded swiftly, silently and obediently down the family ranks, like a torrent of water on the mountain side…part of the village norm.

She sometimes allowed herself to think about that first year though. It was obvious he hadn't noticed her. Even though they shared a school building five mornings a week, with less than 40 children in total. Later, she had seen him drift away from his former friends, to take up what appeared to be a very strong friendship with the new boy, Nino. That pain of memory still acute. The awful news of Nino's death. A school community in a fixed state of shock…and yet with each passing week after hearing the news, pupils (and teachers) gradually managing to grasp back a sense of reality, their own previous place in the world. Keeping alight that poignantly pathetic cliché, that life must go on. Shared sadness mutated into a personal dull ache, which, little by little, managed to dissipate altogether.

Not for Pasqualino…apparently.

It was not Brigida but a boy called Gennaro…or Rinuccio as pupils referred to him…who ultimately came to the rescue. A seemingly unremarkable boy, someone who had always occupied the outer edges of school life and as a consequence, the outer reaches of Pasquale's awareness. A deliberate or fortuitous rescue…no one seemed to know. Rinuccio therefore began to spend more time with his emerging friend, even though the 'rewards' of such an ongoing charitable gesture were not forthcoming. Compared with Nino, Rinuccio came across as an inferior substitute…in appearance, character and natural wit. A grainy shadow of his former friend. A few months later, however, even Pasquale had had to admit that this boy had more than proved himself a devoted companion. He wasn't taking Nino's place…no one could do that. Pasquale had not betrayed his onetime soulmate and blood brother. So somewhat grudgingly perhaps, he slowly let him into his world, with the result that he was welcomed back into the earlier, wider and looser friendship groups of the other boys (and girls) in his class.

Rinuccio had nevertheless one talent in particular. More than anyone else, he seemed to know unusual things, things about the adult world, and the more bizarre goings on in their tiny isolated community. Before everyone else. He so often appeared to find himself in or near the focus of any new event or controversy…having a nose for news.

Something to prove useful perhaps in the years to come…

Brigida came to know Pasquale a little better once her mother had given her permission to accompany her to his house, to care for his mother and help carry out the ongoing domestic duties. Her mother being one of the group who so often lent a hand. Her daughter, forbidden to go there on her own, or openly engage in conversation with him. Eyes always cast downwards. To prevent signs, no matter how small or seemingly innocent, which might lead to the loss of a girl's reputation, that perilous, slippery slope towards social banishment. Every girl in her village would have known this. It would have been considered a 'stupidaggine' to relinquish such a precious treasure…and in this case, even more so, for the sake of such an unfortunate young man. It was likely that no girl in the village had ever been encouraged to share a future life with Pasquale. Conversely, in practical terms, there were very few young men around and even fewer worthy specimens. Girls still needed to marry.

It so happened that Brigida was often present when he mooched about the house in the cold of winter and even more present during the warmer months, when he would slink off outside either to make himself useful, or more often than not, to ponder his circumstances. Only once had she followed him, stalked him, some might say, when she had caught sight of his lanky frame lumbering across the fields. It had seemed like an uncharacteristically foolish act on her part, albeit a newly liberating one. She soon felt forced to give up her mission though, as the day was getting unbearably hot. She had not calculated on him going so far. She had already been out of the house too long, inevitably resulting in punishment on her return; a stinging slap or two around the face and shoulders. Chased by a wooden spoon and the 'cucchiara'-wielding mother, adolescent hair tugged from the roots, so hard as to provoke tears…and further restrictions set as regards her (already limited) freedom of movement. All delivered by way of a spitting anger, a wealth of the worst swear words, and through gritted maternal teeth.

Brigida had continued running, knowing she just had to get home.

Pasquale had eventually come to notice her, but not on that particular day. He wouldn't have remembered when exactly. Clearly a young girl amongst a gaggle of older women. He saw that she had a nice face, that her young arms were strong, the outline of which he could make out through flimsy summer sleeves, rolled right up to her elbows. That they were beautifully shaped arms. An outer circlet of hair shining copper in the sunlight. She wore black, of course, like the older women. Other than face and hands, showing no more flesh than two ankles in the summer months. These would make an appearance only when she pulled up her skirts to avoid the mud or those times when she stretched up to retrieve something from a high cupboard. He also caught a glimpse of a long neck, noble almost, whenever she attempted to tie back her hair into a makeshift bun.

Then, after a couple of years, came the day when she found out that Pasquale was leaving home, to receive an education from the Franciscans at the Convento di San Rocco. How strange. What was this all about? No one else had gone at that age, unless he had received a calling. Something perhaps to do with a plan Nonno Giulillo had devised for him. Brigida didn't understand because no one else in the village could make sense of it either. Again, theories abounded.

Someone even joked that Pasquale must have robbed a bank! That the heat must have affected his brain.

Unperturbed she continued her silent and invisible pursuit of him. He hadn't left the village as such…and he would surely never leave while his mother still drew breath. She was heartened that he was home most weekends, that she could still catch regular glimpses of him even if their eyes still hadn't properly met. Sunday was the best day of the week for that. He still trailed behind those women on their way to church. She positioned herself a few benches behind where she thought he might sit, but on the opposite side of the aisle, from where she could comfortably study his back and profile, follow his movements and check as to whether he was closely following the mass or uncover what else might be capturing his attention.

He had become almost handsome, she mused, if one bothered to see beyond the lankiness, the awkwardness of stance. The dark eyes, inherited from his father, apparently. She took comfort from the fact that only she noticed these things. It meant that, in a way, he was already hers.

Chapter 10
An Unexpected Visit

"Buongiorno, sono la Signora Franceschini, Matilde, posso entrare?"

Pasquale had only just lifted himself out of bed a manifesting all the characteristic signs thereof...dishevelled hair, sore, itchy eyes, still not quite remembering which day of the week it was. It was unusual for someone to knock more than once on their door...the village women always letting themselves into the house.

It had definitely been a tough few months since the passing of Nonno Giulillo. Only a year ago, on imagining such a situation, Pasquale would have already left the village and taken up the life he had so often dreamed of, a life to which he felt wholly entitled.

Something had changed though. It had remained dream, unrealised. He now felt unequipped to make the move. Trapped by some inexplicable force. Maybe next month. Each month came and went. He was no further forward.

He continued to frequent the Convento for tuition, though a little less often than before, his education now centring on the study of history, religion and literature. He continued to borrow books on a regular basis. Father Bernardo had once or twice brought up the subject of his future, even offering to help him find employment, due to a somewhat surprising wealth of contacts and acquaintances that priests accumulated, especially someone in his position, as Padre Guardiano. Priests and even the humble friar still held a key role, and a significant place in the hearts of many people, across each of the social classes. Every Christmas and Easter priests, monks and friars received many gifts. For the most part poignantly simple offerings, from villagers and townspeople alike, their preaching and power to hear confessions covering a wide area. Many such gifts consisting of local produce or items that were hand made by the village carpenter or blacksmith. Wine, salami, 'caciocavallo' and so on. The ubiquitous and highly prized packets of ground coffee.

Pasquale's current, albeit polite, lack of enthusiasm for any of Bernardo's suggestions was undoubtedly interpreted as part of a prolonged period of mourning for his grandfather.

"You know who I am, don't you? You've probably seen me at the Convento. My son is a seminarian there. He is very devout and wants to train for the priesthood. Filippo. I have come here because I happened to find out, just the other day from Father Bernardo, about your mother. We live in the city, and so I know very little about life here in the village. Though I always come to visit my son at least twice a month, sometimes every week…well I was wondering if I could help in some way. Well in a particular way, in effect…could I sit down? Thank you. No, no don't worry yourself; this is fine. You see, we have a vast library of books at home. Inherited from my husband's family. Filippo and I are the only ones to have ever taken an interest though…and yet, I've always been of the opinion that everybody enjoys a well-crafted story, especially if it's someone else reading it to us…or even better, poetry itself. I would like to pop in sometimes to see your mother and read aloud to her. It could be more efficacious than the pills and potions she has needlessly been prescribed. Where is she? May I see her?"

Pasquale somewhat dumbfounded by such a bold and unexpected visit led the city-sophisticate around the corner of the room and pointed out his mother, ever supine on the settee. Their neighbour having already helped wash and dress her, and fed her that day's 'prima colazione'.

"This, Signora, is my mother Maria Rosaria. She hasn't walked or spoken in more than ten years. Books were never of any interest to her I don't think. She could barely read or write. It's very kind of you to think of her but no medication, or prayers come to that, have ever made any difference to her condition. She is locked into…her own darkness."

"Ah, so we have nothing to lose then. I will return…with a book or two…at the end of the week."

She lingered a while, her gaze settling not only on the horizontal woman stretched out on the threadbare settee, but also on the modest furnishings, and the general bareness of the place. This gave Pasquale, who always held back in such situations, the chance of studying her own appearance. Yes, now he remembered that he had seen her before, maybe even a couple of times, in one of the small side chapels at the Convento, except that on those occasions, a black veil had covered her lustrous hair. He didn't find her beautiful as such and yet he was unable to pick out any feature on her face that was not classically perfect. A woman of medium build and height, and wearing a two-piece dark red suit.

To have a mother like that; young, attractive, elegant, articulate…she had, like Padre Floro, wafted in from another world. Had her son's reported vocation perhaps grown out of maternal devotion towards him?

La Signora Franceschini, having refused the somewhat belated offer of what was bound to be a cheap chicory-based coffee, finally took her leave and left Pasquale to work out for himself what it all meant. She didn't appear mad or deranged, just a little eccentric perhaps, with her perfectly rounded vowel sounds and crisp consonants, her crazy offer definitely signalling a certain strangeness. Would she ever return? Did he care one way or the other? It was obviously going to be yet another waste of someone's time.

After a few days, she did return as promised, however, dressed in a similar suit as before, but this time in emerald green, and lost no time in drawing up a chair and started to read to Pasquale's mother…from page 1 of I Promessi Sposi.

"Quel ramo del lago di Como, che volge a mezzogiorno, tra due catene non interrotte di monti, tutto a seni e a golfi…"

"That branch of the Lake of Como, which toward the south between two unbroken chains of mountains, presenting to the eye a succession of bays and gulfs, formed by their jutting and retiring ridges, suddenly contracts itself between a headland to the right and an extending sloping bank on the left, and assumes the flow and appearance of a river. The bridge by which the two shores are here united, appears to render the transformation more apparent, and marks the point at which the lake ceases, and the (river) Adda recommences, to resume, however, the name of Lake where the again receding banks allow the water to expand itself anew into bays and gulfs…"

Pasquale had meant to leave the two women alone, la Signora Matilde having already dismissed the dutiful neighbour, stating with self-imposed authority that it would be better she return later to clear away the dishes. However, he found himself rooted to the spot, entranced almost, by a voice more mellifluous now than when giving orders, as it floated, like the water of the lake in question, through Manzoni's words. He was beginning to see what she had meant by the power of the written word when lifted from a page of flat, monochrome print. In this case, by a voice which itself touched on the heavenly.

Her visits continued. Whether or not Pasquale happened to be there. The locals also got used to seeing her arrive and depart, always carrying her briefcase of books, and quickly becoming the latest focus of attention and tittle-tattle. What a strange woman…why would someone like that bother with such a lost cause…was she up to something…but what? What did she need that she didn't have already…an elegant Signora from the city? There was also much laughter at her expense amongst a usually whingeing, joyless community. The women commented on her appearance and ever-changing outfits; they made fun of her class-ridden accent, with its hint of an 'erre moscia', (almost French sounding) and tried with varying degrees of success at aping her, her voice, her walk, the movement of her hands. The men of all ages, unbeknown to their wives, made lewd jokes amongst themselves about what they would like to do to her if she turned up at their door. All fascinated by this exotic and alien creature but at the same time inwardly hostile towards her, due to her city status, apparent wealth and privilege. She greeted each villager she encountered with elegantly clipped phrases and perfect manners, resisting any opportunities however to engage in lengthy conversations with them. Many others looked on with half-gaping mouths.

No one was of the opinion that her reading aloud to Maria Rosaria or Mariuccia, as they often referred to that poor sick woman, would make any difference whatsoever…an empty gesture coming from a pampered and silly woman who didn't know how to fill her days. As far as Matilde's son was concerned, few were convinced Filippo had received a true vocation, and many took bets as to how long he would last at the seminary at San Rocco.

Chapter 11
Gathering Clouds

Pasquale looked out of the window from his semi-supine state, finding himself confronted by white balls of puffy cloud suspended, as if from invisible strings. All stretched out across a valley canvas of clear blue sky. A fixed sky scape that continued for most of Saturday morning. By the afternoon, however, an altogether greyer picture was presenting itself, a deeper and creeping grey, which had begun to envelope the five villages.

He had stayed the night at Nonno Angelo's house.

That morning as he dipped each 'fetta biscottata' into the milk, he found himself…unusually…pondering the fate of women. Where night's dreams had perhaps taken him. How, like clouds, their lives continued to transmute as the cruel years passed by. White and fluffy turning to amorphous grey. There were the village women of course, who had always been around.

He recalled their interminable nagging and in particular, their cautionary reminders whenever they saw him (as if it were the most precious advice they could ever hand over)…not to go around without something on his feet.

"Non andare scalzo, mi raccomando."

Stuff like that which they dished out, relentlessly! The only way they knew how to show their fondness for him (or for anyone). Proper meals of course and wise advice. Food and wisdom. Little, by way of smiles or bursts of affection, even when he was much younger. Working indefatigably, a small and tough army of advancing ants, a selfless task force, in their drive to help him and his mother survive another day, a village shared predicament. The next-door neighbour who came every morning and evening, to help him lift his mother and prepare her to face the new day…or carry her back into bed, to welcome the comfort of night's darkness. The ample bowls of pasta, beans and 'minestra' that she would leave out for them.

The others who came, in twos or threes, throughout the day to place a bucket beneath her and then empty its contents.

The entrenched and insular bitterness, which stopped him from ever seeing them as human beings, with their own needs and identities. It was too late to start now. Feeling little in the way of fondness towards them, in spite of all their heroic and unrewarded efforts.

Then, there was the local 'puttana' with whom, by now, he had shared intimacy on a good few occasions. Carnal love bought and sold out of mutual need, physical for him, economic for her. There was also that girl he had noticed at school, who now came with her mother to clean the house. He had in fact, permitted himself a modicum of interest in her. Was she enough to keep him in the village though? A girl like that? He could always take her with him, as his bride…but was that what he really wanted?

He thought he didn't know the answer.

There again, more recently, the regular encounters with Matilde Franceschini, a sophisticate from the foreign world of the city, a place he wanted to be and yet couldn't quite reach. The mother of a boy training for the priesthood. A privileged woman, selflessly giving up her only son to the church…and giving up time to help a fellow mother. An educated woman who must have known that reading aloud to Maria Rosaria was never going to meet with any demonstrable success, so as well as having time on her hands…a woman with Christian principles, a woman of faith.

All these women serving the needs of others. Maternal instincts transcending the basic urge to protect their own children, their own parents or husbands, when sick, weak or elderly. Extending out their care for the whole community.

He was at that moment truly content he had been born male. Sensing a rare flutter of, albeit quickly fading, gratitude.

Every Saturday Pasquale took the short walk from house to cemetery to pay his respects at Nonno's graveside, Giulillo's so-called place of rest. Not the traditional day for family visits, but he didn't like the picnic atmosphere, which characterised Sunday afternoons there, neither did he ever want to engage in conversation…unknowingly sharing that terrible truth that "L'enfer, c'est les autres" (hell is other people)…if it could be avoided. Today, as hoped, there was no one else around. Only the minute figure of the warden busy with his barrow and shovel, in the distance. Before reaching his grandfather's grave, Pasquale filled up one of the available cans from the tap, to change the stale, oily looking water in which the flowers, usually chrysanthemums, had stood dutifully for seven days…flowers he himself often took there. He knew some of the village women would also place a few flowery stems of their own into the spare vases, as a mark of respect for Giulillo and out of affection (or pity) for his grandson. Little silent acts, which spoke.

On this particular occasion, he found an envelope, wedged behind a large stone at the base of a wooden crucifix, from which a primitive image of Christ looked down upon the grave. A temporary Christ attached to the rickety cross he would soon replace with a stone one, once the earth had settled and the warden had given the go ahead for a fixed structure to replace it. Both the envelope and incongruous pebble had grabbed his attention straightaway and after kicking the stone away, as he did with any uninvited debris that might litter this sacred space, he picked up the note. Hardly something carried there by a gust of wind. He delayed his habitual salutations to Nonno Giulillo.

It was from someone who apparently knew his movements.

He stood motionless, entirely taken aback; letters of the alphabet, mainly black and red, still in their perfectly cut out square or rectangular surrounds, stuck down on a limp sheet of paper…from newspaper articles…someone having taken the trouble to make every edge straight. A capital letter correctly selected for the start of each new line of sentence. No handwritten words, no signature, no obvious clues as to who might have been its author. It read in grammatically correct Italian,

So cosa e' successo quel giorno…I know what happened that day.
Ti ho visto…I saw you.
Non pensare che te la caverai! Don't think you will get away with it!

For a few long-felt seconds, he couldn't make any sense of it, but then of course its message became perfectly clear. That life-changing day! The burning hot day when he had raced across the fields and had found Vestrini dead in his chair. The day he had stolen a fortune off him. To seal a brand-new future of his own…an episode he continued to re-live and live off.

But he had been so careful, ever confident in the knowledge that he had not been followed there…or even afterwards on the way to Nonno Giulillo's. He had meticulously covered his tracks at Vestrini's farmhouse, in spite of feeling very unwell. Who was this person? What did they want exactly? A random guess that had hit the mark? Might it refer to something else? A mistake, a message meant for the mourner of a neighbouring tomb?

Was Pasquale's buried conscience merely pricking him at last?

He decided there and then to put it out of his mind until later in the day, when the shock of finding such a note had subsided a bit. With a cooler head, he would decide what to do…and it struck him that was how Nonno Giulillo would have tackled the situation. Still the guiding force.

On leaving the cemetery, he happened to notice his friend Rinuccio riding towards him on an old bike. The two young men had continued to meet up quite regularly, even though their school days were long behind them and Pasquale had started tuition with the friars. He was an easy friend. Ever helpful, never one to make demands or be over critical. In addition, he exuded a lightness of being, a practical young man with a built-in ease as to how best approach the ways of the world…which quickly took you out of yourself, if only temporarily.

"Hi, Rinu, have you been around here long? You didn't see anyone near my Nonno's grave, did you? Like in the last hour?"

"No, I've only just come…why?"

"Oh no reason, I just wondered…some flowers…" his voice fading to nothing.

It so happened that Pasquale made more progress that day with his future move to the city, than he had all year…an authentic plan of action almost formulating itself. Piece by piece, in his head. A plan that could still be changed or adapted but at least something tangible in place. Some days were like that, turning out to be days of revelation. Days, which stood out from the rest. He made the decision he would stay in the village for no more than a couple of years or until his mother's passing, which could of course happen at any time. He would join forces with Rinuccio, who would, he was certain, jump at his offer. Not too big a sacrifice for his friend, as Pasquale would convince him that, ultimately, it would be far more lucrative than his working for a pittance at the family run 'cantina'. Nevertheless, a place to which he could always return.

Pasquale would make contact with his bandit brothers, with a view to getting hold of a rifle or two and some lessons in how to protect himself.

With Rinuccio's help, he would track down the writer of that menacing note.

Once in the city he would change his name to Giovanni, in honour of Nino (Nino…GiovanNino…Giovanni) and in that way create a new identity for himself, as well as keep his dear friend's name alive, a joint 'renaissance'.

Nothing whatsoever to do with Rinuccio.

One niggling question did linger however…about how much to reveal to his replacement friend. At what pace? Perhaps no more than necessary at any one time…Nonno's wisdom still trickling down to cool his now hyperactive brain.

The two young men agreed to meet up at Rinuccio's family cantina that same evening.

It had emerged that, as regards their business, Rinuccio's parents had been duped. A good few years beforehand they had purchased the cantina…a run down and unloved outbuilding (with family accommodation at the rear) from a man from the next village, who was about to emigrate to Patterson, New York. Except that there was an undeclared outstanding loan on it, an 'ipoteca' as they referred to it, and so they had since become indebted to Vestrini, in order to pay it off. They couldn't have it out with the previous owner, as once both parties had sealed the deal, he was nowhere to be found.

Things had started badly therefore in their new venture, coupled with the fact that the person left in charge of their takings, Rinuccio's mother, Elvira, couldn't read or write and that some of the customers would trick her into believing they had already paid their bill or stating that they would be paying later in the week. She tried to keep abreast of everything she sold with a system, which required her placing marks on bits of paper. Her husband, there most evenings, was then free to charm those present into buying more drink and tout for work. As regards his carpentry skills, honourable skills passed down from his own father and grandfather. To bolster the family cantina business. Every evening with Elvira stationed behind the bar, having become yet another fixture in that elongated room. Conversely, her husband making his way from table to table chatting to would be clients of his own. This giving him a ready-made excuse to consume more wine than she would ever normally permit, as he needed to appear jokey and affable.

They organised a party, to celebrate the fact they would no longer have to repay Vestrini. After hearing the incredible news, that the 'strozzino' had suffered a fatal heart attack.

The cantina was little more than a long room on the ground floor, with a kitchen at the back, a counter in the middle, and a scattering of round tables, odd chairs and a few wooden stools propped against the bar. Only wine was on offer to drink, red or white, served up in sturdy ceramic carafes. The walls mainly bare, were of whitewashed stone and housed numerous alcoves, on which were dotted an assortment of knick-knacks, some inherited, some their own. Cantina fare was predominantly savoury and included cheeses, salami, sausage (salsiccia) and home baked bread…all to encourage more thirst and subsequently even more family income.

That evening amongst the regular customers were the two young friends, locked into weighty conversation. Pasquale had only been there a couple of times before, never staying long and only now beginning to understand where his friend probably got so many of his news stories. Of course, in such a place, so many people coming and going, and not only from the local community, with tongues getting ever looser the longer the wine flowed and daylight inhibitions evaporated. A general feeling of bonhomie, which gave customers the privacy and confidence to share local gossip (from a male perspective), which in turn resulted in a melange of often vulgar jokes, old anecdotes and the spouting of borrowed theories about the meaning of life. A place with dimmed lighting and scant female interruption. A place to make hasty promises and broker deals, a place to secure new 'friendships'.

Not in the case of Pasquale and Rinuccio however. They weren't there to drink their fill; they were friends already. They were there that night to cement a brand-new relationship.

Chapter 12
Biting the Bullet

Apart from time spent sleeping, their 'summit meeting' spilled over into the next few days. At home, in the fields, at the cantina, near the cemetery. The two young men, sometimes seated, sometimes walking. Sometimes leaning against Giulillo's farmhouse wall. Pasquale tall and purposeful, Rinuccio shorter, eyes aflame. He had been on board from the very start…just as keen to find a way out of the stagnant pool of village life. To find a life that suited them both, far from the political arena, subservient to no one around them, to no national social ideology. Every man for himself…a do or die way of doing things.

Rinuccio opened up early on in their discussions about his 'fidanzatatina', a girl to whom he had already pledged his love, in spite of their tender ages. Her name was Annunziata, and he called her his little Nunziatella. He couldn't imagine life without her, even though he was now ready to renounce everything for his friend, their new relationship, their plans for the future, EVEN her…if that's what it took. On this matter, though, he was unexpectedly fortunate.

"Marry her then! She will come with us to the city," came Pasquale's reply.

A delighted Rinuccio, sworn to permanent secrecy for every loaded word that now passed between them. A short, memorable rite having then taken place.

Pasquale's thoughts racing ahead, and not wholly confined to the realms of altruism. He would give them an income, which would in time, be generous. Accommodation, security. Annunziata would cook and keep house. He knew Rinuccio wasn't stupid however and must have wondered where his friend had found enough money to be making such plans. A 'contadino' grandfather couldn't possibly have had much to leave behind. Rinuccio didn't feel able to broach the subject. Better to wait and let his friend (and now partner) fill in the gaps at a future date. He had complete confidence in him. Completely won over.

Neither young man uttering Nino's name, though, a deeply sensed no-go area.

However, the subject of Pasquale's former friend did come up quite naturally in fact, when the name of the moneylender Vestrini happened to slip into their discussions. It was when Rinuccio mentioned the fire. The terrible fire that had gutted the whole house.

"You do know what one or two people are saying, don't you? All these years later. That the fire wasn't a tragic accident after all…"

"No, no, what do you mean? What are they saying?"

Pasquale, beginning to stiffen at the news but also realising that he didn't want to reveal too much about his own pain. It would smack of weakness. His face already drained of colour and he had started to crack his knuckles… he needed to know everything but endeavoured, at the same time, to appear cool, unmoved.

From then on, and in spite of himself, he just let Rinuccio do the talking, without further interruption.

The only version of events that had ever reached Pasquale's ears was that a fire had broken out that fateful night at Nino's house while everyone was sleeping…a terrible accident, possibly caused by a stove left on…or by a lighted cigarette, which must have been carelessly discarded. No one knew for sure, but an accident nevertheless. Nino, according to witness accounts, had behaved heroically, carrying each of his brothers and sisters (and theirs was a large family even by village standards), out of the house as quickly as he could…all suffering from the effects of pungent smoke inhalation, some nearly unconscious. It was when he re-entered the building for a final time, to check on his parents in their room on the other side of the house, that a huge chunk of burning rafter, its hellish embers, glittering like evil rubies, crashed down upon him. Meanwhile, his mother and father had both managed to make their own escape from an outside stone stairway, having joined their children at the front, all in varying degrees of shock, all gasping for breath, coughing and spluttering; all the worse for wear.

Where was Nino? He had been there just moments ago.

No one seemed to know. A momentary silence gave way to new panic.

His charred and limp body by now fallen under the showering debris, flung down from above and tossed like a sack of hay upon the hard stone of the kitchen tiles.

So many times, Pasquale had retraced his friend's last moments, picturing his every move, as if in slow motion, feeling and hearing the impact of each laboured breath, his every gasp as he tried not to inhale the thickening smoke, his own heart racing in belated unison, almost as much as Nino's must have been that night.

Could there have been an alternative explanation…as to why their house had suddenly caught fire? Unthinkable…until a few moments ago when Rinuccio's words had dropped so loosely from his lips.

Now Pasquale, still to be re-baptised Giovanni, had to know everything. Every detail. Even down to the level of gossip and hearsay. He had to discover what had really happened, to make up his own mind. He felt the weight of responsibility…it was now down to him and him alone. Only he could avenge the death of his beautiful and idiosyncratic friend, should there prove to be suspicious circumstances, an alternative version of events. Now, it seemed, he had a secure place, in which to channel the grief mixed with a new latent rage, replenishing the store already there, that had continued, silently, to devour him.

"Well, it wasn't straight away, I can't remember when exactly, but definitely after a good few months had gone by, a couple of blokes in their late 20s, early 30s we think…'forestieri', strangers…came into the cantina. We plied them with extra jars of wine, as we do with all our new customers…you know to spread the word, to give them a memorable time while with us. Papa went over to sit with them for a good while, sharing his usual batch of jokes. Well of course the more they drank, the looser their tongues became and they started talking about a house on fire, something they had almost been involved in themselves, but how in the end they couldn't go through with it…some other retard had agreed though to carry out the deed within a matter of days. Such an 'idiota' he must have been, they blurted out, because he left behind the can of paraffin he had used to burn down the place, and that a big noise called Vestrini had sent the two of them…to remove the evidence the following morning. Their speech was by now slurred and the detail of their account becoming repetitive and colourful. They had still managed to convince Papa though, that it all did really happen like they said. They could answer all his questions and not once contradicted each other."

"It wasn't till the following morning that it dawned on him that their story wasn't just a random event. My father had heard the name Vestrini before, and suddenly remembered that, he was the 'guy' he'd gone to, to borrow money for that 'ipoteca' business. You know, ages ago, when Papa bought the cantina…a name spoken in a certain way, given with a certain look, meaning a high up person who spelled danger. How could Papa have been so slow on the uptake? It all fitted perfectly."

"Perhaps, they were unfamiliar with the territory (together with all that wine they had been downing), they hadn't realised just how close they were to the village in question. The fire they'd been talking about was THAT fire, the fire that had killed Nino, 'buon'anima', as he tried to rescue his family. Well once Papa had put 'two and two together', he just couldn't contain himself. He called us all to the table the next morning and recounted everything he could remember from the previous night. He made each of us swear there and then, in the name of his beloved mother, Nonna Sara (may she rest in peace)…not yet realising that he had also spoken out when perhaps he should have stayed quiet, in order to protect us…that we were never, but never, to speak of this to anyone. Matter closed. Dangerous forces were at work. The usual village adage…what we don't see with our own eyes…never happened."

Rinuccio seemingly unaware that he had just broken his word to his father. With Pasquale's world once again turned upside down.

As is so often the way with secrets however, be they old or new, and in spite of sacred family silence (l'omerta'), whispers had begun very slowly to begin with, to circulate around the cantina and out into the village…that perhaps there had been a deliberate attempt to burn down Nino's home after all. His family had gone back to live at their old house and so were now out of the picture. Once again, gossip ran rife. Questions followed by multifarious comments and theories…and then more questions. Had the fire meant to serve as a threat or warning? With no fatalities intended? If so, why had it taken place at night then with the family asleep in their beds? In what way had they upset the local, ever nameless 'powers that be', those men who lurked and operated behind tightly closed shutters? Why target a family so new to the village? Perhaps precisely because they were new…or that there were old scores to settle?

"Oh, and by the way," continued Rinuccio, as he once again interrupted his friend's billowing thoughts, "I found out from that warden, that a few minutes before you arrived at Giulillo's grave the other day, there had been a young 'cristiano', the dialect word for person, hanging around in that part of the cemetery."

"Did he say who it was?"

It was now Pasquale's turn to interrupt, albeit nonchalantly.

"No, he said he'd never seen him before but I didn't leave it at that. He went on to tell me that he thought he might be able to recognise him if he turned up again, and that's because he remembered that he had a slight limp, which became visible as he made his way to the exit. You know, dragging his leg. I didn't let on that I was over-interested, just making conversation really and allowing him tell me what he saw. Quite the detective our old warden. Who'd have thought it?"

Pasquale, in the meantime, thoughts again racing ahead, was now feeling a misplaced satisfaction, in spite of the shocking news. Rinuccio too had (unwittingly) proved himself, having turned out to be a more than competent investigator. He knew how to judge a given situation. He knew how to engage people in conversation. He knew how to take the initiative and when to stay quiet.

How to remain loyal to his new partner.

He was, Pasquale concluded, the right choice as his right-hand man. An early and justifiable confirmation.

Chapter 13
Marital, Filial…and Brotherly Love

During their meeting, Pasquale finally told Rinuccio about the sinister note that he had found that morning at the cemetery. He was even prepared to show it to him. He went as far as to explain that there had been a past incident, to which it could refer. It was better his friend was kept in the dark though, at least for the time being, so as not to become any more closely involved.

In this way, Rinuccio, already on the payroll, could go on and make some discreet enquiries, as to the possible whereabouts of Pasquale's two renegade brothers, Arcangelo and Romano, who might be able to help them.

Rinuccio was genuinely surprised, his friend rarely having mentioned them. It was common knowledge they had left the village some years beforehand, even though it meant abandoning their ailing mother. They had become outlaws, living somewhere in the not-so-distant mountains and off the proceeds of robberies they carried out on travellers and others. Not surprisingly, there arose a difference of village opinion as to whether such bandits were no better than common criminals…or rather self-sacrificial individuals, taking up arms against the rich and the 'powers that be'. Against those who followed Mussolini and even those who paid lip service to his demagogic status. The 'truth', as always, falling somewhere short of the two extremes…and wavering from outlaw to outlaw, from illicit action to action.

It took a while but through the cantina 'grapevine' a message did eventually reach Romano.

However, first was to come a village wedding. Something to bring much-needed cheer and relief from the daily grind…some fresh hope, always in short supply. Annunziata's mother and aunt had been busy for months, putting in the finishing touches to her 'dote', a dowry made up of linen sheets, matching pillowcases, bedspreads, nightdresses, napkins and towels. They had also hand sewn a wedding dress for her, based on a design they had found in a second-hand magazine, complete with inserts of satin and lace. As was the tradition in that part of the world, she would wear fragrant white blossom in her hair, freshly gathered from the orange trees, which grew in abundance, on slopes much nearer the coast.

They were both so young but Rinuccio, her family were certain, would protect his wife, he having on more than one occasion promised both families they would return when possible; they were not breaking ties, they were going away for the best of reasons, a much better life awaited the two of them and future children.

The special day came and went. A sunny and slightly breezy day in late April. Earlier that morning, Annunziata's sisters had gone to collect the crate of orange blossom, fragrant little sprigs which they would soon be weaving into her hair, and had decorated Rinuccio's family cantina with left over pieces of satin, ribbon and lace, which they also draped over the lintel of the main door. They prepared huge brightly painted ceramic bowls and wicker baskets full of seasonal fruit for the central table and covered the smaller ones with string tied posies of flowers they had picked in the neighbouring meadows, with the help of a band of volunteers. Their mother, albeit with initial hesitation, finally agreed there was no point keeping locked her own dowry chest. To the girls' delight, they discovered amongst all the reams of hitherto unused linen, some embroidered squares, to cover the smaller tables, which they needed to rearrange, to accommodate the guests, leaving enough floor space for the musicians and dancing.

After the church ceremony, members of the brass band, smart in military-style uniforms, and exuding an air bordering on arrogance (even ennui), were waiting three deep, ahead of the noisy bridal party. The gleaming instruments beginning to thunder out buoyant and cheeky sounding tunes, the procession at last ready to wind its way to the freshly 'dolled up' cantina. The same band played at all the local functions, by now in possession of a wide repertoire of suitable pieces for each occasion. Once inside, the priest, together with the newlyweds, their parents and 'testimoni' all took up their places at the main table, centre stage. Then between courses and amateurish attempts at speech making, Rinuccio's brothers played familiar pieces on piano accordions with their cousins on flutes and fiddles…throughout the afternoon and into the evening. Bursts of frenetic dancing, mainly couples attempting dubious versions of the local 'tarantella', erupted sporadically inside and out, so all age groups could play an active part.

Five courses, from farm, field and forest, interspersed by characteristic folk tunes and dancing. The latest village wedding.

By the end of the evening, many of the men, as anticipated, began to stagger home much the worse for wear, the wine having flowed freely for hours.

Pasquale, one of the 'testimoni', had also played a conspicuous part that day; newly mature, responsible, attentive and looking particularly handsome in a dark suit, made to measure. With his perfectly coiffured hair, he proved a match for any bridegroom, even for today's happy 'sposo', Rinuccio! He delivered a speech, short and punchy, in which he paid compliments to his friend and to the young bride, making sure that jokes were witty and free from overt vulgarity. The result of all those hours spent apart from the rest, deep in study at the Convento. From monosyllabic Pasqualino to Pasquale, public speaker. He had become articulate and unlike the other speechmakers that day, never needing to slip back into the comfort of their local dialect, unless for deliberate effect. He had succeeded with elegance, yet without offence, to distance himself from the other villagers. He had risen to the top. It seemed he was using his friend's wedding day as a kind of rehearsal or nod to his life to come. None of this lost on anyone who knew him or knew of him, obliged from that day on, to reconfigure their former opinions. Who among them would have foreseen this metamorphosis? The once gangly and unfortunate orphan. The once brooding, rough-mannered and anti-social young man.

Nonno Giulillo…if only he could have been among them that day…and to believers, he definitely was…would have been a very proud man.

There remained two unanswered questions though…just how was Pasquale financing this ongoing transformation? How was he able to offer employment to his friend? Nobody felt inclined to ask him directly, nor even a radiant Rinuccio.

Romano, via a series of coded notes concocted between them, had insisted Pasquale meet him in a secret place in the mountains. So secret a location, he had sent out what appeared to be a skinny 16-year-old lad to find him at a predetermined spot and then accompany him the rest of the way.

The brothers' encounter was awkward on both sides. As to be expected. Pasquale's insides raw, his mind freshly conscious of the years of abandonment; he the youngest, still a child then, the most vulnerable of them all, no father to look up to, presumed dead, leaving not even the account of a heroic death on a foreign battlefield, to comfort him. Left at home with an ever-worsening crisis…his mother…the eventual loss of all communication with her. Presenting a bigger void than he knew how to breach or deal with.

In the early days, he had dreamed that unlike his father, his two brothers would become family heroes. That they would one day make an honourable return to the village, heads held high astride noble warhorses. Feted with laurel branches, whose leaves would encircle their heads (like those of the ancient emperors) and weighed down by rows of shiny medals, emblazoned across their chests. He used to imagine his own role on such a golden day…the boy who, alone against the world, had never given up on his older undercover brothers, with them scooping him up in turns, carrying him high on their shoulders, parading him above the roaring crowds…he sharing in their hero status!

They had never returned however, as far as he was aware. No rumours of their sneaking back home under cover of darkness, nor slinking in the shadows of the steep narrow alleyways, just to get a glimpse of how their mother and little brother were doing. How they were coping. He hated them. He felt nothing for them. He had ripped them out of his young life, like pages from his exercise book. Now he would use them, exploit their skills for his own ends. They both owed him much more than they could ever repay and must have known this, somewhere in their dark inner reaches. In response to the sinister note, he now knew he needed protection. He also needed their knowledge as regards weapons and ammunition. Lessons in self-defence.

Perhaps it wasn't out of love, but Romano, for some buried reason, had answered his call.

There was no backslapping, no big male hug, no tears of love or spillages of guilt. The bare cave-like setting perfectly mirroring their present dispositions, empty of visible emotion. Pasquale unable to recognise any family likeness, as he strained to look beyond the deeply sunburned skin, the unkempt beard and through to the backs of his brother's eyes.

It was a short encounter, in which Pasquale heard just what he had wanted to hear…that Romano was disposed to help him with weapons and training. He and the others were lying low for the present, as times had become more dangerous of late. They had little to do. Just biding their time. Perhaps he was thinking that his young brother wanted to become a recruit. They planned a follow up meeting. Again, a mountain lair of the older brother's choice.

He was unable to give any news on their brother Arcangelo's present whereabouts...he had been missing for quite some time. Nothing new there...just the way they now lived. Pasquale made a point of describing their mother's current situation, regardless of the fact that the self-styled bandit hadn't once bothered to mention her. He had made him listen, though. Romano learned that she was wasting away and that she probably wouldn't see out the year. His face unmoved. A set mouth, which gave no reply.

Surprisingly Pasquale was pleased at this, reassured. It gave him more strength, less inner turmoil. So much easier, so much more justifiable, to go on hating...especially when his brother gave no signs of concern, affection or guilt.

He was in fact making headway in a variety of ways. A week before Rinuccio was due to marry his sweet and sensible Annunziata, she had suddenly become unhinged, on a tiny, crazy mission of her own. A last-minute surge of teenage nonsense perhaps, which took her straight to Pasquale (knowing he was going to be at Giulillo's farmhouse), where she suddenly flung her arms around him declaring her undying love, telling him, through gasps and sobs, that in truth it was he whom she had always loved.

Although somewhat bewildered...not to mention slightly amused...by her shocking revelation, he pushed her away and replied with stiffly controlled authority, never needing to raise his voice. He told her that she was being ridiculous, and that of course she had to marry Rinuccio. Under the circumstances however, he would stay quiet on the matter, through loyalty to his great friend. He would never talk of her behaviour that day.

But that if she wanted to show him some proof of her love, he was quite willing, just the once of course, to see why she had come, what she had in mind.

It was all over in less than twenty minutes. Yet another conquest. This time, though, a delicious secret, far more profound and long lasting than the sex, to exploit and savour.

A done deal. Their lives linked and sealed, secretly and silently, from then on. Her mouth, unlike her legs, firmly shut! She was now completely within his control, separate from the power he already wielded over her soon to be husband. It would serve as a reminder, each time he saw his friend, that like the medieval Lord of the Manor, he had been first to possess the wife of a lower ranking aide.

Maria Rosaria died a week after the wedding. Pasquale let out a long, silent cry, as he felt the heavy and ancient load drop finally from his shoulders. As expected, neither Romano nor Arcangelo made any kind of contact in the days or weeks to follow.

Chapter 14
Heat and Joy

Pasquale and Matilde Franceschini, over the weeks leading up to Maria Rosaria's death, had begun to converse a little. She had even started referring to his mother as Mariuccia like the rest of the villagers. A sign of affection towards her (or even him), together with a bizarre need to dip a toe into their simple foreign ways. Willing at last to play a walk on part in their drama. She had even arranged to buy some of the produce direct from the local 'contadini'; their cheeses and salamis; olive oil and wine; their fruit and their vegetables.

Her popularity now on the rise.

The bedside story and poetry sessions continued as usual.

Like the others, she couldn't fully comprehend Pasquale's situation. A simple young man, born into 'contadino' stock, someone who had (lately) gained an education, cared a lot about his hair and always spoke standard Italian. A poor rustic of course but possessing big dreams. So different from the rest. Father Bernardo at the Convento, speaking highly of him, openly lauding his resolve, both past and present.

Pasquale became aware that over time Matilde's tone had softened slightly towards him, not quite so dictatorial now. Perhaps her involvement in his mother's life had caused her to become a little humbler. It was also likely he, like the others, had misjudged her. She who came from a place not so distant, and yet born into a starkly contrasting world. She who must have felt an innate sense of superiority, the villagers subconsciously supporting the view that they were lesser beings. A mutual undercover hostility, quietly raging.

She had mentioned that she knew of his city plans and wanted to offer him her support. She would ask around and listen out for a room that might become available, or a chance for employment. Her husband of course knew a great number of people. Pasquale smiled back, a wry smile, as he thanked her for her concern, but that it would not be necessary. In order to avoid any resulting uneasiness, the conversation developed more generally, her going on to tell him that someone in their nineteenth-century apartment block in the city centre (or 'palazzo') was moving out…making so much noise in the process…and she was wondering just who would be renting it from him next.

An earnest Pasquale suddenly interjected with the words, "Tell him not to rent it out. I will buy it from him. At a fair price of course…"

La Signora Franceschini was all at once dumbfounded, thinking that the young man had suddenly taken leave of his senses. She let out a nervous laugh to cover, on his behalf, her badly disguised embarrassment. Should she actually tell him the market value of those properties? Surely, he must have had an inkling as to their worth? That they were totally beyond his means.

Pasquale's facial expression and body language remained unchanged.

"I'm totally serious. I have the money. Will you speak to him for me?"

She had no choice other than agree to his request, after recommending that it was best, he first went to see the apartment, to check that he liked it and that it suited his needs. She could then introduce him to the current owner, if he was still in residence. Pasquale lost no time in taking up the offer and the two left within the hour…her driver grateful for the extra money he would be earning that day; for the inconvenience of having to wait outside longer than usual, for carrying an extra passenger and for extra journeys there and back.

How bizarre it felt, sharing a car with this well to do woman who floated in and out of his and his mother's life…today wearing a pale lilac floral dress and matching short-sleeved jacket. Wearing shoes with high heels. He who until recently had walked everywhere, other than when riding Rinuccio's rickety bike or astride a donkey or when hitching a lift on the back of a passing cart. All three of them now heading out towards the city. Events were moving so fast even Pasquale's brain could barely keep up. The empty apartment had provided the much-needed catalyst to set his future in motion. Inadvertently, he had been getting ready for just this moment for the past 24 months.

It only took a few minutes into the journey and he suddenly became conscious, in all that heat, of just how close she was to him. Their warm thighs close to touching, their breath sometimes mingling, as they sat mostly in silence at the back of the car, he looking straight ahead, Matilde sometimes staring out of the open window, her chin tilted to the right. He felt her body warmth creep into his; he breathed in her perfume, rose water perhaps (he had heard the village women speak of it); he looked across at her tiny pale hands without moving his head. In an instant, he felt an overwhelming need to lay that reeling head in her lap and let her stroke his precious hair with those pale delicate fingers.

It was yet another hot sticky day.

He remained motionless throughout.

They finally arrived at Matilde's apartment block. Comfortably set back from the road, along a vast tree-lined avenue, in a style he was later to discover to be an early version of Liberty (the Italian equivalent of Art Nouveau), a building, six floors high, with most of its rooms looking out onto the vast square opposite from ornately curved, wrought iron balconies. The driver dropped them off without properly parking the car, asking if it would be all right if he returned in a couple of hours, to which she gave her consent. Her apartment was on the second floor, and reached by a capacious and elegant lift, which moved slowly and silently. She told the uniformed liftman they would be heading for the floor above, on this occasion, and he, on guessing their interest in the mostly empty property, supplied the information that Sig. Boschi (the owner of the flat in question) had in fact just returned. Pasquale also learned that it was considerably smaller than the Franceschini's.

Within minutes, they had struck a deal, Pasquale handing over a vast quantity of rolled up bank notes he had placed in his inside jacket pockets, serving as a deposit. In fact, there had been little in the way of negotiation…the buyer having offered the seller a tentative first figure, followed by a far more realistic one, which was immediately accepted. Boschi said he would take care of the paperwork and legalities, together with informing the person who thought he would soon be renting the flat, that unfortunately it was no longer available.

This time Pasquale and Matilde took the stairs down to her own apartment. Because of the rising temperatures, her cleaner had pulled down each of the heavy wooden shutters, almost as far as the floor, long before the heat had had a chance to penetrate. The flat, like its marble floors, had therefore remained cool and in semi-darkness, now full of shadows cast by low-lying sunbeams still waiting to invade each room. She ushered him into the sitting room. In spite of the dimness, he was able to make out, little by little, the lines and polished surfaces of the elegant furniture, the glimmer of silver ornaments and then the mirrors and paintings, which seemed to own the very walls on which they hanged. Shiny brass pots of very tall palms dotted the floors. It was like the inside of an oriental palace; perhaps almost as magnificent as the Royal Palace of

Caserta, he had once heard described. Never having seen anything quite like it, never really believing that such places, outside of dreams or fairy stories, actually existed.

She caught sight of the young man, as he stood there, silent and in awe of the unfamiliar surroundings, taking in, in gulps, all that he could in the limited time available. His heart was still beating wildly from the deal that had just materialised...he was getting closer... He watched her remove her summer jacket, which she carelessly discarded on the nearest armchair. She invited him to sit down and on returning from the kitchen, offered him a tall glass into which she poured some homemade lemonade from out of a glass jug; they were both quite thirsty. An apologetic Boschi had not of course been able to open the customary bottle of champagne on reaching the deal...his apartment being practically empty. Matilde and Pasquale now laughing that they were having to drink lemonade instead. Each savouring the swift-moving and heady success of the day. It really didn't matter to either of them, they joked, for the absence of French champagne, something Pasquale had never even tasted in any case, unless we count the glasses of homemade 'spumante' he had recently drunk at Rinuccio's wedding.

He thanked her again for letting him know about the flat, for introducing him to the owner, for accompanying him, for her hospitality. After which it only took a few moments for him to fall victim to the earlier heat and joy of the day. His spiralling self-confidence, sudden loss of inhibitions, and the knowledge that there was no one else around; no husband, domestic or driver. He got up from his chair, pulled her up off the sofa, and thrust her against the nearest wall, feverishly kissing her hair, her face with its soft eyelids, her mouth, her tilted chin, her perfumed neck. At first, she remained stiff and still, seemingly not wanting to respond. Never however imploring him to release his grip.

She would never forget where he had first placed those outspread young hands against the wall...high above her head. She would continue to visualise the place and, no one present would ever know what she was thinking or remembering. Such a frenzied encounter could never obviously repeat itself, yet she now possessed its invisible imprint; they had both sensed the danger, no need for words of explanation.

Afterwards, having sorted their clothes, she seated on the padded ottoman, he kneeling on the rug with his head in her lap, she lovingly fingered her way through the beautiful locks of his dark hair. A playing out of that scene he had craved in the car. A passionate encounter. A mother and son reunited. An orphaned boy and neglected wife. Reaching nirvana.

Both coolly aware, by now, that the driver would soon be coming to take Pasquale back to his village. He told her on thanking her once again and kissing her goodbye on both hands, that should ever they meet again, he wanted her to call him Giovanni. A baptism of sorts, he explained. If she could try to remember…the name of Pasquale soon to disappear into a past life not worth living.

The drive back, silent and surreal, to Via Stella, his house even humbler now, but no longer bothering him, ending one of the most fulfilling days of his young life.

The heat, the city, the shadows, his new apartment, Matilde. Impossible to separate out or try to imagine a more sublime interlude. He had once again acted and grabbed each blossoming moment. A fortunate talent for sensing the right moment…

Chapter 15
Fun and Games

Brigida appeared to be making headway as regards a future alongside Pasquale. They were even managing to meet up alone, sometimes for just a few minutes at a time. Perhaps her mother had been a bit distracted of late, having younger daughters to keep in line or that Brigida had already reached an age whereby she could now be a little more trusted. She would never have obtained permission to see him, without the ongoing presence of at least one responsible chaperone. In fact, it was a common event to see around the village, at various times of the afternoon or evening, a couple of 'fidanzati' out for a walk, followed (about ten steps behind) by a tight knot of family members.

However, Brigida had herself by now stepped over that invisible line, thus behaving with him outside of village norms. What was she thinking of?

Pasquale waited to see where it would all lead, just how far she would let him go. He viewed it all as a kind of light-hearted game, with Brigida's virginity being dangled as a bargaining chip. It involved intrigue, a fair amount of skill, and ultimately, the prospect of victory...and of course, the undeniable (and longer lasting) pleasure of the chase itself. Ingredients, which appealed to his sense of self and vanity; a typical, sexually charged, red-blooded young male. This particular chase, proving to be a leisurely diversion, as he waited for his move to the city to materialise. It provided an easy antidote to the tough training he was getting from his brother Romano, which had now progressed to the business of weapons, how to store and use them. He gave little thought as to how Brigida might fit more permanently into his life. He found her pleasing, cheery and uncomplicated, 'una ragazza simpatica', prone however to being a little too talkative, especially during those times he craved quiet. Over the weeks it had gone from her letting him give her a kiss on the cheek to touching her breasts, but only from outside of her clothing…it was clearly going to take a bit longer till he could claim the obvious prize.

Brigida, on the other hand, was holding out for him to mention a visit to meet her family or to talk of a shared future. Nothing forthcoming, but she would not give up hope. She tried to stay positive and jokey in his company, more than aware that, unlike her, he was now highly educated, well at least by village standards. His presence at Rinuccio's wedding had revealed just what he had become. A rare prize, but she knew she had bagged him long before then…when he was still gangly, awkward and surly. As far as she was aware, no other girl was interested. She tried to make sure that before each frenetic encounter she had found the time to brush her hair and that she was clean, especially around her fingernails, and sweet smelling after spending another day of domestic drudgery, after hours in the fields or farmyard. All without raising any suspicions at home. She also tried, with less success, to work out just what was going on his mind. If SHE was on his mind…or even better, in his heart.

She had never thought about Matilde Franceschini as a possible rival to his affections; that would have been outside her (conventional) way of seeing the world.

He was always nice to her and seemed to take great pleasure in the few, but steadily increasing, liberties she allowed him. Never certain, though, he ever fully listened to her, when she attempted conversation of a more serious kind.

She, in order not to bore him regarding her daily chores, had recently described to him, in full detail, an event the villagers were getting excited about, the latest trial playing out at the Tribunale. He listened with limited interest, and found it easy to predict each of its twists and turns (well before she actually reached them) because, by now, he knew the ways of his people, through and through.

One account focussed on the plight of a local farmer, who had recently paid a widow a substantial sum for the 'use' of her much-acclaimed male goat, with the view to its impregnating his healthy young female. It was October, the optimum time of year for such an event to occur, the goats (albeit domesticated) still attuned to their ancient rhythms and mating cycles. The prize buck arrived in all its glory and stayed for the better part of a week. It was therefore assumed nature would take its course and that the farmer would soon be reaping the rewards of yet another wise livestock investment.

Nothing! No pregnancy; no kid or kids in the making. He had been holding out for three! What could possibly have gone wrong? Well for the disgruntled farmer, also publicly humiliated, as he had boasted widely in advance of the event…the only thing for it was to demand his money back. To which the widow gave a resounding NO.

"O' caprone ha fatto il suo dovere e tu mi devi paga'!"

In effect stating that her goat had done his duty and so the money was rightfully hers. She had loaned him her goat; she (and her billy goat) had played their part in the agreement. It was not their fault if his defective nanny had not conceived. It was as simple as that.

The farmer therefore lost no time in taking this rude and intransigent woman to court, holding out, if nothing else, for a little civic sympathy and a lot of compensation. The villagers, those attending the courtroom, and those at home awaiting news as to the outcome, were more or less equally divided, as to who in effect was in the right.

Yet another farcical story regarding his people, who resorted to the posturing of the playground, in order to save face. The case would inevitably go against the farmer; moreover, he would find himself considerably out of pocket, not merely regarding the money he had already forked out on the billy goat. Would they never learn? Was there, perhaps, also an element of perverted self-enjoyment in the farmer's predicament? The inbuilt desire for confrontation at all costs. The silly pleasure of playing out each domestic scene in a public arena, getting others onside, creating preposterous rifts and ripples.

The logical alternative, Pasquale argued, would of course have been to include a clause, in a previously drawn up written agreement, and witnessed by a third party, concerning the eventuality of her goat not impregnating his. It couldn't have been the first time in village history such an event had turned out that way.

This interlude also highlighted the somewhat surprising power that some of the village womenfolk wielded.

Given the culture of male dominance, shouldn't they all have been humble, passive, and downtrodden, both inside and outside of the family home? Wife beating brought on by drink, rage and frustration being commonplace. Rarely acknowledged, even if everybody knew. Varying degrees of violence, part-and-parcel of day-to-day survival (as every young village child quickly learned). Life was harsh. Discipline in the form of corporal punishment was necessary. At home and at school. How else would children (and wives) learn? A sure sign of parental and marital love, the only way to imbue and sustain moral values, to show one's power, to keep control, and to educate. The women also appearing to concur.

Likewise, the catchy and rhyming 'Mai mettere dito fra moglie e marito', a commonly spouted adage backing up such behaviour, which left married couples to sort out their own domestic issues. No woman, regardless of her circumstances, would ever have considered leaving (well, not for more than a few days) the man she had promised to love and obey, for better or for worse…and subsequently the father of her children. Neither would he ever think to leave her. Such hard love continued regardless.

Marriage requiring man and woman to become and remain one person, as we are reminded of Friar Lawrence's lines in Romeo and Juliet, "Till holy church incorporate two in one." Therefore inseparable.

Where would a woman have gone in any case? It would have meant abandoning her children. Who would have taken her in? Definitely not her parents…when two heads lay on the same pillow, they belonged to each other, would have been the blunt reply, she therefore placed beyond and outside of past parental responsibilities, deprived of all compassion. She should just try harder to be a good or even better wife…never giving up hope that she might one day transform her husband's behaviour.

For centuries, many women had, in spite of all this, managed to create ways of turning their inferior position around to their own advantage, society often leaning towards the matriarchal. Especially when menfolk were away at work or war.

Such a system (and mentality) had, paradoxically, given way to an otherwise unexpected breed of tough, stubborn and mouthy women, who just like Nino's mother and now the widow with the goat, could hold their own in many situations, both at home and in the public domain.

They could clearly look after themselves and others when males were in short supply.

It only took a few more encounters and quasi-romantic phrases, and Pasquale finally got his 'wicked way' with Brigida and on more than one occasion; in the fields; up on the hayloft; atop Nonno Giulillo's creaky old bed. He hadn't even had to resort to a tenuous proposal of marriage.

Then, unsurprisingly perhaps, another anonymous note, with the same neatly cut out coloured lettering, arrived at his house in Via Stella. It contained an even more intimidating message than the last…that he should start to watch his back.

Unfortunately, Rinuccio hadn't made any more progress as to who was behind it, all his enquiries leading frustratingly down blind alleys. Pasquale had therefore felt compelled to fetch back a cache of weapons that he'd purchased from his brother, dividing them up between his two village homes; assorted knives and guns, together with lengths of rope, chain, tape and blindfolds. He sensed he would be in receipt of a visit from the person in question and wanted to be ready for him. It was just a matter of time. With a view to finding out before killing him (if that's what it was going to take), just who he was, what he knew about that day in question, if he had told anyone else…exactly what it was that he wanted.

In the meantime, still trapped in that name, still to become Giovanni, he did as the note advised him; he watched his back at all times. He now had his precious gun and knives at the ready; he alternated between staying overnight in Via Stella and at Nonno Giulillo's old house. He examined the outside areas every night before going to bed. He rammed into position an old chest or other bulky bits of furniture against the main door. He placed the gun under his pillow. A big black dog he had borrowed from Rinuccio's parents, one with a loud, aggressive bark, also lay in wait in an outside kennel.

No nocturnal, gun-wielding assassin did turn up however…and for the time being, there were no more threatening notes.

Instead, the day arrived when Pasquale received an (unannounced) visit from two men dressed in dark suits, each sporting leather briefcases and courteous white smiles.

Chapter 16
Two City Slickers

"Buongiorno. This is the 'Avvocato' Andrea Toffoli and my name is Gaetano Gentile. We are lawyers representing a highly prestigious client, whose name I'm afraid, we are unable to reveal on this occasion. Could we come in?"

For a split second, Pasquale had thought that it might have to do with the purchase of the city apartment. He very quickly changed his mind.

They exchanged brief nods and polite handshakes, after which Pasquale allowed the two strangers into Nonno Giulillo's former home, buoyed by the knowledge that Rinuccio had turned up a little earlier and would therefore be at the ready, yet out of sight, should anything untoward come to pass. They were totally prepared for a range of dubious scenarios. The loyal Rinuccio by now fully aware of his friend's role in the events concerning Vestrini and the stolen money.

From the doorway, Pasquale had spotted a big black car parked opposite. A uniformed driver at the wheel.

Surprisingly, he almost welcomed such a visit as it fed his desire and need to discover any link, no matter how tenuous, as to the identity of the sender of those anonymous notes and links with Vestrini. Perhaps this encounter could offer up the opportunity to do just that. It seemed that things were moving at last. If so, he and Rinuccio were more than ready. Confident his life wasn't in immediate danger, as there was something he had that somebody else wanted! Only he knew of its whereabouts.

Pasquale would let them have their say…never openly reacting to anything he might hear. Never bother to interject. He would merely look on and listen. With a mere hint of a sceptical smile and possible touch of ennui, released from hooded young eyes.

During the meeting, the three men sat around the kitchen table, looking in on one another. Gaetano, the one who seemed to be doing all the talking, lost no time in offering their joint condolences regarding the recent death of Pasquale's mother. This served, not only as a polite gesture…but also delivered the covert message, that they were indeed fully up to date with his personal circumstances.

It was however now down to business, as soon as Pasquale had placed onto the table, two tiny cups of already poured coffee, 'gia' zuccherato', from a small ceramic tray. As was the custom.

"We are busy lawyers and haven't come here to beat about the bush. We are fully aware of your situation. A number of years ago, you stole a considerable sum from a certain Signor Vestrini…at his country home. It is possible you also murdered him. That's of no concern. What perhaps you don't realise, is that a large amount of that stolen money did not actually belong to him; he was only a moneylender after all. It belongs (verb clearly expressed in present tense) to our illustrious client and you are dare I say it, a very fortunate young man, in that he also happens to be a somewhat wise, compassionate and generous individual. Yes, he understands entirely what compelled you to carry out the robbery. Things must have been very hard for you all. It must have taken a great deal of courage. He well remembers the mad passions of his own youth…"

The lawyer then adopting a more serious tone of voice said,

"He is also, of course, au courant with news of Maria Rosaria, 'buon'anima', her long-term condition and subsequent death."

At that point, he stood up, made the sign of the cross (in a slow and overtly played out manner) on his forehead, chest and shoulders and then proceeded to remove his jacket, folding it carefully in half, inside out, while attempting to brush off some invisible dust or fluff. The jacket revealing a white, silky lining, as it lay across the armchair. All while the 'avvocato' Toffoli remained seated, jacketed, and silent…devoid of all facial expression.

Once installed back at the table, Gentile again took up his monologue, delivered in his slightly menacing, now thick, syrupy voice.

"And so, all he requires is for you to give him back what is rightfully his…you will find the precise amount set out in this envelope. Open it once we have gone. We are certain you will feel a strong sense of relief that our client is not planning to pursue matters against you in court. No one wants to spend the rest of their lives looking over their shoulder. These past years must have presented you with an awful dilemma. Do as we say and you will be free to go about your business in the village. You are a young and apparently healthy young man. All this must have been quite an adventure."

"A decent future surely still awaits you, in spite of…well, we appreciate you might need a little time to get used to your new situation. So, expect another visit from us in, say, a couple of weeks…have the money ready of course. Let me repeat that. With the correct sum of money that we will expect you to hand over to us."

After a long and dramatic pause, Pasquale never lowering his gaze, staring at each of them in turn, replied with the most quietly authoritative tones he could muster,

"I have listened attentively to all you had to say. I am, in truth, deeply offended. Under the circumstances, I hardly see the need to give a reply, other than to say, (and here he let out a short, cynical laugh) I don't have any recollection of stealing an amount of money, large or small, or of murdering someone I've never even heard of. I think, *You must agree, being of sound mind, I would have remembered.* I have never taken part in criminal activity of any kind. Your accusations are both insulting to me and preposterous. Such a bizarre story. Clearly your 'illustrious' client is suffering from some kind of delusion or, at best, I've been the victim of mistaken identity. You can give him this message on your return. I too am busy with things I must attend to, so if you don't mind…"

After which he rose brusquely from his chair.

The two lawyers said no more as they also got up, faces possibly more pinched but definitely paler than when they had first arrived, Gentile deftly slipping his jacket back on and Toffoli shuffling out behind him. They had not expected this. Pasquale escorted them…in silence…to the front door, which he shut firmly (not resorting to slamming) behind them. The envelope, containing the figure they had mentioned, lay conspicuously on the table. Within a minute of their departure, Rinuccio made his own appearance. The two young men now clearly with a lot to discuss and new plans to draw up. They had each long anticipated some kind of turning point. This was it.

They knew just how important it was to stay calm as their initial ideas and comments bounced across the table. First needing to acknowledge that (at least) three other people now knew something of that day's events. That in all likelihood, it was Pasquale, who had stolen money. That they were able to track him down. That the client in question had made him an offer via the two lawyers.

A gift of some remaining money and a promise his crime would remain unreported. Pasquale still finding it incredible that someone had seen him or followed him that day; he had been so careful and vigilant, in spite of falling victim to a vicious, summer sun.

Had he been of a different ilk, now may have been the right time to 'surrender'. An unknown, apparently 'kind' hand was reaching out to him. He could have placed into it the requested amount (and still have some left over), returning to the life that had been mapped out for him in the first place. Peace could return to his soul. Yes, it had been a long and exciting dream, an adventure they had called it. He had shared it, intimately, with his Nonno Giulillo. As a bi-product, it had brought them ever closer, his grandfather subsequently making a good death. In addition, Pasquale had received an extended education, from learned men who shared a deep spirituality…an experience and privilege he had somewhat enjoyed. Father Bernardo would be more than happy to find him a respectable position, maybe even in the city, whereby he could finally sever ties with the backbreaking farm work of his ancestors. The constant fear of self-sacrifice…for scant reward…no longer relevant.

He now knew that Brigida Amato was also madly in love with him and would be quite happy to take him. "For richer, for poorer."

Within a couple of weeks, if not sooner, guilt's iron grip could disappear from his conscience, if it had ever been there. For some, it would surely have been an attractive proposition…a kind of closure.

For some perhaps. Not for Pasquale however. He had invested every sigh and sinew into this project for three long years. There would never be another opportunity. He had no way of knowing whether the lawyers were speaking the truth in any case. A lot of guesswork on their part, perhaps. Agreeing to their request did not after all guarantee his safety…two pretentious puppets sent out on a mission by a seemingly ruthless individual.

The two young men discussed the above as a possible option, but in effect, it took no more than a few minutes. They dismissed it out of hand. For tough practical reasons, as well as for their ongoing dreams. After all, they only had an unknown stranger's word that he wouldn't bring legal proceedings. A veneer of respectability concealing at least one foot firmly rooted in a corrupt shadowy underworld. The stolen money had probably NOT even belonged to him in the first place.

Pasquale and Rinuccio had already entered the war zone. All that they had gained, they now needed to cling on to, even more tightly than before.

Chapter 17
Carmelina

Pasquale was now Giovanni…and Rinuccio had taken back the formal version of his name, Gennaro. Even when just the two of them. They had left the village of their birth. They…and Annunziata (from now on always Nunzia) were living in an airy city apartment.

It was not the flat on the third floor of Matilde's elegant 'palazzo', nor even in the same city. They had felt it wise, under the circumstances, to go further afield.

A lot had happened in the intervening weeks and months.

Giovanni was (paradoxically) in the process of following in Vestrini's footsteps and setting up a money lending business of his own…not even a stolen fortune lasts forever.

Whereas Gennaro was currently on a completely different mission, which involved negotiations with the parents of Brigida Amato.

As we discovered, and yet another paradox, the nanny goat in her story had not become pregnant as planned, but Brigida, its narrator, was now herself carrying a fragile new life, a consequence of her couplings with Pasquale. They had not been destined to marry…she had got that bit wrong and was now paying the price of not adhering to the rules of a young woman's time and place in the world.

In the end, Pasquale had gone to her house, as she had always hoped…just once…but unhappily never to propose marriage. It was a formal meeting, which took place between him, Gennaro…and Brigida's parents; their daughter nowhere to be seen on that particular evening.

She had been adamant about one aspect of the 'situation' however. She had dug in her heels from the start, categorically ruling out a visit to the local (or any other) abortionist, the woman who took care of that sort of thing in the village.

A role, which incidentally helped, more often than not, older married women already struggling with vast numbers of children, rather than young girls like Brigida. It was supposed to be a secret place…but everyone over the age of about 12 knew something of what went on, in a certain room on the upper floor of her house.

Perhaps Brigida was already thinking of a future date when she might go and reclaim her child. Perhaps that's what was keeping her sane. In any case, she would not allow the baby's annihilation. Her parents finally coming around to her way of thinking. For completely different reasons. The more people who got involved, the higher the risk of the pregnancy scandal becoming public knowledge. A powerful argument.

That evening there was some banging of fists, a lot of shouting and even a couple of blood-curdling threats filling the air, but the 'gang of four' still managed to strike a deal within the hour. As far as her parents were concerned, Brigida's condition had to remain hidden at all costs. If not, dishonour would fall on the whole family (especially on her younger sisters, innocent bystanders in this sordid affair) and a tainted Brigida never able to find herself a husband. Giovanni, while putting across his case, in the coldly detached manner he had by now perfected, simply stated that he had absolutely no way of knowing whether the child was his, with that well-used and ignoble argument, that if she had been weak or foolish enough to succumb to him, she was just as likely to go with others.

He was, he concluded, the potential victim here.

He also stated quite clearly (and truthfully now) that he had never declared his love to her nor even hinted at marriage. He now lived elsewhere. His life had radically changed. However, that because he was a generous man, and very grateful for all the help Brigida's mother had given him and Maria Rosaria over the years, he would do what he could to help them out of their current predicament. The mother, in particular, astounded that the once pitiable orphan was speaking with such authority; so much so, she barely recognised him now.

They discussed various options, more often than not, rejected. Time was not on their side, however. Decisions had to be swift. In the end, a solution was found and it was agreed, that her daughter would deliver the baby a fair distance away from the village, with the explanation, should anyone enquire, that she had gone to look after an ailing aunt. In the meantime, Gennaro would make discreet enquiries as regards a temporary 'safe house', as her shame became visible. He would take it upon himself to look for childless couples (outside of their province), who were considering adoption. Brigida could return to the village, shortly after the birth, as soon as the baby had a new home. No one, simply no one could find out or even suspect. At the mother's request, they all swore, by laying their hands on the dog-eared Amato Bible that they would each keep this knowledge to themselves.

It was an awkward time all round, even for Gennaro and Nunzia, as they too were expecting their first child and a hormone-filled Nunzia, in particular, couldn't stop herself from thinking about the fate of Brigida's baby, and what kind of life awaited it. She also thought about Brigida, unable to imagine what it must be like…to have your baby ripped away from you. She pleaded with her husband to find the best possible family for 'sta povera creatura' (the poor little mite).

For Giovanni, it was more a case of seeing the situation as a minor, yet messy inconvenience but alas one, which deserved priority; as if he didn't have enough to contend with at present! Gennaro continued to follow up a number of leads, with the help of the mother superior of a nearby nunnery.

Giovanni paying his associate handsomely for his talents and efforts, for his ongoing loyalty.

He knew he didn't have feelings for Brigida; he had quickly grown bored of their predictable encounters, once the thrill of conquest had subsided and he now had no plans to marry in any case. He found himself quietly detached from the situation, in fact. Likewise, fatherhood remained a concept he hadn't even begun to explore. Neither did he feel any connection with his child, boy or girl, the new life, which grew day on day inside her.

Brigida, he concluded, was in fact fortunate that through all their efforts, her reputation, unlike her virginity, would remain intact. Like him, she could also make a new start.

He hadn't been back to the village in quite some time and on the rare occasion when he did visit, he was sometimes struck by certain images that had always been there, but ones he'd never really internalised. The difference in height between the villagers and his new people, the city dwellers. His being tall by 'contadino' standards. He also noticed just how bowed most of the women's legs became (and some of the men's, come to that), once they reached a certain age. Was this due to continued intermarriage? An inherited weakness therefore? The Church always spoke out against marriage between first cousins, even though there were few opportunities for young people to meet people from further afield. On the other hand, as regards the bowed legs, perhaps it happened, because they regularly carried heavy weights on their heads. He knew they protected their skulls, as best they could, by folding a piece of cloth to buffer the impact of a deep copper pan or basket. Buckets of water they repeatedly carried, with great elegance in fact, from the 'fontane', a series of taps dotted around the villages, from which poured water directly from the natural spring. Baskets full of fruit or vegetables, carried back from the market, bundles of washing to and from the little river.

He was then reminded of a story he'd been told in his childhood.

As with many such stories, he couldn't remember the precise details or even whether it came with a moral message. This one had something to do with a boy from his village, who had become obsessed with the appearance of a certain woman carrying a bucket of water on her head. Every time he saw her, he would fall into a trance-like state calling out repeatedly, 'Mo cade, mo cade', the Ds being pronounced as Rs as the rules of their dialect dictated (it's going to fall, it's going to fall). And no one knew how to cure him of this affliction. Until years later, on returning to the village and seeing the same woman carry water just like before, he once again burst out with the stream of 'Mo cade, mo cade', at which point a visiting stranger instructed the woman to just let the bucket fall from her head. The combination of the gushing water and crash of the bucket as it hit the ground resulted in an immediate cure, with the young man emitting a very long, almost tangible sigh of relief. His irrational fixation finally assuaged.

It was unusual for Giovanni and Gennaro, when together, to raise their voices in argument. There really wasn't a need, theirs being a sound relationship, each knowing exactly where they stood within it at any given time. Deep knowledge of what made the other tick. This didn't mean that they were always in agreement though; debates were lively, with Giovanni's ideas not always winning out. As well as the mutual respect, each man possessed an awareness of the other's shortcomings…so all in all a tightly effective duo. Gennaro having now long passed a prolonged stage of hero worship.

Something then happened which completely turned everything upside down. Gennaro had uncharacteristically misread a situation together with bad timing…or even bad luck; Giovanni had reacted to it in a way not even he would have thought possible.

There came the time for Brigida to deliver her baby. Everything was going to plan with Gennaro keeping Giovanni abreast of any new developments. Just the facts; yes, no; good, bad; where; when. There was no soul searching, no discussion. Definitely no idle gossip on the matter. Brigida had been in the care of nuns at a convent ('monastero') and a childless couple had been found for her offspring, who would be delivered, like a parcel, to a new home at the tender age of 12 weeks. Yes, she had given birth to a healthy baby girl and they had even allowed her to select a name for her. Carmela was the name she had chosen, for reasons of her own. It could have been after an aunt or cousin. Two or three of her former school friends also shared that name. No one knew exactly.

So, what had gone wrong? It was just a small last-minute change. Instead of picking up the new baby directly from the convent, the adoptive parents asked, with a convoluted explanation, if they could collect the infant from Giovanni's apartment in the city instead, to which Gennaro subsequently agreed (Giovanni was not due to be there in any case). He would simply collect the baby, take it home with him (safe in a carrycot on the back seat of his car) and the heavily pregnant Nunzia would look after it until the arrival of the baby's adoptive parents. With the whole procedure probably lasting no longer than a couple of hours.

Only that Giovanni was already on his way back, earlier than planned, from a trip to the north. As he climbed the staircase, which led to their apartment, he was surprised to hear the agonising cries of a newborn (nature's perfect stratagem), blaring out. He bounded up the final set of stairs, feeling a sudden and altruistic rush of happiness…if only for his friends. It had not been a particularly good day but at least it now meant that Nunzia had given birth; there was something to celebrate…a healthy new life. He was genuinely happy for them.

Wasn't she supposed to have returned to her mother for the birth though? The baby…haha…must have wanted to make an early arrival.

Quite a different scene awaited him. In the spacious vestibule of the apartment.

Yes, there was a baby. In the arms of a strange woman. It continued to scream, throb and sob as the 'grown ups', seated in a semi-circle, looked on, each handing out to the inexperienced mother, bits of their own easy wisdom. Gennaro, a huge and concerned Nunzia…and the man, who in the last five minutes, had become the baby's father.

For Giovanni, reality coming quickly into focus.

He took an instant dislike to the woman. Purely a gut response. Although seemingly doing her best to stop the red-skinned baby, his baby, from crying its tiny heart out. He ignored the man completely, even though he looked kindly and concerned. What the hell, were they doing in his home! He turned his head away from the tiny 'bundle'. A baby Brigida had named Carmela. Oh God, Mio Dio! He had never seen a baby up so close.

But now the urge to look at her, to scrutinise that little prune face…could there be a trace of his in hers, or perhaps much more than a trace…the urge to count and examine the constantly wriggling, miniature fingers, to stroke the all too visible mop of dark hair, overcame him. To scoop her up and put a stop to the incessant sobbing. An almost overwhelming urge. He dealt with it the only way he knew how, by removing himself as quickly as possible and slamming the door behind him. He headed directly for his own suite of rooms. He couldn't remember whether he had said hello or goodbye to any of them, or how long he had stood there welded to the spot. Neither did he care. It had seemed like a lifetime, too many invading thoughts, triggered by raw emotion. To those present, he had remained thick-skinned, unmoved and poker-faced.

Later that evening, after Nunzia had returned to the village, Giovanni ordered Gennaro to join him in the room he used as his office. There followed a terrible row, which left each of them reeling from the after-shocks. Too early to know if this signified a permanent break in their relationship but it definitely coloured the way they each lived, worked and felt over the next few days.

Giovanni outraged that after all the possible scenarios they had discussed, Gennaro had deliberately taken power into his own hands and invited a couple of total strangers into their home, into their personal space. A place where they kept their affairs private.

What he had not divulged, of course, was the other reason for his outrage, perhaps the real reason; the fact that he had come face to face with his own flesh and blood…in the arms of inept and undeserving strangers who had come to take her away. This should never, never have happened. He would now be left with tangible memories, images of recognisable faces and voices, and Carmela's agonising cries, which would never release their stranglehold.

Chapter 18
The Gift of Observation

Giovanni was under a lot of pressure, above all, pressure on himself to make a success of his new life. The money lending was going well and as a business, already expanding. He enjoyed the running of such a venture. The network he was forming. That sense of power that often charged through him, reassuringly electric! He was now well into his 20s but still wouldn't allow himself, quite yet, the luxury of the villa overlooking the bay.

His days were structured and started early. More often than not beginning with a stroll to a nearby bar for a first 'colazione'. There he would exchange pleasantries with whomever he encountered; barmen, trades people, suitably attired professionals and an assortment of others on their way to work. He always came across as a cultured and courteous individual, never overly chatty...far keener to listen to what others had to say. In fact, the bars and cafes proving to be excellent training grounds for observing human behaviour. An ongoing education in how people think and behave. Whenever on his own, to listen in, head tucked between the pages of an outspread daily newspaper. Back at the apartment, he would down in one deep swallow, a second espresso with Gennaro, to which he usually added a few drops of Sambuca.

Fortunately, the blazing row hadn't caused any lasting damage...It had in fact been a powerful learning experience on both sides and any lingering hostility gradually softened with the news that Nunzia had given birth to a baby boy, whom Gennaro had named Alfonso, as expected, after his father. It hadn't been an easy delivery, but she was now back with her husband in the city.

Giovanni shared in their happiness but from a keen distance and promptly donated a very generous sum of money as a nest egg for the child's future. He often heard the baby's cries (and later bubbly laughter gurgles) but kept to his own rooms in the main, rarely entering their domestic set-up. This also worked well for the married couple and their little Alfonsino, giving Gennaro, in particular, time away from the dubious world his friend and partner was now occupying. Nunzia was besotted with her baby son. Each time she appeared to accept, with a brief nod, the droning village advice never to kiss or hug him until he was asleep, for fear that, it would affect her future control over him. Causing her to appear weak and causing him to become spoilt. Once back in town, however, she would smother him, throughout the day, in a rapid succession of tiny kisses starting at the top of his head, especially when he was fully awake. It was just easier that way, to pretend to listen and obey. Her people spoke and gave advice with rock hard certainty, handing out dire warnings and stories of what awful things would otherwise occur…removed from them now and as Alfonso's mother, she just did things her way. Responding to Mother Nature's urges.

Never having acquired the habit of cooking for himself, Giovanni would let Nunzia know, well in advance, if he required her to prepare something for him. Gennaro cooked just as skilfully, if not even better, having watched and helped his own mother prepare meals from childhood, as was the case for many of the village boys. It was therefore quite usual for the three of them to have lunch together during the week, but at weekends, Giovanni was more likely to lunch or dine at one of the local restaurants, small, family-run affairs. Sometimes Gennaro would go with him, when not back 'in paese'.

Giovanni was beginning to rub shoulders now with a more varied set of people and was learning to adjust his behaviour, if only slightly, when in their company. Not out of a sense of deference but for his own desire to merge in with each group, appear urbane and affable at all times.

He also remained in constant touch with his brother (yet another 'type') via intricate forms of coded messaging and meetings. He had come to realise that since their reunion and in spite of an ongoing lack of physical or verbal affection between them, Romano had not failed him. Each time, he had kept his word, never needing to make excuses for a job not done, even though Giovanni, the younger brother, had initially presented himself in a hostile way and making many demands on his time, energies and personal safety. Romano was after all a wanted man. He had patiently trained him in a range of paramilitary skills; had supplied him with weaponry; he continued to furnish him with sound advice. This too was a form of love then…a hard love displayed by concrete actions. Consequently, his older brother having proved himself a loyal comrade.

Giovanni looked around him, to those closer to home, at the so-called successful men in particular, those that interested him most of all. Some of them were his clients, and he was intrigued to discover, bit by bit, that a number of them (rarely acknowledging it) had fallen victim to personal weaknesses. It manifested itself in their habitual presence in bars and nightclubs, their erratic drinking habits, and for some, involved illegal drug use. Consequently, growing problems on the domestic front. It also became clear that in powerful circles, it was possible to access many 'pleasures' about which he had no prior knowledge. He learned that all desires, no matter how bizarre or perverted, could be fulfilled, illicit fantasies carried out…by closely observing these individuals, and in spite of their superficial shine of success, he also learned that it was possible to 'buy' anyone, if the 'price' were right. The biggest mistake would have been to see himself as different from the rest, outside or immune from such behaviour, to conclude that he would never fall prey to such forces. We all had weaknesses and aspects of our lives we intended to remain hidden. Some hidden even from ourselves. It was therefore important to know oneself, the good and the bad, and act upon those findings. To stay forever in control.

As far as he was aware, he had no such depraved leanings, his desires, as far as he was concerned, merely natural and healthy ones; the desire for great wealth, an elegant home, exquisite food, fine wines, and of course, for an unending supply of beautiful women.

A hard, cynical and cruel world was thus slowly manifesting itself to him, coming more and more clearly into focus. A putrid underbelly; a secretly collapsing world of addiction and self-destruction, propped up with indecent amounts of money. A world set apart from that of the villagers, whose tight-fisted grasping ways now appeared innocent and artless, charmingly folksy by comparison.

None of this put him off. The city was what he had sought. It contained all that he wanted. He could never go back to how life was before. It existed to serve his purpose, not to swallow him up.

Unlike others, he was steering a deliberately different path, needing to prevent any kind of tumble by the wayside. Singlemindedness, courage, self-discipline, patience and the ability to think and plan meticulously, such strengths would sustain him…and the fact that he wasn't intimately 'involved' with anyone; he loved no one other than himself. Always a great advantage.

He did acknowledge the fact that he had, in past years, encountered love and attachment, however. Even laughing to himself that, paradoxically, there had been no women on that tiny list. The child Nino (whose full name he now wore), his ancient and wise Nonno Giulillo, still somehow looking down on him, and lastly Padre Floro, whose near perfect image he had felled instantly from his heart the day he had read the parting note.

He might also have included Matilde Franceschini on that list. Her visits. Her elegance and mellifluous voice. Their conversations and the story reading. That crazy postmeridian encounter, whereby for just a few hours she had become both, perfectly, his mother and his lover. A hot, lilac perfumed afternoon in May.

That was poetry, not love, he concluded. His former life had owed him that.

Some thoughts too painful, too complicated to navigate or unravel. Too debilitating, unnecessary, ultimately destructive.

A range of growing dependencies had therefore become a feature of the lives of many of his new acquaintances to such an extent, that it became clear many couldn't properly handle the day without reaching out for glass, bottle or pipe. The colourful and cautionary image of a trembling hand stretching out for yet another slug, sniff or hit, before its owner could struggle out of bed, stayed constantly with Giovanni. For a few, this process had happened quickly, no doubt to those with fragile personalities, a psychological addiction conspiring with the chemical effects of the alcohol (and or cocaine) consumption. He realised just how insidiously the habit could start; the thrill of trying something new or illicit, something exotic, the social context, the need for escapism, that cosy feeling of your inhibitions gradually dissolving, that your levels of self-confidence were growing and growing…your imagination soaring.

He needed to protect himself against all this. Otherwise, it could destroy him too, lead him into situations, which could prove to be dangerous, impossible to resolve. He had to remain on guard.

Never drink alone, no more than a glass of wine or champagne at lunchtime, no more than a few drops of Sambuca in his espresso, no more than two shots of grappa at the weekend, or as a reward for signing a new deal. A rigid programme that he created for himself. Always open to adjustment. He was fortunate in that Gennaro rarely drank, he also knowing how important it was to keep a clear head.

They naturally kept all they knew about this murky world away from Nunzia, who, as a typical village female, had herself never taken up the habit of consuming alcohol. Whether through innocence, ignorance or a deliberate act on her part to stay out of their business affairs, neither did she ever ask any awkward questions.

Then came the day that Giovanni received a request of a different magnitude. Highly dangerous, yes, but coming with a reward beyond even his imagination. One act and then over! Should he take or leave the 'offer'? He had to think about it carefully, not even wanting to consult with Gennaro until he was certain. Any planning, should he agree to the venture, they could then carry out, together. This time it would require organising a series 'middlemen', human links in a deadly chain, each pawn knowing nothing other than their own move, keeping the main players separate, and therefore permanently safe. He gave himself three days in which to make up his mind.

He believing he needed that amount of time. A life changing decision. He said no in his head and then replaced it with an emphatic yes. It continued like this for each of the three days and three nights. Until he awoke on the fourth morning fully aware, he had been totally committed to carrying it out from the very start.

Chapter 19
A Layer of Summer Snow

Santa Maria was the short version the people used whenever talking about one of the five villages. Santa Maria della Neve to give it its full name. 'Neve', the Italian for 'snow'.

Tradition has it that a miracle occurred back in the Dark Ages when a childless couple from Rome decided, despite their sadness, to give up all their material wealth, in order to build a church in honour of Our Lady. Mary in turn appeared to them in a dream, indicating exactly where this should happen. On arriving at the hill in question, the young couple found the ground covered in a fresh layer of snow, notwithstanding it was a blazing hot Italian summer.

After many years, someone from the south, perhaps a bishop, inspired by this faith-heavy story, named a newly built church and hence the village growing up around it, Santa Maria della Neve, in honour of the miracle. Mary, the most important saint of them all, protagonist of a thousand miracles, mother of Jesus and mother of the universal church. The villagers, then and many even now, believing that she would always look down upon them and wrap them in ever-loving maternal arms.

In times of misfortune, she would empathise with their suffering…she who knew all about that, having placed one heavy foot after another along the Via Dolorosa, alongside her tortured Son as He approached the awaiting cross…and would intercede on their behalf, answering prayers and supplications. Each year, during one whole week in August, they would venerate her in a special way, showing their gratitude for her continued care and protection…all culminating in the Sunday feast day celebrations.

People would stream out of their homes, each playing their part. Those, who were ill or those who could barely walk, would install themselves on front balconies or little terraces to watch the long and winding procession, all the way from its colourful head through to its straggly tail. Everyone sharing in the familiar hymn singing and prayers, applauding as the statue of Mary passed and throwing down coins (or low value notes) into strategically positioned baskets. The children would absorb the party atmosphere and general lightness of mood, enjoying it all in their own fantastical ways. A day that stood out from the rest. A long day or them, but whenever it began to drag, they could look forward to a huge festive meal and the evening's programme of events, organised in and around the village square. There would be musicians, singing, dancing and groups of visiting stallholders, all plying their wares; a mix of regional delicacies. One particular favourite being 'o' muss ro puorc', (pig's muzzle), upon which they squeezed drops of lemon, eating as they wandered around. Then there were all the different kinds of nuts shovelled into cone shaped paper bags, the long bars of 'torrone' (a hard nougat), and other sticky and brightly coloured sweets, in frustratingly short supply for the rest of the year…and of course the inevitable religious knickknacks. The culmination of hope, saintly comfort, Christian devotion, together with an overwhelming need for sweets, taste, colour and show.

One of the villagers, in more recent times, had written a special prayer dedicated to their protector saint, which they would recite on the Snow Mary's feast day every year from then on, during morning mass. It included 'puffed up' phrases such as 'guiding star in our darkest hours' and 'turn your merciful eyes towards us' and so on, ending with the lines,

"May the experience of our forefathers, who with holy pride passed down their faith, give us the courage to implore you to watch over us all, for yet another year."

Faith poured down the generations, rarely questioned or analysed. Watertight. Together with the indescribable pride of belonging.

Upon waking, Giovanni had decided, all of a sudden, that Santa Maria della Neve was just where he needed to be that day. He rarely returned to any of the villages. Some of the locals would probably recognise him, of course, even though this wasn't where he was born and he looked and dressed differently now. In spite of the geographical barriers dividing each little community, and a deep sense of village rivalry, there was always a lingering interest in what was going on in each, and who the key movers were at any time. The same type of feast day event took place at different times every year in each of the villages (each with its own 'santo patrono'), and served not only as a day of public devotion, but also as a showcase as to how well each of them was faring. There had been years marked with good health and harvests, high numbers of births and baptisms…but also many years punctuated by death, struggle and hardship.

Far away, on the world stage, however, it was a particularly complex and sensitive time…and no more so than in the Kingdom of Italy. Nationalism, as in other parts of Europe, was rife. It appeared that the lessons of the Great War had not served any long-lasting purpose after all. Something ugly and yet still unimaginable was brewing. Something about to fall out of the flames of Fascist dictatorship.

In many ways, it appeared that life in such out of the way villages remained untouched and unscathed by those decisions carried out on a global scale. Laws issued by those, who were physically and emotionally detached from the ways of isolated rural communities, for whom life was still stuck in a seemingly medieval void. In effect, not always a disadvantage…a parallel subculture, left alone, free to follow its own traditional ways.

However, when WAR was the outcome of such major decisions, the 'powers that be' became 'pied pipers' once again leading simple folk into that bigger reality, beating out with their mesmerising rhythms, the heady message of glory and patriotism. In times of War, governments needed soldiers…a continuous flow of soldiers and many of the young men conscripted came from villages such as these. The painful memory of destruction, injury and loss would return to the women's lives. The absence of husbands, brothers and sons, often far from home in remote, foreign sounding places; a loss of income, skills and labour; the permanent loss of loved ones if this 'mad adventure' ended in death.

So often it did.

As regards the sacred statue of the Snow Mary (usually housed in the little church, which bore her name), a group of men had recently fixed it on top of a wide plank board of dark wood. Her annual airing. Morning mass had just finished and as for the parish priest, it meant a long and arduous day ahead. A flutter of gowned 'chierichetti' (altar boys) surrounded him, as they took up their positions at the head of the procession. The priest dishing out in whispered bursts his last-minute instructions. Eight of the village's strongest men, spanning a range of ages, had the backbreaking task (but also the honour, for which they remained ever proud) of carrying the statue for the approximately three-hour procession. Upon willing, sacrificial and well tested shoulders. They too were organising themselves for the way ahead, having already manoeuvred their holy charge, today festooned with a myriad white flowers…down the front steps of their church. That was a spectacle in itself, with the usual groupings of villagers witnessing every pant and sigh the statue bearers emitted. The route, always the same, covered each accessible road or public space. Each villager playing a part and showing due reverence to their mother saint. Each year the priest would in return bless the home of every family they passed.

Giovanni looked on closely that day. He saw everything, each breath-taking little detail, with and through new eyes, cynical eyes perhaps, which blocked any room for nostalgia. Struck by how much effort and community spirit went into pulling off the mammoth annual performance. There, but detached, passive, invisible. An event that he had grown out of, once reaching manhood. Village pride and patriotism. Religious fervour. The old traditions. Today, it was as though he had noticed, for the very first time, the age-old and yet very familiar statue. Completely European in design, and reduced to the vulgarity of an oversized China doll, with its matching China doll Gesu' Bambino. The Mary effigy managing, simultaneously, to both hold her son and proffer open hands to the crowds, as she stood high upon her perch, looking down on her people and the day's proceedings. She wore her familiar party garb…a highly decorated gown of white and gold, a cloak of sky blue, reminiscent of heaven and a golden crown wedged onto her China head. The Baby Jesus an almost comical, miniature version of His doll mother.

Giovanni's thoughts had of course taken him back to his early childhood. How he had once believed the statue really was the Madonna. How on these feast days, here and in his own village, he and his preadolescent friends would take bets on the statues falling and how the poker-faced adults (so pious, at least on that day of the year…no swearing today!) would shout and shoo them out of the path the eight muscle-bound statue carriers were treading. They had often seen Mary (or the other saints) wobble slightly, but as far as they were aware, she had never come crashing down, never to leave a spillage of China pieces, a trail of tiny flakes of snow….Only their imaginations had shown them images of scattered streets.

His thoughts were suddenly interrupted by the sight and sound of a young American woman (well, she looked American judging from Hollywood films he had come to watch at a local cinema) calling out to herself in English…as if there were no one else present, uttering something like, "Oh isn't this all just so cute?

Just wait till I tell Mom and Pops about this…It's like, it's like…being on a movie set."

Who knows what she was doing there? Who she was. Where she came from exactly. Her presence annoyed him profoundly. He wasn't even sure why. He just wanted her removed, for her to go back to where she came from. He was probably the only one to have understood the meaning of her silly words, even though everyone had turned to face her. The villagers part hostile, part in awe, all definitely curious. It was probably the first time many of them had seen red hair (in any of its shades), which they wasted no time in linking with evil, the work of the Devil. In any case, she clearly had no place amongst them.

It dawned on him later that day, that if he'd seen her or someone like her in the city, her presence wouldn't have affected him at all!

He watched the ingenuous young woman, as she gradually passed out of view with the others, the only one unable to join in with reciting the rosary, the only one with fair, reddish hair, snow-white skin and light blue eyes. By the time he'd caught up with them, she had…thankfully…disappeared from view.

Towards the end of the day, a few of the better-behaved children (or more accurately, those with connections to the mayor) were given the go ahead to throw a handful of white petals over the head of Maria della Neve. Symbolic of the manifestation of summer snow in years gone by…before the statue's return to its habitual niche for another long span of twelve months.

Chapter 20
Obliterated

A couple of years beforehand Giovanni, with Gennaro's help, had successfully tracked down the lawyers, Gentile and Toffoli, shortly after their visit. The search had also led them directly to their mysterious client. A powerful man who knew (or suspected) too much, a man who had political links, a man after Giovanni's fortune…and therefore someone they needed to remove from circulation, and as quickly as possible. They discovered that like many others of his type, he too inhabited the world of undercover business deals and public respectability. Giovanni and Gennaro concluding that his 'disappearance' would also serve to silence the two lawyers, without further recourse to violence. They would be too terrified for their own lives (and the lives of their dear families) to continue pursuing the would-be perpetrators. Nevertheless, after the deed, Giovanni would go on tracking their movements very closely.

Within ten days of their visit, he had fled the village, while Gennaro continued to work at the family-run cantina.

Giovanni, with more than a tinge of regret, had decided against buying the apartment in Matilde Franceschini's 'palazzo'…it was just a little too close to his village. He now needed more room in which to operate and in which to lie low…having severed most of his past ties. Plans were therefore afoot to find a more secure and suitable base.

In fact, this turned out to be a very wise choice, as the 'illustrious' client, they soon discovered, kept an apartment of his own, just a couple of blocks away from Matilde's. It meant of course that Giovanni had lost his substantial deposit, but that, he concluded, no longer mattered…merely part of the world he now inhabited. Decisions needing to remain flexible. Accepting philosophically that not all investments met with automatic success.

Gennaro proved to be highly efficient in the tasks he was set, each carried out with a rock-solid determination to get it right. Partly due to personal character traits and partly because Giovanni never gave any snap or sloppy instructions. After all, Giovanni's continued success guaranteed his own. Every angle, every option was thoroughly explored before a course of action was decided upon. Every plan had at least two back-ups. In the meantime, Gennaro had become masterful at adopting a growing range of disguises and behaviour quirks...nothing too dramatic or obvious, just tiny changes such as a dyed moustache, a slight lisp or limp, a growing collection of regional accents, different ways of parting his hair...whenever approaching a stranger for supposedly innocent information. Most of the time he simply needed to blend in with the crowd. He took his work very seriously and with great pride. With Giovanni's help, he became adept at entering into conversations with people he'd never previously met, in order to discover significant bits of information. The two often practised role-play. The investment in time, practice and attention to detail was definitely paying dividends. All the skills needed for an investigative reporter, a scientific researcher.

Giovanni had learned from his time at the Convento how the most successful students, weren't necessarily those everyone considered to be the most intelligent or the most erudite, but those who quickly ascertained what it was their teachers or examiners wanted, and even more importantly...where not to waste their energy. Top students allowed sufficient time to prepare selected material and revise thoroughly. In a totally focussed manner. A blend of single-mindedness and near-perfect timing, as well as the necessary brainpower. Now he realised, he was doing just the same, applying the same methods, but now operating in a far-removed unholy world. He learned from every situation that presented itself. No matter how seemingly insignificant. Always open to take something new from each person he encountered.

He and Gennaro never carrying out their plans rashly...but with clear heads, spurred on by their pure desire to hold on to everything they had so far amassed...to gain even more.

They also discovered how easily the majority of people could be 'bought'. It just took courage and determination. 'Bought' in the form of their silence, their deaf ear, their blind eye...and that very few, in any case, ever relished the idea of helping the authorities with their enquiries, probably having their own shabby little scams and dodges they wanted to keep under cover. Reporting a wrong could turn the spotlight on you, with your name appearing in police files. Never arouse unnecessary suspicion, a characteristic already deeply ingrained in the ancient village mentality.

The most important lesson of all taught them never to allow links in a chain to form…nothing that connected deed with culprit, culprit with deed. No chain, no trail.

They planned to kill him in his car. An elegant Lancia. Symbolic of his shiny success. Over several weeks, Gennaro had stalked him and recorded all his movements. They now knew where he kept and parked it and the times, he normally chose to get in it. It appeared he didn't employ a regular chauffeur to take him around, indicating that he enjoyed driving the impressive vehicle himself. They examined every aspect of his life, his daily routine. Of course, he was their sole target; this was not an act of vengeance, merely one of cold necessity. As far as they were concerned, his wife and children were no part of his (or their) sinister world, and so it was important to keep them out of the picture.

On the other hand, if their time should also have been up that day, a last-minute change of plan, any detail impossible for Gennaro to have uncovered, well…their dual (and warped) conscience would tell them that they had done everything to avoid it.

With the help of Romano, his older brother with anarchic leanings, Giovanni was able to get hold of the necessary explosives and expertise as to how best to deploy them…never caring to reveal the target, neither did Romano ever ask.

The outlaw brother told him that it was a relatively straightforward task. Most farms of a certain size would already be in possession of dynamite and that he knew a couple of women, who worked in factories, where it was produced, somewhere in the north.

On hearing that word…dynamite…Giovanni experienced a warm rush of satisfaction, as he suddenly remembered a random fact picked up from Father Bernardo. Over time, they had spoken on a range of topics, and on one occasion, this had led to a comment about the Swedish chemist, Alfred Nobel. Bernardo told the then Pasquale, who had no idea, that the great man also happened to be the inventor of dynamite, the deadly explosive, and word from the Greek meaning 'power'. They had shared a chuckle or two about this, with the wise 'padre guardiano' adding, somewhat ironically, that, as well as for physics, chemistry and medicine there were also Nobel Prizes awarded to the creators of the finest literature and to the world's peacemakers.

Creation and Destruction, such a paradox. Power in the form of an explosive. How decadent. How timely. How poetically appropriate.

Now Giovanni would be using this same explosive to kill a fellow member of the human race. It didn't matter…they would be ridding the earth of a corrupt specimen, after all. A fleeting reflection perhaps, yet another flicker of solitary pleasure he would keep for himself.

The killing took place with clockwork accuracy. Obliteration of car and man. The car smashed to smithereens in an instant…and the body pulverised. As a newsworthy story, it seemed to rage on and on, spattered over the front pages of every daily and regional paper. Multifarious theories were on the rise; his possible links with the Camorra, talk of embezzlement and double-dealing, the extra-marital, possibly homosexual relationships…someone who had inevitably created enemies for himself, whose actions had hollered for revenge.

It also signalled a booted kick in the face of Benito Mussolini who had launched a robust programme to defeat organised crime and racketeering.

The Carabinieri did their best to track down the assassin or assassins. However, they could find no evidence linking the murder to any of those notorious 'families', who brazenly and famously lived off the proceeds of criminal activity. Nothing seemed to stick.

However, a number of die-hard reporters, driven by the spectacle of the exploded Lancia, and the image of a powerful man erased in seconds, also got a taste for the hunt. Men in high places kept their distance, not wanting to be associated in any way with the story…having their own reasons to stay quiet, especially those who had enjoyed past dealings with the murder victim.

Unknown to the law enforcers, Giovanni and Gennaro kept likewise quiet. To the outside world, everything appeared the same. The habitual trips to the bars and restaurants; always affable in their dealings with others; unremarkable in many ways, which was just how they wanted it. Going about their business in the normal way. Nothing that pointed to them. No possible connection. They would sit this one out…and of course, eventually…there would be another item of news, something fresh and equally, or even more salacious or scandalous, to capture the grisly attention of readers, and the police themselves. The killing of a 'pezzo grosso' with possible links to the criminal underworld. He would have known the risks. He getting his just desserts. Those who lived by the sword…

The masses would predictably tire of feeling their initial outrage. A loss of momentum.

That is exactly how things panned out. The case had to remain open but without leads, clues or evidence, gradually losing its newsworthiness. Giovanni and Gennaro never spoke of it, not even when alone, and the silence helped them to distance themselves and their consciences even further from any involvement, aiding the process of self-denial. It might still come up in conversation in a bar or club… people merely needing to cling on, to have their say on the killing, to make guesses as to who the perpetrators probably were, to speculate upon a possible motive and so on. On such occasions, Giovanni would listen with inner amusement as they spun out their theories, spurred on by the presence of others and at how each theory became more and more fantastical as the night wore on. That need to hear one's own voice, that need to express an opinion, especially when drunk.

A mark of stupidity, as far as he was concerned.

Chapter 21
Unfinished Business

Giovanni, having become a successful entrepreneur, and by now also dabbling in the buying and selling of objects from antiquity, had never forgotten the fate of his inseparable friend. Nino. How could he? He wore his name with an immense pride each day; he had 'assumed' him, he believed, just as Mary's body had been assumed into Heaven. It meant that, in just as mysterious a way, it was as though his friend continued to exist, to breathe, somewhere alongside or even inside of him. They were not separate.

A conjoined force.

This didn't mean, however, that Nino's killer, the monster behind that fatal house fire, could go unpunished. Unthinkable to forgive and forget.

In spite of Giovanni's time spent at the Convento, where he had also sat through what seemed like a myriad of homilies on the theme of forgiveness and reconciliation. He put to good use, his own use, however, everything he had learned there, and how, when necessary, to 'work' the truth. Surely in order to forgive someone, the sinner himself must first repent and apologise, which only then might lead the way towards absolution. In this case, the perpetrator had clearly never thought to crawl out of his dank dark hole to confess and seek forgiveness from Nino's heartbroken family.

A uniquely beautiful life extinguished by evil. An acceptance of the murder would have been way off Giovanni's concept of justice, with or without faith in the sacrament. As he had learned to interpret the world, that would have made him a traitor. He would take the matter, and the man, into his own avenging hands, quite literally.

In his own way. At his own pace. Once again, the law of the land had failed. It was ever inept.

He had to get the right man though. Giovanni was not a police chief having to content the masses, baying for blood, during a nationwide manhunt…for whom any name would do. So that the case could draw to a 'successful' conclusion. No, this was deeply personal. Inky records still clinging on to the lie, 'death by misadventure', besides Nino's name. The misfortune of having risked his own young life by returning, repeatedly, into the smoke and flames of a solitary home, set apart from the huddle of sturdier stone-built houses overlooking the square…with the one overriding thought; to rescue each member of his family, blatantly disregarding his own safety.

Giovanni's blood boiled and then froze, boiled and froze, even years later, whenever he took thought journeys back to the string of events that awful night. Even when he still believed that the fire had been a tragic accident…still ridiculously (and repeatedly) holding on to the possibility of a different outcome, if he went over it all in his head, just one more time.

The day finally arrived when Gennaro was able to relate to him, that one of the men, who had spoken to his father with knowledge about the fire, had finally returned to the cantina. The stranger had agreed to disclose all he knew of the matter, this time with a clear head. He also agreed to make contact with his former friend, the other man present. Gennaro naturally making it worth their while. After much toing and froing, several interviews (sometimes with each on his own, sometimes together), names of people, places, and dates being gathered, an almost complete picture was emerging for the very first time.

Together with a credible motive for the fire.

Vestrini, so it appeared, had merely followed orders. Given by someone who would never take no for an answer. One of those men in the dark and high places of village consciousness. There was nothing for it other than to agree, no matter how abhorrent the task…the moneylender even trying to convince himself, with a fleeting flurry of pride, that he had been hand plucked to carry out the mission! What he knew deep inside, however, when vanity abated, was that when someone had something on you, a knowledge of past misdemeanours or a weakness of character, a so-called secret, a favour needing instant repayment…whatever it happened to be…that person had power over you. Saying no would mean they would come for you, or even worse, for a person they knew you loved. Because they had already discovered your Achilles' heel. You knew the day was coming…and in the meantime, you continued to buy their silence at a price they always dictated…always uneasy, waiting for contact, in the form of a personal visit or 'pizzino'…that dreaded tiny slip of paper.

Giovanni was almost ready to swoop…when, all of a sudden, he learned just who else the man behind Nino's murder happened to be. It stopped him in his tracks. The trail had led him to a Don Salvatore. From his childhood days, he had doubtlessly absorbed bits of whispered conversations about the infamous 'uomo d'onore', the 'pezzo grosso', who, oddly enough had in his own youth, set out on the lifetime mission to shield his lowly people against such 'monsters'. In fact, he must have sold out quite early on, if that were the case. Only to become such a man himself. The continued thirst for power and Mammon, deeper, higher, greater. Don Salvatore, far more powerful than the by now diminished Vestrini, who turned out to be yet another pawn on the human chessboard. More powerful than the 'illustrious' client Giovanni had had blown up in his sleek and beautiful car.

It turned out, that Don Salvatore also happened to be…the natural father of Matilde Franceschini.

She had taken the name of her husband and had never spoken to anyone about her family origins. Don Salvatore had fathered so many children, in any case. Was she herself even aware of his dealings, his silent notoriety? Women, in their narrow roles of wives, mothers, aunts, nuns and daughters, were shut out from such goings on…it was now practically the same for Nunzia. In the female interest, of course, it being convenient for such men (or men in general) to continue generating the myth, that their female counterparts had no head for business of any kind. Too emotional, too volatile, lacking the necessary clarity and ability to reason. They couldn't keep secrets either; they gossiped. All this meant they had learned not to ask questions. Better by far to go on playing a purely domestic role…their limited power operating in kitchen, nursery and bedroom, behind closed male owned doors.

Yes, Giovanni had heard mention of him and his legendary exploits but like the other villagers, had absolutely no knowledge of his family. Father and daughter, this meant a sacred blood tie…he was certain she had never referred to it, not even by allusion. He found himself once again sifting through their past conversations. This information now shining a different light on matters. Was her husband also somehow involved?

It perhaps also shed new light on why her son, an only child, had answered an early call to the priesthood. A means of escape from the hereditary nature of such criminal bloodlines. The church offering him a total break with his past, he concluded.

Giovanni finally had to accept that his actions might cause lasting pain and torment to the woman, who had patiently read aloud to his mother, and who had shared with him, two or three of the most intensely beautiful hours of his life.

She the woman who had filled his heart and mind with a shaft of love (whatever love was or meant), one sultry May afternoon.

On making the discovery, he decided there and then to postpone the killing. Only perhaps for a week or so. It wouldn't of course erase all the diligent work he and Gennaro had been carrying out in the lead up. This was their most challenging and prestigious 'project' to date. One with no financial reward, purely personal. However, now Giovanni needed more time to think and breathe. He proffered a couple of uncharacteristically weak excuses…something to do with feeling tired, having pushed himself too hard of late…to a somewhat perplexed and frustrated Gennaro; his friend, for some unknown reason, seemingly out of salts, somehow altered.

Gennaro suggested that he should go cheer himself up, perhaps go and stay somewhere a bit closer to his brother's whereabouts, certain that a bond was growing between the two of them. He could definitely manage on his own for a few days. Giovanni wouldn't hear of it however. No question about it, he would be staying put! Instead, accepting that what he needed was a change of scene, he decided to 'try out' a new club he had heard about, just a few blocks away from the apartment.

No more so than in the present moment, did he cling to the need of a world within a world. Where outside forces could not easily penetrate. It suited him better than any other landscape. Certainly, for now. A secret place, emerging at the bottom of a steep flight of stone steps. Of a tall building. No passer-by could know what transpired there, unable to peer in from the outside. Most people oblivious to alternative possibilities, of other realities.

Then a narrow corridor…dark and winding; becoming sweetly perfumed. Leading to a dark red centre. People and objects gradually flickering into consciousness.

The thin tinny chink of glasses, the release of echoing laughter, human faces brought to life and made beautiful by candlelight. A world of adults only, inhabiting a smoky nocturnal space, all their own, appearing to have nothing in common with domesticity or the brutally regimented world above. A severed world. Out on a limb. Therefore, vulnerable. Trapped but mercifully hidden away, even if temporarily from the Dictator's thugs…and others. Here time either stood still or just flowed differently. The air gauzy. A beguiling world therefore, running parallel to the one above. His glance now wandering to the intimate recesses and little tables, the claret-coloured velvet couches resplendent with silky pillows. Men in dark suits whispering into the ears of pretty girls. Lines of bottles on counters made colourful by their magical contents.

Band members taking up and playing their polished instruments on the tiny stage. Oozing unfathomable mellow sounds, intricate streams of primitive and life-giving rhythms. All a semblance of ease and leisure. Hooded eyes, dreamy smiles, fluid body shapes. Things and people perfectly unarranged, appearing to remain exactly where they had first alighted. Club members and musicians; a different species. Nocturnal creatures. Gradually writhing back to life.

It was here Giovanni was first to set eyes on Iolanda. Introduced as Jole, her stage name. She wasn't there on that particular evening…still waiting in the wings, but Fortuna was planning a big return.

Meeting Iolanda would strangely allow Giovanni to perform, more easily now, the execution of Don Salvatore.

He would feel the weight of an ancient burden (like when his mother had passed her final breath) loosely slip from his shoulders.

Giovanni did finally avenge his friend's murder. Clean, to perfection. His only regret…that he couldn't confide this to members of Nino's family. To tell them that it had not been an accidental fire but an act of attempted murder. That the perpetrator, Don Salvatore, was now dead. That Pasquale, now named Giovanni, in honour of their son and brother, had tracked him down and killed him, slowly sucking the life out of him with his own avenging hands.

Chapter 22
Mountain Air

Another killing therefore took place, for which Giovanni was responsible. He had taken it upon himself to strangle Nino's murderer with his bare hands. In much the same way, he had strangled poultry, geese and rabbits throughout his childhood.

He now had to deal with the mental and emotional aftermath. He was still human. He headed for the mountains. Not to be with his brothers however.

Gennaro had supplied him with an assortment of village clothes, the kind of thing he hadn't worn in a good while, topped off with an old black 'coppola', the ubiquitous flat peasant cap. Wide-legged trousers with braces to hold them up, a few coarse shirts, woollen sweaters and woollen underwear, which covered arms and legs, and a long shapeless padded jacket for the evenings, when temperatures dropped drastically even before the setting of the sun. Nothing, which might draw attention to him while outside of the house. He grew a thick black beard.

Giovanni was now staying at the home of an elderly couple, who had, so Romano told him, allowed their older brother Arcangelo, to hide out at least a couple of times, in the hayloft. They lived there alone, far from civilisation (their children having fled the nest, or lair in this case, many years beforehand), and like the two bandit brothers…hated the Fascists.

The woman insisted on washing and ironing Giovanni's clothes, which he recovered each morning, from a neat pile near his bed.

A good place for Giovanni for the time being, his head in full swirl for what he had done…and for what he had now become. This, he felt, was quite different from the other murder. This one deeply personal. Opening up to his vulnerabilities, he even allowed the couple to admonish him when on the second day he turned up very late for supper. He felt all at once contrite. They had waited and waited, refusing to eat themselves until their guest was safely back with them. They were right of course to be angry...used to having their meals at exactly the same time every day...and he made sure it didn't happen again. It was, after all, the only house rule they had laid down. It was obvious to them he needed time to himself and they chose not to ply him with questions. They had been very fond of Arcangelo...and this was his young brother.

To Giovanni, the husband and wife appeared weather beaten and probably old beyond their years. The loose leathery skin on their hands and faces, skin turned nut brown within its deeply grooved folds, testament to a tough life in the mountains. They were however as fit as fiddles. All down to fresh air and hard work of course. They got up early, were always busy, inside and outside of the house...and ate sensibly. Never between meals.

They ate everything they could grow, pick, conserve, transform and rear. The humble tomato, the basis of nearly every meal. Milk became cheese, 'ricotta' and 'provolone' in the main; pork turned into hams, sausage and salami. Hens and ducks provided them with all the eggs they could possibly need, and then, in the surrounding forest, there was the 'cacciaggione', game, of all sorts and especially wild boar, rabbit, baby (dove-like) pigeons, whose meat was more easily digestible than that of its older counterpart, and quail. Mushrooms, ideally picked in the damp early hours following a full moon, another free and local delicacy. So many varieties of wild herbs to forage...oregano, garlic, flat-leafed parsley, rosemary, celery, mint and bay leaf. Dessert, a simple sampling of the fruit each season would yield, and hazelnuts, roasted chestnuts, almonds all freshly picked. Cheese was always on the table, ever enhanced by the last dregs of the wine. Any surplus foods stored and conserved 'sott'olio' or in vinegar, in the cool darkness of the barn. Other produce, such as flour, grain or pulses, they would buy or barter for at the nearest market, their donkey always on hand to bear the burden.

They went without things they would have considered useless, a waste of time and energy; all capitalism's giddy glamour...fashion, travel, big screen entertainment...or the never-ending pursuit of impossible dreams, non-existent in their case. The glass or two of red wine, which they each drank of an evening alongside supper, definitely not a luxury...'il vino fa buon sangue', they would have retorted...wine makes for good blood! Therefore, health giving, so becoming another of life's necessities. Local, foot-trodden wine.

Few opportunities for social mixing or merrymaking. Funerals were now more likely to be the order of the day.

Each aspect of their existence linked to place, custom, religious feast days, soil and the seasons. Birthdays, rarely celebrated, only 'onomastici', their saints' days. People having lived this way for centuries. Such members of the older generation, who although uneducated in the formal sense, were all committed to the stone set advice they handed out, the wisdom they passed down. No room for self-doubt or hesitation. They had practical solutions for every situation. Often backed up by a proverb or maxim. A ready answer for every question that touched on farming and food, family and health. What else was there? God certainly, who had breathed life into them in the first place. Well, the priests took care of that sort of thing.

Giovanni now constantly reliving each stretched out moment that led up to the deed, as if in slow motion. The accompanying sounds and smells and then, the deed itself. No regrets of course. It just had to be so. In that manner and carried out by him, alone. Two murders to date and a new lifestyle, marked by a capacity to undertake shady deals, even usury and yet all draped with a silk-lined cloak of refinement. Both murders essential, of course, one to seal future success, the other to right a terrible wrong. What was he now? A survivor? A monster? An ancient mythical hero bravely following his destiny? A destiny, which was permitting him the freedom, at least for the present, to carve out for himself.

When previously, life had dealt such a rotten hand.

He knew he had to face these nightmarish thoughts and feelings, which were battering his brain (and possibly his soul), not blank them out. As painful as it was, he instinctively knew future sanity depended on it. He would deal with each thought and each feeling…and when they returned to haunt him, he would deal with them again and then again. He would use his ability to reason, to defend his watertight sense of right and wrong. He was also discovering something else about himself in all this horror. A positive thing, no doubt about it. That he had taken no pleasure at all in the act of killing. Moreover, an immediate revulsion for what he had done and witnessed. A step into unknown territory. It could have transpired that such an act might open up in him a concealed, primeval urge to repeat the performance. To enjoy the act. What did he now have to lose?

This was not the case…and it gave him some unexpected comfort.

Every so often, he forced himself to look down, once again, at those offending hands; they seemed larger than before, darker. First spreading them out on his lap and then lifting them slightly. Clean, firm, purposeful still, no sign of tremor, freed and innocent once again. Justice had washed away any spilled blood. He remembered studying scenes from Macbeth with Padre Floro, but knowing straightaway, that he was not like the Macbeths. They had murdered not only a king, but also a noble friend. It was for this, he concluded, that had caused their dual yet diverse descent into madness.

His own crime having rightly taken place, in order to avenge the wilful murder of his own loyal friend.

He turned them over to examine the more offending side, the palms. Hands, intended to guide, support, to comfort, cleanse, love and create. Hands he had used to destroy. Hands and eyes…an eye for an eye.

He did not envisage having to use them in such a way again.

Knowing exactly where the power had sprung from, to throttle his nemesis. From the pain of loss. How the pain had surged and stayed. How he had fed it and fanned it. How he (and only he) could have carried the deed through to the end. In real time, it had only taken about five minutes, but it had felt as though time had stopped completely. He had to be sure that the process was complete. It could have happened just after a minute or two…when the life force had finally extinguished itself from the body. Different each time, his brother Romano had said. Who would have known the precise moment? Giovanni had waited and waited. He had then, trance-like, spent an unknown amount of time staring blankly across at his handy work.

This process of a tough self-analysis was also permitting him the luxury of seeing, once again, that villa overlooking the sea…yes, the time was about right. By day and by night, the dream returned. He would tell Gennaro.

He spent these days of self-imposed freedom wandering…following tricky and tortuous mountain tracks, exploring the thickly wooded areas, stumbling across half-hidden streams, never encountering a fellow human being. Listening out for the sounds of the wild, sharply keen like never before, to witness the animal world around him. Crawling, clambering, scampering, whirring, blowing, sniffing, snuffling, rummaging nature. The magic of flora and fauna. The impact of the wind or rain. All this enabling him to face his demons, to restore his peace of mind, even reinvent himself, once again. Implausible, if he had continued as normal in the city. Not even with the panacea of the nightclub. That place existed to blot out world and personal pain…he knew, for certain, that it was not a cure.

He was of course planning return visits there. He had only just fallen under the spell of the voice and stage presence of a tiny female singer. Jole. Dark dress; dark hair geometrically cut. With what looked like emerald eyes. Tiny in stature, yet perfectly proportioned. Why her though? The club, like his new world, was full of beautiful women, women he knew he could so easily possess and then discard, if he cared to. So why had she left such an impression on him?

Still to present himself to her, and yet rock certain it was just a matter of fate picking the optimum moment.

Perhaps it is possible to feel destiny at work when you let it play out unaided. Like when you lie on your back on the surface of water, a pool, a lake, the sea. All you need do is stay blissfully afloat and watch the sky. Everything just appears to happen in and around you. Present tense. Being. Living and breathing in present time. Quite different from the power of hindsight, special though that is, when you finally make out the links in the chain laid out for you. Giovanni was living in the present now. As much as was possible. Once back in the city, he would return to the club and sit, watch, listen and wait…just like floating. Watch and wait. Follow Jole's movements, imbibe her silky voice.

Giovanni slept well in the mountains, heavy dream-crammed sleep. The villa, the sea and Jole. Clear, hard dreams, nothing fuzzy, which could throw him off course. He would return, cleansed and energised, to resume his city dealings. He remembered that just before the murder, Gennaro and Nunzia had announced they were expecting a second child (a life for another life, perhaps) such happy news for them, and it struck him that they would, in old age, merge into the married couple he was staying with now. Like them, they had inherited the wisdom from their own families that fresh air, wholesome food, and above all family, were at the root of any earthly happiness. They might be living with him in the city for now, but in their hearts, he could already read a future desire to return home. By then, much better off financially and with a deeper understanding of life's opportunities. The best of both worlds, perhaps.

This was their desire though, not his. His own family had not passed on those things to him.

Chapter 23
A Different Kind of Woman

Giovanni returned to his club several times before Jole was to perform there again. He discovered, she wasn't a permanent fixture, perhaps singing at a range of local or regional nightspots. He could easily have tracked her movements, sending Gennaro to find out about her. Yet this wasn't what he wanted. He wanted the pages of their future story to unfold naturally, refusing, as always, for her, or the club for that matter, ever to control him. Neither did he want his friend to know about her. Well, not yet! She wasn't like the others he habitually escorted, whose names he quickly forgot, whose attempts at conversation he found tedious. Jole shone out from the rest…he had already started to read her whenever her beautifully proportioned frame was dominating the stage.

Gennaro was likewise happy. With how things had turned out. How life, and theirs in particular, had its risks but now the worst was over. Relieved that murder was no longer the order of the day. Only the two killings then, both crucial, and now neatly folded away in the cupboard of the past. Never to be aired or exhumed. With no suspicion falling on Giovanni. None on himself. No criminal record and nothing, which could possibly pin their names and faces to the rapidly growing police file on Don Salvatore. Provided the two cantina 'witnesses' didn't speak; he had paid them generously for all they knew, himself divulging very little about the person who had sent him in the first place.

He would continue to keep them, as for the lawyers, under surveillance.

He then turned his thoughts to his dear Nunzia. How she was, of course, oblivious to their shady activities. How he and Giovanni now occupied a world created exclusively for men and by men, a parallel world, and one, which freed women to get on with the important task of running homes and raising families, the crucial stepping-stones towards civilisation. Both worlds important, both separate but also strangely interdependent.

Until that far off golden day, when life might become fair and equal for all.

Gennaro had loved her for as long as he could remember, each one made for the other, two interlocking pieces of the village jigsaw. He didn't really envy Giovanni's freedom to select women, at will, with their red lips, perfumed wrists and necks, their tapered nails, only to discard them as soon as he got bored. Yes, they were elegant and glamorous, and of course, he would have gone with any one of them himself, if the opportunity arose and if he thought he could have got away with it…not worth the risk though, just for a short-lived thrill, believing that his Nunziatella was worth so much more. Solid, loyal, a traditional wife and mother, and now proudly carrying another baby, their second child.

In truth, when he thought about it, Giovanni's women disgusted him.

With Giovanni away, he too had found himself taking stock of his present situation. The past few weeks being particularly fraught.

Such usually uncharacteristic thoughts were soon interrupted by the arrival of Alfonsino, as the little boy, choosing to run rather than walk, teetered and stumbled his way into the kitchen, all the while giggling and gurgling, followed by an out of breath Nunzia, who continued to utter pleas of 'Vieni qua, monello! Ma che devo fare con te?' Come here, you little rascal. What am I going to do with you? His son having learned to toddle at the tender age of ten months.

On seeing his son on this particular occasion, he caught an instant glimpse of how he must have appeared at a similar age. It cut like a knife. What if Alfonso discovered what he and Giovanni were up to and wanted to follow his father's path? An unthinkable prospect. He needed to come up with a plan. To keep his son as far away as possible from their activities. He had of course known this all along in a vague sense…and yet had it hadn't properly dawned on him until this moment. He suddenly didn't feel quite so self-assured, more than a touch uneasy in fact. It was crucial he begin to create an alternative route for him.

What he did know was that he didn't want to involve Giovanni in this process.

He also noticed that recently his wife was looking just a little out of salts, and on this occasion, her face sweaty, with her hair falling out of its bun, a splattered apron, not properly tied. She appeared pasty and tired. Well, it was of course due to the pregnancy…he had seen it take its toll on many of the village women. In just a few years, many appeared quite different from the carefree images of themselves displayed inside photo albums. Not so much a spurt in the ageing process, more of a piecemeal letting go of the dregs of their youth, of a girlhood they no longer felt. What did that matter now? Life had entered another stage. No looking back. Life only went forward. Motherhood, he'd heard the women mutter, was a gruelling business, on top of running the home and seeing to the needs of a husband. Attention to hair and clothes, to appearance in general, rapidly lost its urgency, but was rarely a deliberate choice to just give up. In spite of the physical wear and tear, vanity would still return on special days, such as for weddings, Baptisms and Holy Communions…the rare, brimming pleasure returning, once again, that pride in looking one's best. Each generation of young women, fast turning into their own prematurely ageing mothers before them.

He would speak to her, perhaps buy her something pretty to help delay the process…he couldn't help but compare her once radiant face with how it looked today…even though she was still young…and living in the city.

"You know, Gennari, I think we should start going to mass again. Poor Alfonsino still hasn't been baptised. Papa and Mamma are out of their minds. You did say. You can't use the excuse of this move to the city forever. I just don't get why it's such a problem."

Her frown stubbornly intact and a sense of frustration etched into the drooping corners of her mouth.

He let her have her say. He'd heard it all before, word for word. *Every so often, like all women,* he thought, *she just needed to unburden herself of mounting worries but the baptism situation clearly wasn't going to solve itself.* He wasn't against it. What he hadn't worked out yet was what he would say to Giovanni. There was probably an expectation that Giovanni would be the little boy's godfather, 'compare', in their language, it being a title which signified great responsibility. It meant, heaven forbid, that should the little boy lose his parents in an accident or some other set of tragic circumstances, it would be down to the godparent to see to all his future needs, perhaps even taking over the parental role.

To be fair Giovanni had never mentioned or even alluded to it; he never referred to religion and wasn't even a churchgoer now. Gennaro just didn't want a criminal career for Alfonso or for any future children, come to that. He'd willingly and knowingly jeopardised his own claim to sainthood…but there it ended. This was not going to characterise THEIR lives, determine THEIR futures. He needed to protect his children, especially sons, from all this, but wasn't sure Giovanni would understand. The best thing was probably to announce one day soon, quite nonchalantly, that he had asked his younger brother (who had recently married) and his new wife to fulfil the role of godparents…Giovanni would probably be relieved, or not care one way or the other.

Nunzia was right though, they as a family needed to resume mass attendance. Their souls now in a state of mortal sin, with Gennaro deeply feeling the need for absolution. Neither was it fair on their families; not fair on Alfonsino. There was also a new baby on the way. He would speak to Giovanni on his return. A good time…Giovanni clearly having many other things on his mind.

Songs of a love gone wrong, of betrayal and pain; songs, whose words exposed hypocrisy and exploitation; songs of war and injustice; of the impossible search for individual happiness…songs about men and women swimming against the tide. Themes, deep and dark, merging with the bluesy music, releasing a dreamy flutter of images into the mind's eye. Each club guest or member sensing, that these were sultry songs, radical songs, part and parcel, of a potentially risqué world they were choosing to inhabit.

Jole, by popular demand, once again, bringing the night to a close, with her own bluesy version of Bella Ciao, a song whose political impact and importance was still to spread to a much wider population. In the dark, aniseed sweet and smoky atmosphere, which hung low into the small hours of the morning, the audience would gradually join in…some by then, believing naively that they were singing goodnight to the enchanting woman in front of them, others with a more realistic grasp of its message. Her velvety voice singing back at them, 'bella, ciao, ciao, ciao' from the stage. The song would continue, each verse repeated countless times, in different styles, and at different speeds, no one wanting to leave, to slot back into the system of the world above.

The politically engaged, mindful of this song's simple potency, and of many of the other songs in her repertoire. Anything they could construe as anti-fascist was acceptable. Mussolini the common enemy.

Three hours beforehand, Iolanda had arrived at the club, alone, slipping through a back entrance just before her first song was due. It was just possible to make out a black dress, which seemed to cling to her, half hidden under a long trench coat. She was puffing on a cigarette. So difficult to give up the habit, though she was trying to reduce the number she smoked each day. Knowing instinctively that if she continued, smoking would one day kill her voice. This voice, God's gift to her, so they continued to remind her…a gift, which needed to be cherished and polished, daily. Nicotine, however, helped her relax before each nightly performance. Without it, the nerves never releasing their crab-like grip, in spite of the audience's growing adulation. Knowing, however, this could change at any moment. She dealt with it as best she could. On her own. It wasn't fame she was seeking in any case. Merely the ability to be in paid work for as long as possible, to express herself authentically and spread her gift for the pleasure of others, offering them too, a temporary escape route from the pain of living. She sang the songs, whose music and message she believed in. The songs, whose words she tried to live each day.

Singing enabled her to pay the bills. Work enabled her to live as an independent woman, in a society where this was next to impossible. This, she believed, ennobled her in a way no other lifestyle could.

Chapter 24
After Pasquale

Brigida was now safely back in the village with her family. If anyone had taken the trouble to notice, finding her just a little thinner than before, her gaze slightly more distant. In many ways, though, it was a case of slipping back into her previous role within the household, and as the weeks passed and merged, it came to feel as if she had never been away. She had even taking up crochet and embroidery of an evening, following in her mother's footsteps, following on from the year that never happened. Helping her mother in the house, supporting her younger brothers and sisters with homework or supervising their own farmyard duties. Paradoxically, she was also charged with the responsibility to keep an eagle eye on the sister closest to her in age, (if not in character), as Anna Maria had started 'seeing' a local boy from the neighbouring village. 'Seeing' meaning that he would visit the family most evenings for up to an hour or so, and often at the weekend, always trying to catch sight of Brigida's very nubile sister, and even snatching a few minutes in her company.

The older children, especially the girls, knew there could be no repetition of Brigida's behaviour and the turmoil that had followed in its wake. From their parents' perspective, ongoing vigilance and a fresh determination for the daughters to marry as quickly as possible would quash all irrational, carnal longings. Waiting just the necessary length of time. Doing things properly, in the right order. They no longer in a position to urge the younger ones to wait, in order to find a more suitable spouse, someone who might better live up to their (relatively speaking) once lofty expectations. Husbands for their daughters and to a lesser degree, wives for their sons. For the children to settle down, or as they expressed it...'sistemarsi'.

Such a pity their eldest daughter was still on life's lonely shelf, after all their efforts to restore her to a virginal state. Giovanni (Pasquale) had even paid someone who said he could stitch back the missing hymen. As a result, still no replacement husband, however, unearthed from any of the five villages. No one waiting in the wings, in spite of the fact their secret shame hadn't found a way of seeping out. It appeared to them later, that by temporarily removing their daughter from their part of the world, Brigida had lost her place in the queue of eligibility. With few visitors to the house (or village), each day wholly rooted in the family home…and the latest (relatively young) village widower having just proposed to the 'spinster' daughter of his next-door neighbour. Under the circumstances, he would have been a good catch, but the news had happened so quickly, they hadn't had time to make a move of their own.

No one in the family spoke of the events of the past year. Be it in front of Brigida or behind her back. Once again, their way of doing things. If they didn't talk about it, it never happened. All properly buried in the past, in settled earth.

Brigida had found a way, at least for the time being, of coping with the loss of her own daughter. Another silent subject. Poignantly believing she had been fortunate in all the support she had received…before and after.

Each afternoon, during siesta time, instead of falling asleep, she would dredge up first the face and then the rest of her baby girl, the tiny hands and tiny feet, the soft dimpled shoulders, as it skimmed the clear waters of recent memory. Almost certain that she could still make out bits of her own face in the little one staring back. Her own creation, her flesh and blood, remembering how it felt to give birth, cradle her in her arms, to rock her, to deliver up half-remembered lullabies, to feed her milk and love, milk and love…around the clock. With these images in place, she would then start to talk to her in a gentle whisper.

Never shedding any physical tears, not the family way.

She told Carmelina how much she loved her. How she would always be with her. How and why, she had chosen her name, what kind of future awaited her, how she, her natural mother, would look after her from afar, be her guardian angel…how she would think of her in a special way each year on her feast day, the day of Santa Maria del Monte Carmelo and imagine how her new family might celebrate it with her. She would almost certainly be much better off! She told her about her grandparents, her aunts and uncles and about life on the farm. About some of the little animals…the chicks, rabbits, ducklings, kids and piglets, she might have played with one day, had life turned out differently. Only time and place separated them. As if that were nothing at all. They could together overcome all this. Her mother's love flew to her directly, to fortify her. She felt the love pour out of her soul, like the milk that used to empty her breast during feeding. One day her daughter would know. She might somehow know already. One day perhaps return that love. Brigida would end each mental 'encounter' with one or other of the little prayers she had learnt and recited from childhood.

Sleep would then come upon her…she would be at peace until the need returned the following day…as her milk once did, in response to the next violent scream.

What she never did, however, was imagine that she might one day to go in search of Carmelina; to watch her from a nearby hidey-hole, to try to speak to her face to face, or even to snatch her back into her life. Not in her wildest of dreams. These were thoughts beyond Brigida's power of imagination, their absence perfectly in keeping with that village mentality, developed over hundreds, possibly thousands of years, which signalled a deep resignation to one's fate.

When alone in the shuttered room, she would speak in whispers to her little daughter and if Anna Maria or her younger sisters were to join her, the monologue would continue regardless, this time entirely inside her head, as she lay facing the dark blank wall.

She had long abandoned any thoughts or yearnings for Pasquale, her baby's father. That was how it was for men. She was over it…and over him. Without the need of science, Brigida had reached the conclusion that most men, including Pasquale, were surprisingly weak creatures, driven and ruled over by the all-encompassing urge to procreate. Leave bits of themselves behind. As many as possible, in fact. Once fulfilled, they could then walk away unscathed. They had performed their function. It all stopped there. Then move on to the next encounter. The chase and then victory, the hunt and then the kill. Sewing their seed. Biology. Women having to lay traps, through meals and seduction, to get them to stick around…the trap of marriage and children. It didn't always work though.

A woman's life was completely different. In their world, she knew she had overstepped the mark, the point of no return, and unlike Carmela's father, would continue to pay the price for her actions. Loss, pain, absence, injustice. Once driven only by her love for him. Was this also biology?

She felt no animosity towards him, now only dryness and emptiness. Resignation. He had at least returned to help find a solution for the baby he had fathered. For her sake, she had every reason to be grateful. Looking on from a slightly open door, Brigida had witnessed every twist and turn of that night's proceedings, every desperate shout, curse and sigh, had absorbed each weighted and weary word…displaying no desire to intervene. It was as though they were talking about somebody else. About someone else's predicament.

That was the night, she was almost certain, that she had felt her then still unknown baby give her first gentle flutter.

For Brigida, it was a sign that notwithstanding her own lack of autonomy, she had acted courageously. That night they finally agreed she could carry her baby for the forty weeks it needed, to give it life. She had stood firm. The only acceptable outcome.

The question as to whether she would go on to marry one day, have more children, rarely surfaced in her mind. Start again, as her parents anticipated. She couldn't bring herself to care. One way or the other. Neither did she feel that anything might change. Building a new future seemed irrelevant now, so exhausting…and for what purpose, to have yet another person impose their will upon her, telling her how to live, branding her with their own needs and expectations, checking that she wasn't straying from society's unbending rules. Creating another set of life's stormy chapters. Whether she realised it or not, she had lost all sense of time or of self, perhaps an involuntary defence mechanism against further suffering.

Three months or so, after Carmela's birth (if not much earlier), it became clear that something big had finally died within.

Nothing mattered while, in the semi-darkness of the room where she lay and rested of an afternoon, she could go on speaking out to her beloved little girl.

Chapter 25
For Sale, an Old Palazzo with Sea Views

"Buongiorno, Signor Sebastiani. I hope you found us without too much difficulty. Oh, that's good, very good. I only arrived ten minutes ago myself. Yes, yes, do come this way. I think it's best to begin the tour from the side entrance, over here on the left. Then we can gradually work our way to the top. Leaving the best until last, I believe. Did you happen to catch any of the view on the way up? Sublime isn't it, the little village clusters, the hills, the sea and there again on a day like today. At night, it's different again. I don't think I shall ever tire of it…even I manage to discover something new every time…look I think you know already that much of the place is in quite a state of disrepair. I must therefore ask you not to wander off. The worst bits we have cordoned off, or laid down planks for would be buyers, but there's no knowing what else there is that could be about to crumble or fall. So, keep an eye on what's going on above you as well. No accidents yet though, thank God."

Giovanni was quite happy to follow (mostly in silence) this proud, cultured yet amiable young man, who was so conscientiously showing him around. Alessandro Valli turned out to be a mine of information, as regards both the crumbling Palazzo, a kind of castle-like structure, and the various branches of the noble family who had resided there over generations. There was also, Giovanni detected, a lurking sadness about him, which he was doing his best to conceal. Something about the eyes, and in his tone of voice, which occasionally gave way to a deep sigh. He encouraged Giovanni to stop and ask questions whenever he felt the need. It turned out to be unnecessary though, as his 'guest' was absorbing, amongst the floaty grey sheets of ancient cobweb and ragged velvet drapes, far more in the way of information, than he would have been able to ask.

Giovanni acknowledged the fact that his guide was leaving quite an impression on him, a rarer event these days. He could learn from him too, from the mature poise and self-confidence he exuded; the detailed knowledge he possessed, well beyond the needs of the day. The way he dressed…the very choice of clothing, material, cut and style, which when put together expressed a classic image of understatement, relaxed good taste, someone at ease with himself. In other words, someone who had nothing to prove to the wider world…a man, who, albeit graciously, pleased himself.

Never forgetting that his inner story might have read quite differently…an outer shell of composure, concealing unknown pain and turmoil.

They must have been close in age, each walking with his head held high above well-shaped shoulders, as they made their way around the grand historic structure. With very different upbringings, the potential buyer presumed. Valli, Giovanni guessing, the product of parental love, wealth and privilege. His own pathetic childhood set on a starkly different route. Did this day mark them as equals? Well, the thought did occur to him, as he tried to suppress a wry smile…that he was now the one in a position to buy the neglected Palazzo…it seemed his knowledgeable guide was not!

Furthermore, that it was very likely Alessandro Valli had links, near or distant, with the very family, whose lives he was now chronicling. The image of Fortuna's wheel ever present on Giovanni's horizon.

Giovanni's search for a second home high above the city had started only a little while ago and had already consisted of inspecting a few newly built villas, some still incomplete. There was also the opportunity to buy up a portion of prized land and employ a team of architects and engineers to come up with the perfect design for a villa from scratch. Professionals whose plans would obviously take maximum advantage of the views reaching out towards the glittering turquoise sea.

Plans that would appeal to Giovanni's sense of rising self-importance.

It had only taken him a few moments, however, even before entering the Palazzo…to know that this was what he wanted to buy. Once parts were habitable, it would serve as a second home, a weekend or summer retreat, somewhere he could pursue solitary interests, reading, music, research, taking solitary walks…an escape from everything that had become part of his life in the city. Also, as a place where he could entertain a few carefully selected acquaintances, females in the main, and bask in their (anticipated) reaction to it.

He now wanted to find out even more about the aristocratic family in question, to discover how they had once achieved greatness…and what was even more crucial to him personally…how they had lost it.

Such a lengthy restoration would inevitably throw up myriad problems but even that appealed to his sense of adventure, of mission. The challenges to overcome…more than he could begin to calculate, the persistence and patience that would be necessary, the seeing such a project through from start to finish, in spite of all the obstacles. He didn't want a magic wand for instant transformation in any case. To pour money into a complete renovation, only to return on completion. He wanted to watch it slowly resurrect itself, bit by bit. He wanted to be there every step of the way, mentally and physically. Firstly, to fix the main areas of roof and the plumbing and drainage system. Next, see to all the resulting practicalities…then a room, a feature, or wing at a time. At least, the bare bones of the structure were in place. He decided there and then to keep all the signs of the family, who had had it built, wherever possible. Ripping nothing out that he could find a way to salvage…proud, idiosyncratic signs and symbols, which spoke of past grandeur.

He would be continuing their line…an ongoing act of reverence and gratitude, the Palazzo surely having chosen him and so no need for blood links, he concluded with further wry amusement. It was as though this once highborn family was in the process of adopting the orphan. They were entrusting him with the work they had not been able to complete or preserve, probably through idleness or the pursuit of pleasure. The type of family he had ached to be part of, when still a child, as he kicked stones around the messy yard, as he watched his motionless and horizontal mother from a safe distance.

It also unlocked once again, those painful memories of how he used to dream of his two absent brothers returning home as heroes, of their parading him around the village on their shoulders…a life touched just for an instant by victory, power, glory.

The child that still lurks within…returning to remind us who we really are and where we come from.

Adults? We are no more than overgrown children.

Chapter 26
That Simple Pleasure of Talking Deep into the Night

"And so, my hope is that, just occasionally, a word, a phrase, a feeling…linked to a bit of melody…gets really stuck, you know, like that bit of apple in Snow White's throat, and that it causes them to think, to begin to change, and for the better. In spite of the haze of alcohol. That could even be helpful…like a powerful dream we will suddenly one day remember. I also use my voice for this."

"It sounds like a mission you are on, bordering on the political…"

"Well, if I knew how to write a book, I'd probably do just that…if I knew how to deliver great speeches, the same thing. Singing is MY gift to the world. I've always known it. It's also a release. I'm trying so hard to save it…down to five cigarettes a day now…Life's pretty hard for most of us, especially women, you know…or maybe you don't…a daily battle…" the voice in question now reduced to a whisper.

"So, where's all this come from? Where are your family? Who cares for you?"

"Who cares for me?"

At this, she let out a short shriek of laughter.

"I look after myself, of course. I always have, even when my grandmother was still alive. In fact, I looked after her, especially towards the end. She was great, a formidable woman, 'una forza della natura', we all said. I live the way I do predominantly because of her. Well, I'm trying to carry it on…but she was so much more courageous…she could stand up to anyone, whereas I don't cope quite so well…yet…with confrontation…"

"So, you don't have any other family, no brothers or sisters?"

"Oh yes, dotted here and there. You see as I said, we come from a large family of performers, street theatre, circus type routines and so on. Going back generations. We've got some French blood too, somewhere along the line, apparently. Travelling around the country, staying for a season at a time and then moving on…again. Cities and provincial towns. It just worked out that I found work here and the time had come, I thought, for my grandmother to have a more settled lifestyle…"

"Aren't you ever afraid? Just how do you cope with people, well I mean men I suppose, those at the club, who might want to exploit you, a young woman, it must make you vulnerable, working at night…living alone?"

"Men like you; you mean?"

She laughing now through emerald eyes at her own quick and witty response, he remaining poker faced.

"I think there's a lot of guesswork going on in your head. It's not that bad and I never said I live alone or that I am afraid…I merely meant that life is a constant battle. As it is for everyone (at that point looking back up at him, before adding), well nearly everyone. I'm fortunate now in that I know what I'm prepared to put up with and where I must draw the line. How to deal with awkward situations even before they arise. I work to earn my own money…"

"No one keeps me or has power over me. I manage…just…to pay all my bills each week and month. Even the dresses, shoes, my hair…not luxuries, just part of the image and magic, my manager calls it, I'm expected to emanate. My grandmother, Rosalia, was her name, used to make some of my gowns, but I like to go for a less fussy look these days…to show how serious I am about the songs I sing. Even the more light-hearted ones. I will continue for as long as I can…while I still have a voice, a voice, which allows me to sing the songs that I and a certain kind of people want to hear, and the songs I find important…while I am still fit and healthy…after that, who knows?"

"And have you never fallen by the wayside? You sound like you've got life all tied up, with all the religious resolve of a nun, in fact…in spite of the obstacles."

At that, she let out a second rare laugh…a refreshing sight and sound, piercing a very pleasurable, yet otherwise intense night's proceedings.

"Well, of course I have made mistakes, made wrong choices, even found myself in some very sticky situations over the years…that is how I have learned. I mean I've never made the same mistake twice, just new ones. That's how I've come to understand the world. Always backed up my Nonna Rosalia's wise words and stories."

At this comment, Giovanni's own thoughts flashed briefly back to Nonno Giulillo and all that he had done to create (and safeguard) a viable future for his grandson. His focus then quickly returning to the lovely and unusual creature by his side. Her words she had powerfully delivered but he just couldn't accept that she looked after herself so closely…like now in fact, how would she be able to defend herself against him? Alone together in these early hours of the morning, as they spilled into a brand-new day. Far from other people. Amid a still, cloaking darkness.

Perhaps Iolanda believing, instinctively, that she was safe in his company.

Her speaking voice was quite different from the one she used for singing, Giovanni decided. He had tried to gage her accent, wanting to pinpoint a town, province or even a region but of course, this turned out to be a futile task, she having travelled around since babyhood, continuously rubbing shoulders with people from a mix of places, other countries, even other races. Like him, but even more so, she belonged nowhere and to no one; no geographical roots to hold her firm or call her back. Was solitude, or even loneliness, the price she also had to pay then for clinging on freedom, or at least her notion of it? He couldn't make too many assumptions. He was merely on the receiving end of information she had seemed all too happy to impart. It could have been a well-rehearsed act or smoke screen. A theatrical yarn she spun out with each new encounter. Yet to his well-honed ears and eyes, it all smacked of authenticity. He needed it to be authentic.

Far too soon, to capture or assimilate the whole story…and we never really uncover all of that, not even our own.

He looked down at her from their seated position on the wall, as she stared out into blind marine blackness, and wished he had a blanket or something similar to wrap around her defiantly exposed young shoulders. Even though she had tried to convince him that she was much less vulnerable than she looked.

At the click of his fingers, he could have helped her, even temporarily, erase her continued financial struggles…it would have meant a very small sacrifice on his part. So much to gain…and enjoy. He was about to open his mouth to offer something smaller in the way of support but the words just wouldn't form and silence prevailed. 'Buying' her, in whatever kind of deal, he knew, would have reduced her to the level of the others, would have made her no more than his latest plaything. She probably wouldn't even have accepted. He didn't know why but he just didn't want it or need it. Not even the thrill of the chase had its usual appeal this time…this was all about present tense.

They took up their walk along the 'lungomare'.

Giovanni and Iolanda had been chatting together in this way for well over two hours, having earlier shared about half a bottle of wine, with neither conscious of the passing time. She having learned far less about him than he about her. This didn't seem to matter much. She had been initially surprised, however, that he hadn't turned up with a lavish bouquet of flowers, the inevitable bottle of champagne, two tickets for the theatre. She usually saw them coming and knew what it all meant. Giovanni arrived empty handed, without the gifts or the sleazy charm. Didn't seem to be playing the usual game. She couldn't be sure though. Had he just changed the rules around, to catch her off guard? She found herself quite curious to see where this would all lead. He appeared genuinely interested in her life…her ideas. She already felt at home in his company. She liked him from the beginning.

It was only about three months ago, when Iolanda had begun to recognise him at the club, to pick out his face among a small sea of mainly male faces. She didn't know his name and would never have asked. Sometimes on his own and sometimes in the company of a female (or two), women which she thought were different every time, but couldn't be certain. He occupying the same alcove, which housed a couple of claret-coloured sofas and 'old gold' fringed satin cushions. Her eyes eventually anticipating his presence there. She was struck by the fact that he never joined in with the customary singing at the end of her performance…he would merely sit back, watch and listen to all that was going on around him. A seemingly elegant and cultured young man. For some bizarre reason, she was grateful that he never appeared ruffled or affected by drink, always leaving the club with his head held high, regardless of the time of night or his chosen company. She felt happy when he was there, uplifted…then there were the gaps and she could never work out a pattern of attendance. Perhaps, less happy whenever there was a woman in tow. This was merely how she felt at that moment, unconscious of implications; no thoughts analysed or even processed…no future dreams for the two of them in the making.

She then happened to bump into him one evening on the steps, which led out onto an annoyingly unexpected wet pavement, he asking her if she would like to go for a quick coffee…to which she found herself saying yes. The tiny bar in question, Bar Gaeta, was only a few metres away, opening up at an unearthly hour to catch the odd nightclub member or two, hoping to sober up, before making their way home. It was a slightly awkward meeting, she being tired, feeling a little out of salts. It did give Giovanni, however, the opportunity to see, for the first time, her face in close-up. Her eyes were definitely emerald in colour, as he had expected, big soulful eyes, beautiful in spite of the obvious fatigue, which came with each performance and in an atmosphere of thick smoke. Hooded, eyes with shadows underneath. Eyes, which spoke of late hours and a solitary lifestyle, having to give so much of herself during each performance. The club. Her nocturnal habitat.

It all took probably less than ten minutes but she hurriedly agreed to meet up again soon, maybe go for a walk around the public gardens.

With each fresh encounter and there had by now been about five…they both learned a little more about the other; in the case of Iolanda, this involved detailed accounts of past places or experiences, many of which he found quite comical, beguiling and sometimes bordering on the bizarre. Whereas Giovanni was unsurprisingly more reticent about revealing much from his own acorn store of memories. She decided not to pry however, even enjoying the slow process of uncovering his thoughts and character traits from the little he was prepared to divulge…especially from his silences and seemingly no-go areas. It didn't take her long to realise that his life wasn't quite as straightforward as she had first surmised. Far from it. She detected a brooding quality, in stark contrast with his outward trappings of ease and early success. Neither had any idea where this unusual relationship, a kind of unlikely friendship, was heading. They were living in the present moment, for as much as anyone is able…each so different and yet each struck by a deep desire to work out, absorb, to understand the other.

Equals.

Giovanni continuing to see the other women, who also furnished his other spaces.

Chapter 27
The Winds of Change

At around this time, it appeared that the Kingdom of Italy was fast becoming a Totalitarian state, an all-embracing one-party reality…headed by a paltry and self-acclaimed Fascist god, who by casting wide his net, took possession of millions of lives and minds. Never quite reaching, however, the predominantly silent few, those of independent means or independent thought…those simply paying him lip service. Against a backdrop of raging propaganda. Individualism stamped on and stamped out by sturdy black boots…nearly everyone serving (or appearing to serve) that amorphous and intangible entity, the State. Inward but at the same time outward looking, Il Duce's desire to recreate a second Roman Empire around the Mediterranean. Foreign expansion. Following the example of other key European nations. Power over other peoples, not just his own, getting a foothold and then stranglehold in new places, especially within the vast continent of Africa.

In a war that was about to erupt all over the planet, an even more evil replay than the last, it was inevitable, nonetheless, that there would be those who would come to benefit.

However, for the great majority, it would leave ongoing physical and mental scars, with so many people losing everything or nearly all they once knew or owned. Worst of all, there would be the millions who would lose their lives. Once again, and just over twenty years since the last time, the wiping out of a vast cohort of young men. Families suffering the empty pain of lasting separation. Towns and cities undergoing full or partial destruction, homes reduced to rubble. In the main very young soldiers, carrying out orders passed down from much older, 'wiser' men in high places. The bitter fruits of war, those comfortably ensconced political leaders playing their manic games of chess with millions of human pieces. Unbridled lust for power and expansion, and in Italy, veiled by the showy success of the trains, now apparently arriving and departing on time. Was this yet another myth?

The romance-packed image of a new unfolding epoch…golden lies fed wholesale down the throats of the hungry masses.

People sorted and graded; so useful when the state needed scapegoats. Divide and rule. The human finger pointing so easily at 'the other' in times of despair and ruin. Dire consequences for those who clung on to the notion of individual freedom, or those who now led double lives, only to risk public humiliation, torture, death. Signs of dehumanisation at every turn. In such circumstances, who can criticise the vast majority who merely follow the ants' blind flow? We are programmed to cling on to our lives, no matter how shabby, even when the hero inside is crying out in protest. When the gift of life appears far from noble or sacred.

We have survived thus far and so go on clinging…because we might still…find ourselves, one day, on the radar of Fortuna's golden smile.

In the months leading up to war, change at the club was likewise underway, albeit slow at first. Fascism now also beginning to trickle down into the quiet cracks of hitherto hidden places. In particular, those nocturnal spaces, where people went to enjoy a few hours' respite from the pressures of the over ground, away from curious ears, peeled eyes and vicious tongues. Where the small club owners made a healthy living, as they continued to supply their clientele with everything they craved.

In such a political climate, venues like this were considered hotbeds of anarchy; places for the nurturing of liberal ideas. Tainted minds massaged by sex and alcohol and even worse, by American style jazz. Enemies of the state, a state, which would sift them out, by the gathering of tangible evidence (found or fabricated). Vile amoral types, creatives mostly or intellectuals, who by leading debauched lives, corrupted the state's pure heart. The subhuman; experimental artists, drug users, aspiring and practising homosexuals, the occasional transvestite, foreigners…those, who wouldn't allow themselves to worship at the feet of an unhinged demagogue. No place for them in the vision of a new Empire. 'Il Duce' sending out bands of his own young men, all baying for blood and retribution. Such behaviour was, of course, acceptable; his recruits upholding sound socialist principles, fighting to support the state, not undermine it.

It meant that performers like Jole and her jazz musicians had to change their repertoire. Fast. Songs vetted for ideas that might not fit the current model of

Fascist thinking. Lyrics and tunes becoming blander. Miserable compromises. At first, these changes would spring into force only if the 'camice nere' (Blackshirts) were present but then there were his spies in civvies also beginning to gain membership. It spelled an abrupt end of avant-garde music. The end of songs whose words, motifs and refrains courted protest and revolution. Iolanda hated the changes and hated the 'Squadristi'. Their thuggish lack of courtesy, their lack of artistic appreciation, their narrow mindedness, their open-mouthed leering. Eying her up and down, ever suspicious. All men together, in uniform, manifesting their basest traits. The way they arrogantly installed themselves at the bar. The way they lounged back on the sofas, arms folded contemptuously behind their heads, legs splayed menacingly apart, as though they were now the new impresarios. Appearing to share a constant flow of infantile and bawdy jokes about her and the members of the band.

A different and unwelcome clientele.

She had of course already encountered her fair share of drunks and libertines. All part of the necessary world she occupied, but with the owner-manager now firmly on side, she had grown more capable (and more confident) in how to deal with such tricky situations, she felt protected…he quietly but firmly informing such customers that Jole, his prized performer and their singer, was not up for grabs, of any kind.

The presence of the Blackshirts inevitably reminded her of those early humiliations, club owner after club owner thinking it quite normal to rub his body against her whenever she found herself alone and vulnerable, on the stairs, in a side office, after hours. The grabbing and grasping hands, the sweaty brow. The whispery crude and uninvited jokes, the vulgar comments. The glassy eyes and set, wet smile, with its decayed, uneven teeth. The approaching footsteps in the kitchen, in her pre-singing days, where and when she merely washed the dishes. The stale garlicky breath covering the back of her neck. The auditions, nearly all with strings attached. The oily promises…and partially masked warnings. Then returning to her grandmother, reassuring her every time that all was well.

She had thought all this belonged to the distant past.

One day…seemingly a long time ago now…she had somehow dredged up the courage to tell her present club manager, that he should be ashamed of himself and his wandering hands, in that he was father to a daughter about the same age. To her surprise, this sudden and unexpected outburst had had an immediate effect on him…just as though she had poured a jug of iced water over his head. Her words had loomed large, now lodged uncomfortably, in his brain or little used conscience. An inner alarm bell had sounded. Her outrage having taken him aback, his face drained of all colour, and as a result, he stopped immediately. Had he never recognised the link for himself…that someone could be treating his own precious daughter in a similar way? Was it that unthinkable? Not Iolanda's fault she was alone in the world. Not her fault at all…he acknowledging deep down that she had never led him on, that she never knowingly exploited her physical 'charms'.

For whatever the reason, simple or complex, she had clearly stopped one man in his tracks…it marking the start of a new professional relationship between them, born out of a new respect. She had never considered him a bad man in any case. She also knew however that she could only get away with such a protest because he needed her to sing. Her only worth, her only form of power. The club needed her. She was now in demand. It had taken time to get to this point, requiring a good deal of patience and self-sacrifice. A never letting go of hope. Together with all the hard work. He was even in the process of getting her to perform there four nights a week.

Something she had little grasp of however (which in turn made the trait even more attractive)…was that she possessed a rare quality, which enabled her to reach out to young and old, male and female. An easy quality, which engaged and fascinated those in her company, whether on stage or while going about her business. Even the worldly wise and cynical Giovanni had found her captivating, mesmerising. Was she brittle and heartless or warm and passionate? Was she happy or sad? She was of course all of those, and when necessary, everything in between. Difficult to read or pin down. Perhaps this is why the Blackshirts hadn't taken kindly to her…a shady nightclub singer, no doubt a slut, but one who at the same time, made them feel just a little uneasy about themselves.

They desired her and detested her in waves.

Her mind also sometimes wandered back over the love affairs she had enjoyed. Mainly with fellow musicians, one or two very intense relationships. Authentic, equal. Nothing lengthy or permanent of course. Easy come, easy go. No rules, promises or ultimatums. Each spanning its natural course. Sometimes interrupted by a move, and sometimes just a melancholy but quiet falling out of love.

Of course, she knew that not all the men wearing those infamous black shirts were the same, but it was hard to think of them individually, when they appeared together in their tight groups, all looking identical, entering the club often with that (as she thought) ridiculous black fez fixed to their heads. In groups of about four or five, they usually came for an hour or two once or twice a week, but never on set days, so that it became necessary for those who frequented the club to be ever on guard. Jole continued to perform but it was obvious there were some clients beginning to feel the need to stay away or turn up less often. Conversely, a few of the regulars expressed a firm desire to go on as usual, as that in itself signified an act of defiance. To stay away spelling a further surrender to the state, another defeat in the ongoing and undeclared psychological battle.

There was talk of numerous beatings and worse. Especially upon those with links to such clubs and meeting places. People disappearing, leaving no further trace of whereabouts. Others too afraid to ask questions about them, fearing they might be next on the list…or members of their own families.

Giovanni too was now spending less time at the club. His business dealings, in particular, keeping him greatly occupied. Often working late into the night. He also broke links with its more conspicuous members, never wanting to draw unnecessary attention to himself.

He continued to see Iolanda, however, sometimes going to pick her up in the early hours, or spending time with her during the day. Neither could stay too long from the other. A passion that burned by day and by night. A passion of bodies, but also of a shared and silent universal vision. He took her to see his Palazzo, to the surrounding woods and hills, to hidden coves and forgotten beaches. She took him to see some of the places where her family had performed in the past, or to other haunts where she had once sung out her life, where they shared intimate meals in tiny family-run trattorias. It seemed as though everything they had ever experienced led precisely to these shared moments. Together they wandered through tranquil cemeteries, visited baroque churches and the ancient sites; they spoke to ragged children playing in the streets and squares…until the moment came…when like watching…at the end of the day…the few remaining children run off into the distance…Iolanda also vanished.

Neither of the two having spoken of marriage, but both knowing, in that secret place, that even their relationship would, one day, fizzle out or end abruptly. Domesticity not part of either's world…Giovanni with his dream of wealth and power, Iolanda with her need for freedom and authenticity. No one, not even Giovanni (had he so wanted) could wield any power over her. It was love that bound them, nothing else. A love which, for the present, tied them body and soul. A love that had allowed them a more than just a glimpse of heaven.

Chapter 28
Looking for Iolanda and Beyond

Gennaro had, over time, come to know about Giovanni's relationship with Iolanda and had found himself left with mixed feelings about it. On the one hand, he was secretly amused that his 'boss' had turned out to be human after all, even though that big word 'love' had never been voiced. Instead, all the signs were in place; muffled and awkward conversations, poor appetite, weak excuses to his friend, "I'm just popping out for a few minutes" and so on.

On the other, this unexpected state of affairs had left Gennaro feeling a new and strangely raw vulnerability.

It had long been a blessing, perhaps one he had stupidly taken for granted, that Giovanni appeared…even from their first proper encounter…so invincible, so unlike and beyond everyone else. Never a person ruled by sentimentality. The stronger Giovanni was, the stronger he felt about himself. Giving him a genuine sense of lasting security. As two grown males, they were as close as their culture and background allowed, and so he had therefore assumed his own position (and that of his growing family) would always be rock solid, even in a world about to fragment into another great war.

He didn't approve of women like Iolanda because he didn't understand them. A solo female singer? Hardly a respectable way to earn a living and where was her family? How could they allow it? Then there were her open and easy ways, her friendliness, her performing in clubs…frequented predominantly by men…late into the night. The fact that she…a woman…held (according to him at least) dangerous political views… There again, he had to admit, that she was always very charming and courteous to him and his family, and especially whenever taking time to play with Alfonsino.

She liked to sing the boy a range of little 'filastrocche' with accompanying gestures. She would often change some of the key words to trick him, when he tried to join in with her, which made him laugh and laugh in happy frustration. When taking the toddler to bed, she would tickle him on the way, each time she caught up with him, until he could no longer speak and then once under the covers, tell him a fantastical story, which always drew him in and made him sleepy. Nearly every time, on arriving at their home, she would place into his chubby hands a surprise gift; something like a big juicy peach or a brightly coloured puppet from her own family collection.

Nunzia had also tried to despise her and what she stood for…but it was impossible. Iolanda had in effect won them all over within two or three unforgettable visits.

Then suddenly she was no more. No gifts, no smile, no big emerald eyes! What in God's name could have happened? The Blackshirts? Not very likely, even given the current circumstances… Gennaro had nevertheless made immediate and undercover enquiries, as to their recent activities. No tangible motive or connection surfaced.

She needed to sing. She needed to work to pay the rent. She had only allowed Giovanni to foot the bill, on those few occasions when they had gone out to eat. Only once and because it was her birthday, had she accepted a bottle of perfume from him, Joy by Jean Patou…drops of which she spread, each day from then on, across her neck and wrists.

Giovanni also racked his brain, revisiting their more recent conversations, always in search of missed or deliberate clues. None of it made sense. Why hadn't she just told him she needed to go away? Yes, he would have been heartbroken…but like this, it was tearing at his soul. Had there been a new sadness around the eyes, which had escaped him? Had she spoken in code? Was it something he had said or done that had caused her to flee?

Was it to do with the war?

The image of the dark green dress, which she had worn at their last meeting, refused to leave his mind's eye. Ludicrously, he focussed his thoughts on all the gifts he would have wanted to bestow upon her. If only she had accepted the diamond and emerald earrings…to match that dress and those eyes! He was beside himself. Never having hurt this much, a pain far more acute than the never-ending dull ache of a tragic childhood. He tried with little success, to nurse, by himself, this new and open wound. He spoke to Gennaro in a way his friend had not thought possible…of the extraordinary emotions he felt. Of what she had meant to him. It just poured out one evening…just that one evening…over a strong, ever supporting shoulder and a few too many glasses of his favourite 'grappa invecchiata'.

In the days that followed, there appeared no recovered body…no named or nameless young woman dragged out of the river or washed up on a nearby beach.

It was once again, thanks to the presence of Giovanni's ever loyal friend and no doubt to that long, mawkish outpouring, that they were able to slam shut their file on her soon after. Her disappearance having consumed them both for over three weeks. A lifetime. Having exhausted all attempts at tracking down known Fascist squad members and their sympathisers, they had done the rounds of the regional clubs and halls, made contact with people that they thought might know her, all trails which incidentally led them up blind alleys…nothing!

They came, therefore, jointly, to an abrupt and logical conclusion. That since she had always been in possession of an untamed and openly free spirit, Iolanda had merely decided that the time was right to move on. Perhaps to answer the call of a past nomadic existence. How she would have wanted to handle it. No lingering, no pleas for second chances or shabby confrontations, no staggering on towards an inevitable break up. No pathetic, semi-muttered, empty excuses. No hankering after what might have been…a big no to domesticity.

Giovanni then moved on too. He willed himself, as quickly as clicking his fingers, into a new place. He had done it before, a good few years ago, when Floro had walked out of his life. No looking back. No more self-recriminations. No more pain. He had instead learned a powerful lesson, one no one could have taught him, one he couldn't have taught himself; he had lived it, lived in the present moment, in nearly each and every moment since knowing her…and now made the promise never to find himself in that position again. In any case, he had done it. So why want to repeat it? Another item to tick off, on the rapidly filling page of accumulated experiences.

It turned out to be a good feeling, a strong feeling…surprisingly boosted by the fact that he had no wife, no children and no parents with the power to bend his behaviour or compromise his ongoing ambitions. He was in effect just as free a spirit as Iolanda, no, much freer because, unlike her, he snickered to himself…he had lots and lots of money.

From then on, Giovanni and Gennaro entered a new industrious phase, both working indefatigably…to boost and further develop the moneylending business, the antiques and artworks sales, the making of new and important contacts. Files growing ever fatter with information about key places and key individuals...money therefore continuing to pour into their numerous and ample pockets. Making wise and forward-thinking decisions in the oncoming shadow of war.

Gennaro, even more so than before, took a renewed pride in his growing young family, which allowed him an escape from the pressures of work...a busy and yet perfectly healthy balance. Alfonso was finally baptised, Giovanni unasked and never expecting to become his godfather, something now outside of his world or thinking. So, no problems there. There was also that heady scent of anticipation for the arrival of their new baby. Not long to wait now. A heavily pregnant Nunzia having got her way at last, she, Gennaro and Alfonsino attending Sunday mass at the local church, presenting the comforting image of traditional family life, each week the Holy Family recreated. Kitted out in their best clothes. Nunzia making more of her appearance, if only on the so-called day of rest (especially as regards her hair) all of which was beginning to pay off.

He realised more and more that whereas he would always work with and for Giovanni...their lives even more inextricably linked...he didn't want the same things. Although both business-minded, he planned to invest his well-earned money in land; land in his village; on which he would build an impressive country style villa, with surrounding orchards. To spend more time, when possible, with the people they had always known. Their people. To bask from then on in the sun of their admiration and the new family he and Nunzia were creating.

Having already saved a substantial amount for this very purpose, as well as looking after his parents, financially.

As for Giovanni, work on the ancient Palazzo was underway, with him playing an active role at every stage of its restoration. Progress always annoyingly slow due partly to bureaucracy and partly in the search for those with the necessary expertise. He even spending the occasional Sunday there...alone...still drawing energy from its ruins, its faded, cracked and timeless elegance, still getting excited about his future plans for it. He had in effect become king of the castle. All that he had ever wanted. He had more than achieved his own 'villa on the hill'. Fully accepting Fortuna's rare and generous gift... a gift never to be forgotten or underestimated. He had invested, heavily, in time and patience, education and training, he had put his God given intelligence to good use. While always endeavouring to keep his dealings within the law, in order not to arouse unnecessary suspicion. The two murders having of course been necessary. He now had money, power, but also the desired degree of anonymity. He was young and healthy enough to go on enjoying this bounty for many years to come.

Unlike Gennaro, to bask in his own self-created glory.

From the Palazzo's ancient roof tiles, he looked across and down upon what was now his universe…an azure sky, the gently sloping terraces with their patterned vineyards. The citrus trees, dotted here and there, showing off their gaudy orange and yellow wares; fruit which dangled from densely packed, leafy branches, nature's gifts to a now neglectful clientele. The meandering ribbon of mountain road, which, playfully and continuously, reappeared in sudden snatches only to disappear again. Then the vast sparkling sea itself…he felt a rush of warm blood pass through his head and upper body; and he knew that it was good.

All was about to change, however, once again. Not only in the wake of Iolanda's disappearance but also with the arrival of impending war.

Part Two

Chapter 29
Floating in Darkness

The room that enveloped him, if it was a room, was so dark that it was impossible to make out its contours…no edges, corners or angles upon which to fix his eyes. He was definitely lying down. That was clear enough, but it almost felt as though he could have been floating in space. A few centimetres above ground or up where the birds fly. He wondered…no birds however or planes screeching across the sky of his impaired vision now. So perhaps much higher still, merely suspended or caught up somewhere amongst the tangle of gravitational fields. Between Earth and the other planets, between Sun and moon. Impossible to know whether he was alone or for how long it had been like this…no whites of eyes staring across at him out of the darkness, no moving lips or flash of teeth, or pale hand stretched out towards him. Maybe he was dead and this is what happened afterwards, the waiting room. Life and death, was there really such a marked difference between the two?

Such deep, dark and stretched thoughts tired him quickly.

The young man had therefore lost touch with all sense of space, time and reality. Had he been like this for years, months or a mere matter of hours? He didn't know the answer. He wasn't even sure who he was…where he was from or what had led to this. So, tantalising the sensation, that just as it appeared he was on the point of recalling his circumstances…some tiny memory flash just skimming into view, its crucial spark extinguished upon arrival, his truth, once again snatched cruelly away, together with any once familiar images.

He believed that if he moved, it would hurt, overwhelmingly. His instincts told him to lie still at all times, to prevent further damage. Even if he were able, he decided that he didn't want to reach out and touch body parts, in case they were no longer there. Did he even need them now? While floating. Such strange thoughts. It was probable however, that he could no longer move anything, and that he was somehow all strapped or bound together…like a bundle of sticks or pieces of model aircraft that still needed gluing together. He was certain of one thing though. The lingeringly addictive smell of wood smoke, always there, sometimes more pungent and sometimes less so. Always there. He liked it. Its presence was helping to hold him (or at least his brain) together, in addition to any magic glue.

Mostly it was silent in the room. He still couldn't quite work out the dividing line between sounds stored in a dream-filled head and those on the outside of his being, that found their way into the room. External sounds were the ones that woke him up. He was convinced of that. Of the impression that he slept and dreamed, slept and dreamed most of the time. Probably good for some kind of recovery, if that's the road he was on, if he wasn't dead after all. With the passing of time, still no memory at all, of the circumstances that had brought him here, only void and blackness. He really did want to know, though, and from now on set his brain the ambitious task of trying to distinguish what was real from that which he imagined. Easier said than done. The closest he got was the perception of a scraping stool…surely that wasn't coming from within his head…and perhaps some distant whispery voices. Someone was definitely helping him. Why did he or she, or they for that matter, only make an appearance when he was drowning in a deep sleep?

Yet it could all have been the sound of the wind whistling through the trees.

It wasn't only the distant or more recent past that was causing him difficulties but he was afraid that he was retaining no present time either. Accumulating void upon void of missing facts, connections and experiences. A lot to carry on his now surely frail shoulders.

After a while, other bigger sounds arrived, frightening sounds, real or imagined, but which by now, didn't matter quite so much. He was entering a new and terrifying phase. No more of the pleasant, quiet floating…instead now besieged by shuddery noises, which reverberated in his head, resembling the inhuman sounds of the battlefield, both isolated explosions and continuous blasting, some of it very close by. Others more distant and yet terrifying all the same. The persistent jerky, vibrating throb of machine gun fire, the intermittent and distorted screams of desperation…undeniable words coming into earshot, in the form of curses and bits of remembered prayer, rising awfully, out of the chaos. Sounds bombarding and piercing his eardrums. Followed suddenly by a merciful yet equally ringing silence. The constant fear and worry a new set of blasts would soon be returning…like the fears of a woman in the later stages of labour, as she anticipates the horror of the next contraction, always longer, stronger than the last. More painful…impossible to ride out or navigate. The short silent bits in between full of anticipated anguish.

What he couldn't have known, was that there was a solid band of volunteers, from the 'other side' all working to keep him alive. To support and comfort him during his nightmares. To hold his trembling hands. To wipe his forehead. From the children, who on finding him, had run like the wind to contact the only locally known 'doctor'…to the women who took it in turns to sit in the shadows, and report (at changeover) on his latest condition…the sighs, grunts, screams and ranting he emitted when asleep…or if he was still showing signs of fever.

They also tried to feed him milk, coarse bread dipped in soup, or pureed vegetables, when he seemed to be in a state of near-consciousness, some of which he even managed to swallow without choking. He retained no knowledge of their labours, never raising his eyes in gratitude nor communicating in any other way. Locked away inside himself but still they made no judgement upon him. An older woman with presumed nursing skills had taken it upon herself to wash him, as best she could, and she rediscovered the forgotten maternal pleasure in the slow passing of a wooden comb through the beautiful waves of his (no longer matted and lice-ridden) hair, while her husband kept his rapidly emerging beard decently trimmed. A nod to civilisation. As politicians and soldiers were fast tearing the world apart.

The stranger's name they had made out on a couple of tattered documents that had fallen out of a jacket pocket. Amongst other words that meant nothing to them. A foreigner, not one of them, even though if they had thought about it, they shared the same very dark hair and very dark eyes, the olive-toned skin and longish faces, all classic southern European features.

There again, such a young man, no doubt once healthy and strong, whose life must have held much promise, had he not been caught up in war. A young man, whose family would be missing him, praying for his safe return. They detected something noble and refined about him, even though there was little to go on, as he lay there helpless among them. Something they had all sensed.

However, it had been easy to guess what he had been doing there…in such a uniform, which also caused their blood to freeze. Confirmation as to why he had come to be on their land. Not quite so simple therefore to comprehend their own efforts, the personal sacrifices they were making on his behalf, as if life wasn't arduous enough. All manner of danger lurking everywhere, and now food shortages and the other problems winter delivered, with or without war. Their sons and brothers fighting on the frontline, with little hope of messages arriving back to reassure family that they were safe. A vast and cruel waiting game…a game that could change for better or for worse, from one minute to the next. Quite simply down to luck in nearly every case.

This man, whom they were helping to restore to full health, was therefore a stranger, part of an alien army, carrying out ongoing acts of aggression. Some children had chanced upon him…cold, hungry, delirious and battle weary. As people, they had followed the example of the biblical woman from Samaria. Perhaps in all of us lies the deep-rooted urge to rescue a stranger, a fellow human, in spite of our own fears, something that almost defies reason. A mere thought, flashing through their heads, that if it had been their brother, their son or grandson, there could be someone on the other side likewise willing to care for him, in similar circumstances.

On the other hand, was it just something about this one that had touched their communal heart and stoked their imagination?

A couple of the village girls came each morning, always together, always cloaked in black, to say prayers for his recovery in the darkened room. Young and nubile, with beautiful hands and skin. They whispered comments about him, far from the ears of the adults. Through him they were able to create their own little world, within a world…slightly more removed from prying eyes or vicious tongues. Although, just like the others, they wanted him to make a full recovery, they didn't relish the idea of going back to their old way of life, that is, before he had made his appearance among them. While he lay there, practically motionless, he was of no danger to them at all. The girls continued to enjoy these strange new freedoms.

The weeks staggered by and the young man's memory did begin to come back, if only in fits and bursts. He was also physically on the mend and starting to eat a little more.

Something he now relished (as well as the next meal, no matter how basic), was the wondrous arrival of a matronly bosom, property of a woman who regularly came to care for him. Two breasts, solidly packed, upholstered, bolstered, and then tightly clamped together, forming in effect, one colossal entity. Captivated by its vastness, which proudly pointed in (almost) every direction, downwards, sideways and out in front, he held his breath in wonder whenever she sat close to him on the bed, to feed him his meals or to wipe his face. The voluminous structure seemed to enter his very being, he absorbing its massive comfort. Causing him once or twice to experience a huge wave of claustrophobia…collateral damage. One day, he laughed to himself, he would surprise her by ripping open her dark blouse and setting each of them free.

She smelled of firewood and the kitchen.

The time came when his carers told him (or rather showed him) who he was from his documents they had found, and little by little, he started to build a hazy picture of where he was from.

Chapter 30
Dreamscape

Everything in the vast sky was suddenly of a twirl, in the form of whirling darts of light; silver, green, magenta. Some pale and gauzy. Others like bright flashing swords, which ripped to shreds the very air.

However, a little earlier in the day, down at ground level, a young man, seemingly oblivious to any hint of potential change overhead, was enjoying a still purring breeze, always warm around his neck and shoulders; an invisible shawl. More confident now, as he was surely far along the unchartered path. Becoming neither cold nor wet, in spite of the rain spray, released from intermittent showers or from any follow-up gusts of wind. Merely re-energised. At last, he thought he caught sight of it in the distance, still far out of his reach; and yet something he knew he wanted and had to have. It had at last made an appearance.

Dressed in a velvet coat with white lace at his throat, silky hair flowing behind upon the waves of wind and sound, he continued in pursuit of whatever it was…there was indeed no going back now. Followed by two other figures, much further behind, older, more seasoned and keeping an ever-vigilant eye, but this was his mission. His soft leather boots leaving no tracks as they swished him through the long blades of gold and green grass. On and on…taking him, so he believed, ever closer to the object of his desire, driven by a craving that just wouldn't release its metal grip.

He had been travelling for hours, he suspected…through field after field, green upon green. Stopping for only a few moments at a time, by the crystalline lakes, to take of their waters from perfectly cupped hands. Once again fully refreshed, and thus ready to continue his journey, the mission he had set himself taking much longer than first anticipated. Yet still he carried himself as though there were a crown upon his head. He had forded rivers, sometimes even swimming across and, where there was ice, sometimes skating, still in his boots. Never cold nor wet, and no stumbling or loss of breath. All of nature paying him homage, paving his royal route with ease.

The soon to be moonlit woods, just skimming into view, would become his resting place for the night. A long, necessary night of velvet darkness. For at the rising of the sun, he would be up and ready to go…after a breakfast of berries and the remains of some bread and cheese that he carried in the soft leather bag hanging across his chest. There was, however, still about an hour of demi-light to snatch out of the present day. The going albeit a little slower now…before he allowed himself to bed down for the night, oddly unintimidated by the arrival of distant howls, scratchings, the fluttering of seemingly huge wings and all the manic screeches, which made up the forest's music, already audible. Its nocturnal soundtrack. The elusive creature draped in green still darting or floating in and out of sight, always slightly ahead. He rested his sleepy head upon a mossy cushion of earth at the foot of an ancient pine tree, cosily ensconced between the long and tapering fingers of two of its exposed root structures. A pony, which came and went during his journey, he tethered to a nearby branch.

He was soon dreaming a whole reel of little scenes, played out or relived conversations from his childhood, so many playful and harmless interludes, which seemed, at the time, to border on true adventure. Light-hearted brush strokes of a past life, fuelling his hopes for the following day.

Certain he was getting closer. Well over halfway now, surely! Another 24 hours, perhaps.

The new day turned out to be the same as the first. Except for one thing. As evening twilight approached, he stumbled across a ramshackle cottage or chalet, the first he had seen, just as he was leaving behind the thick knots of snow-packed trees, part of the wood's border with the fields. Smoke was curling out of the chimney and since hunger pangs were growing cruel, there was nothing for him to do but go knock at the door, to ask the owner for some provisions, which he would happily pay for, out of the sovereigns he carried in his belt. No amount of foraging in this forest could provide him with the necessary nourishment for his quest and in any case, it would have amounted to an act of sacrilege killing any of its noble creatures. The gleaming dagger remaining unused in its sheath.

Nevertheless, some powerful force seemed to be looking after him.

To his happy surprise, the old couple who lived there welcomed him warmly, almost as though they had been expecting him, into their little home and with open arms. Well, if arthritis, had allowed them the opportunity of raising them high enough. They wanted nothing for their hospitality, so overjoyed they were to share whatever they had with such a visitor, and the three talked long into the night, in spite of age or need of rest. Their guest revealed bits of information about himself, but never to a point where he might divulge ancient secrets, or say more than he had intended. He then listened with keen interest to their stories, agreeing, in the main, with their generously given lashings of ancient wisdom. They spoke of their desire to see him married one day…to a beautiful village girl (there were a good few in fact, to choose from)…and wished the future newlyweds a host of healthy children. At which point, they got so excited that they practically forced him into promising them that he would return one day with just that family…neither ancient husband nor wife realising that their days were surely numbered and that there just would not be time for them to place a blessing upon them all.

Nor did any of them appear to catch sight of the willowy creature draped in green, as it repeatedly circled the cottage, peeping in every so often through its tiny mullioned windows. The young man believing, however, on at least a couple of occasions, that he had felt a strange icy shiver travel the length of his spine.

The simple meal turned out to be one of the finest our 'hero' had ever tasted. The sweet wine leaving a magical taste on his mind as well as his lips.

However, his adventure or that part of it then ended, abruptly. As though someone had just stood up and switched it off. Creating a blank screen, a new state of darkness. Then like a change of channel, suddenly replaced by something else.

The continuing darkness of the night now working its way onto a completely different landscape. Its thick blanket still covering nearly everything, which turned out to be a blessing in itself. Nonetheless, or perhaps because of the poor visibility…he soon managed to detect a chill in the air, as well as acknowledge the awful pangs of an empty stomach.

The soon to be revealed scene was to defy imagination.

As night abruptly gave way to day, he found himself wandering, alone, through a vast undefined area of stony scrubland. All the while stepping over, not bits of rocky outcrop, but what turned out to be human bodies. More precisely, body parts. Words and images out of Dante's Inferno creeping into his head and echoing in the distance,

"Men once were we,

That now are rooted here."

Young male hands, fingers, arms and legs, flung hither and thither. Dirty pale hands with cracked, yellow fingernails, one or two still loyally sporting wedding rings. Black humour. Scattered arms and legs, some showing signs of gangrene, some still burning, some still part-wrapped in ragged bits of military uniform, khaki drill; life size puzzle pieces, randomly tossed or exploded, patiently waiting like toys, for someone to match them to their owner bodies and rediscover, catalogue and finally announce their identities to newspaper reporters. Spilled guts and brains leaking onto the frozen earth, already starting to feed the local population of busy rats and other vermin. A matted messy carpet of congealed blood on glued-down hair; gaping fish eyes that still saw the horror, once bright young eyes turned ancient in seconds. Mouths still silently shouting the word DESPAIR. All this amid the rest of the mud, blood, shit, vomit. Human waste spread manically around the glorious war dead, whose families would from then on refer to them only in heroic terms, proudly accepting rows of shiny medals dangling from brightly striped ribbon from the faceless powers who had sent them there.

At first, the beautiful young man looked around in an almost detached manner and guarded himself against inhaling too much of the rotting human stench, as he went more cautiously now on his way, but he didn't really see the horror of it all…his mind on other things. Looking forever ahead, head held high, gaze aloof, still looking for his girl in green. She had clearly passed that way, perhaps only minutes beforehand. He bent only to pick up a coiled length of pale green chiffon that must have recently dropped from her ivory shoulders. It smelled nothing like the battlefield. It smelled of sweet lilac; it smelled of her.

Did he ever catch up with her? Did he? He just couldn't remember, and he quickly tried to slip back into the first part of his dream, the one he had been starring in for days. Yet he was more awake than asleep now, little chance of finding out what happened in the end, alone in the room they had set aside for him. As the seconds rolled by, the more he tried to slide back in, the further he felt himself drifting away…such is the way of beautiful dreams. Perhaps if he had merely relaxed, tried to stay calm, then it would have been possible to take up his part in it again. This was no ordinary dream after all, this was practically real; this was his life; surely an episode that really mattered.

However, the battlefield did return. Its sight, sounds and smells. Continuously. Repeatedly. Far more brutal than that first time around, when from inside the dream of our hero's head it had seemed uncannily remote, a minor obstacle or ugly distraction. Night after night. The sound of its silence returned. The stench this time filling up his nostrils, ears, mouth and brain. Day after day. Reliving the 'adventure' now as one fully human, as he brutally kicked at those stick limbs, those gobstopper eyes, which littered his way. Now full of remorse. The magic had moved on.

He now knew it was his own shouts and screams punctuating his sleep now. His body covered in a layer of sweat, in a state of convulsion.

He gradually learned to cope, even with all this. Devising tiny and patient strategies and coping mechanisms. His strength of mind growing alongside his physical recovery and he let the two work together, without the need for further intervention. His carers continued to look after him.

In his head, he now knew he had to prepare himself for the long journey home.

Chapter 31
Away

Gennaro, whose three brothers were on active military service, remained with his wife and two sons in their little village, to see to the needs of remaining family members. His father, Alfonso, also playing his part alongside the invasion forces, deployed, as far as anyone was aware, somewhere along the Greek/Albanian border. An invasion, which appeared to be taking much longer than anyone had anticipated. Considered too old to fight, he had gone to serve his country with the task of distributing food, driving makeshift ambulances and scooping up the dead or injured from roadsides and mountain passes. Albeit never himself far from danger.

Somewhat surprisingly, Giovanni…temporarily re-baptised Pasquale…had also joined the war effort.

What was going on? What could possibly have provoked this? Gennaro, in particular, was and remained dumbfounded. Where were all his friends in high places? People who could have provided him with a safe passage as far away as the USA, if that's what he had wanted, in order to escape the current dangers…or at least furnish him with a completely new identity. 'Friends' who could have rubberstamped a whole range of medical conditions, which would exclude him, definitively, from far-flung battlefields. Had they just abandoned him? The answer was no. Giovanni had never made contact. Going off to war, merely something, it turned out later, that he needed to do.

In fact, nothing could make him change his mind, so with heavy heart, Gennaro promised to oversee his (and their) affairs, as best he could, while his friend was away, seemingly on a manic personal mission, as crazy as the invasion itself.

They also put plans quickly in place in the event of his never returning.

Something had certainly snapped inside Giovanni's head. What was it that had provoked such lunacy? Perhaps he had been working himself too hard of late, drinking too much or not eating properly? Gennaro, however, hadn't noticed anything out of the ordinary or out of character. Had dark memories begun to play havoc with his conscience for past misdemeanours? Yet again, a sign that he was not as strong as he had once believed.

It might have been down to the fact that Giovanni hadn't accepted Iolanda's disappearance after all. With nothing and no one there on the horizon to replace her…but there again, to abandon his Palazzo?

This going off to war nonsense, with or without a rational explanation, was definitely an act of self-destruction. What had happened to Giovanni's colossal ego, his desire for wealth and autonomy, his need of liberty (in all its forms), his attachment to the ancient palazzo? His rejection of taking unnecessary risks? Unthinkable that he would ever have considered allegiance to a political ideology, movement or faction, let alone become a party member.

Did this also mark the end of his 'pact' with Fortuna? Well, Gennaro knew nothing about that. That would have been part of a dialogue playing out between him and her only, somewhere inside Giovanni's complex brain.

It would appear, however, that if this were the case, he was now putting HER to the test, stretching even her possibilities.

Therefore, as far as Gennaro or anyone knew, it was Giovanni alone who had decided to sign up. Responding perhaps to a flash of enlightenment or to something, which had surfaced in one of his dreams, early on in the war effort. In spite of his own political leanings and opinions (or manifest lack of them). Of his own free will, he had turned up, on a certain morning at a distant and makeshift recruiting base, to go where military authority saw fit. No negotiating, no personal preference for place, no particular skills to offer… or none that he willingly divulged. Offering up youth, height, a good physique, sound health and a positive outlook. No privileges…a privately enrolled would-be soldier, ripe and eager to undergo any rigorous training programme. He deftly passing every test they set him. That, more or less, being the case for nearly every would-be soldier, under the circumstances! The ongoing need for freshly selected cohorts of young men; an abundance of brawn, a disposition to obey every command, to serve as cannon fodder! It was not clear whether he ever truly envisaged going to a premature death…or if he was looking anywhere beyond the present moment.

It had been Gennaro, who had pressed him to think about the future. Giovanni, characteristically, having discussed his plans with no one, not even with his friend.

A mere case of where he needed to be at that moment in time. To slot quietly into an amorphous human mass. On equal terms. Invisible to the outside world. Standing shoulder to shoulder with the others, no matter who they happened to be. All levelled by khaki and very short haircuts. It also required, Pasquale decided, a rapid return to the dialect of his village, which, to be fair, he had never really forgotten. He needed, for the first time in his life (or that he could remember), to be one of the boys. 'Nolens volens'…some aspects of our lives impossible to overthrow completely.

He later discovered that things turned out to be far from what he (and no doubt the other recruits) had first anticipated. Even for those who hadn't anticipated much at all. When considering who was at the helm. Past tight efficiencies now going haywire. Emerging all too soon after the troops' fateful departure for the Hellenic coast. A hurriedly put together mission, with overoptimistic objectives and an unrealistic timescale. Misjudgement of a besieged people's resolve. A leader who was looking more to his own grand colonial aspirations, than to the complex, rapidly unfolding European (and world) picture. Only a matter of months before another chilling pact he would be signing, so damaging for those Italian troops stationed (or rather, abandoned) there. Problems with rations, transport, artillery, training, a poor military strategy in what was fast becoming 'una guerra inutile', a useless war. Pasquale also finding himself fighting a war within a war, in which previously underestimated Greek forces were fighting back with all they had. Not part of the original script.

Having to accept early on that he couldn't survive this madness alone…the daily struggle, the never ending cold, the brutal mountainous terrain, the fear of death (or worse) that clung to them all like cellophane, even hunger on many an occasion. He had to permit himself, the unimagined 'luxury' of drawing strength from those around him, those who had just become his comrades. Preposterous but it was all there was, all he had. Notwithstanding the fact that they were a rag tag bunch! Pasquale, surviving alongside the likes of every variant of human possibility. Men, he would never in real life have chosen to spend more than a few minutes with.

However, with only a few exceptions, a tight closeness emerged, almost overnight. An unforced, unsolicited and yet incomparable camaraderie, lightened by the frequent bouts of tomfoolery, farcical impersonations of the officers, a stream of jokes and puerile insults, all of which continued to ricochet off barrack walls. He didn't like the majority of his peers, knew he would never like them, and often felt uneasy about his unfathomable need to protect them, his fellow soldiers. They to protect him, in turn. Not part of his way of seeing the world at all. All of them living, fighting and dying side by side. They were not even his 'people', many coming from different parts of the Italian peninsular, whose looks, speech and history were all quite different from his own. 'Forestieri', foreigners almost, with whom he was now sharing time, energy and his life. A messy and shoddy yet real 'all for one and one for all' culture in the making. Fellow human beings, tightly bound, by their current situation. A set of indelible memories or feelings, some atrocious and some bordering on the sickly sweet, in the making, which would continue well into old age, for those fortunate enough to have one.

He remained philosophical, in spite of everything, trying to see his present life, surreal though it was, in terms of a very long but necessary lesson. There was no one else to blame. He took full responsibility. Not quite knowing where it was leading but taking stock all the while, from the innumerable rich and hellish pickings. He, like the other soldiers, biding his time when there was little to do, smoking for the most part…cigarettes always available and free of charge…or playing cards. Separately or together. Fighting to the death each time battle resumed and for every fatality, stretching his mind once again, to make sense of it all. All the while supporting those around him. They supporting him. All detached from the 'normal'. All out on a limb.

Suddenly you had to deal with a life, which snatched away your privacy, whether out in the open or back at barracks. Day after day. For thoughts or for actions. Ideas we usually tackle or entertain, only when alone. All those little, personal and private acts, we carry out as civilised people behind closed doors. Going to the toilet, washing, sleeping even. There was no escape from the others. Whether or not you were part of any given conversation, it was all around you. Every minute. Like the terrible group silence, when everyone was lost for words. You heard and lived the silence together…loud and inescapable…as you did the nightly screams.

Pasquale soon could pinpoint the different types with whom he was rubbing shoulders. Against a male only backdrop, men who, whether they intended to or not, intimately shared and bared their lives. Their strengths and vulnerabilities.

The would-be leaders, the natural followers, the precious, the shirkers, those who took stupid risks, the fragile, the cowardly and those who deliberately exploited their physicality. The introverts. Men who displayed overblown egos, whose behaviour overcompensated for lack of self-worth, the clowns and the melancholy. All the subtle combinations and variations of these stereotypes as well. Where exactly did he fit into the pack of cards? That he would leave for the others to decide. He thought he already knew a lot about the human condition but continued to scrutinise his fellow soldiers for more and more insight into individual personalities. It gave him a warped comfort, a sense of sly gratification almost…that he was with them under false pretences (he could have avoided all this) and that he was really there to carry out important scientific research into human behaviour and that there just happened to be a war going on. Detachment. Folly. Mental survival.

In the rawness of that bleak and never-ending winter, he continued to watch his own back and that of his comrades. Furthermore, when necessary, to go on taking human lives, the lives of those on the 'other side'…kill or die. Not murder now…you didn't even know them…but all safely rubber-stamped by war.

To those around him, the role he seemed to have given himself (if one was needed), his card in the pack, was that of the quiet man. One who never spoke unless he had something new or significant to impart. A man who could speak his mind though, when pressed. A man who got on with each task in silence. Not caring to participate in the litany of murmurings and mumblings, grumbles, prayers, curses and protests, or jokes even, which punctuated each day's proceedings. A man whose vanity remained hidden from view, his naturally thick, wavy hair kept, for the time being at least, razor short under cap or helmet, but mercifully still there for when he might need it. Never setting out to be leader, preferring to occupy a place in the shadows, the outer edges of any grouping. Yet with time, that is exactly where he often found himself. Dead centre…unwillingly dragged or gravitating towards the limelight. All this aided by the fact that although a 'terrone', a southerner, and to some, bordering on a sub-species, he was taller and cleverer than most. Someone who appeared to know what he was doing and what was going on. With few signs of vulnerability. It had very little to do, of course, with anyone actually liking him.

Pasquale mainly found himself working alongside a group of about five or six others. A tightly knit group, who worked well together. All present and correct, at least for the time being.

Chapter 32
Homeward Bound

Our golden sun, that magnificent hanging bauble…on which we all depend, was once again transforming night into day. Allowing Pasquale (in the process of taking back the adopted name of Giovanni) to catch, at last, the first magical glimpses of land, notwithstanding a stubborn hover of mist. Not just any land rising out of the sea…magical though that is but the land of his birth…emerging to greet the choppy dark waters and any boats heading for its shores. He made out a clump of strange and lumpy masses of stone, which rose out of the sea, all of differing heights. As if guarding the coast itself, their colour bands ranging across every shade from cream to rust. Colours arranged along concentric lines that girded each structure, behind which he could now also see a length of low-lying cliff wall of the same type and colour. Yes, he was only minutes away from terra firma, so close now to Italian soil, as the vessel transporting him crept ever closer to a part of his country hitherto unknown to him…towards a fresh new chapter…of a life he could still not properly remember.

A long, long way from home…still an overland journey to undertake and one he would be making alone. He was cold, chilled to the bone. Suffering from chronic fatigue. Bones and muscles aching incessantly. Yet on detecting land, he felt a slow, warm happiness, trickling, drop by golden drop, deep into his veins. For a good while, removed from the wordless pain of those long months…the daily nursing of wounds, the ongoing battle to survive, the waging of war. His memory was also fast returning, albeit in fits and bursts. The sequence of events still problematic.

Mesmerised almost, by that sheer depth of feeling…in honour of a land for which he had thought he held no particular attachment.

Almost impossible for him to think in terms of the future, when he was still deciding who he was. Still building up the story. Trying to fill in the many gaps.

His memory came and went, like wavelets on the shore, offering up new information, or images, nearly every day, not all of which remained. Like shells or pieces of driftwood left behind. Not always the bits he most needed. He tried not to force or grab too much of it at a time, his instincts allowing him to trust that all was heading in the right direction. A full picture would emerge, eventually. Most of the detail of his life, before his departure, was, thankfully, more or less in place, he felt. It was the last year or two that was most evasive.

As for the physical journey back, he seemed to know, like those phenomenal homing pigeons, in which direction to travel, having learned long ago to tell the time by the position of the sun. Likewise, to calculate oncoming weather. There would also have been a tattered map or two inside his jacket pocket.

Home for him now meant Gennaro and Nunzia.

It had been relatively simple for him (and for the other apparent stowaway), to steal his way from the 'Adriana' craft, unseen. The bustling little port, jammed with crates, trucks and a wealth of other paraphernalia. Easy to crouch behind. With no cash on his person, he hadn't been able to pay for a sea passage, and therefore had had no choice other than to sneak on board an hour before departure under cover of darkness. All which came with its own dangers…that someone might discover his hidey-hole under the heavy folded drapes of tarpaulin. The reality that he might be shot. He could always have continued marching north, trying his luck at some other crossing point. Having weighed up the risks, he concluded it would be a more sensible course of action to leave the Balkan coast as quickly as possible. Rumours of a possible Nazi presence still ringing in his ears…were they now friend or foe? He was alone, out on a limb…the truth shimmering somewhere in the far distance.

"Ma guarda chi c'e', vedi chi e'…Genna'… vieni qua! Subito!" Nunzia screaming out to her husband, telling him to look out of the window and see who had just arrived.

"Ma che e'? Che vuoi?"

He was clearly vexed at the prospect of having to abandon the task he had just started, that is, to mend some tools. He knew that she would not give up.

Then, as his eyes rose heavenward out of sheer frustration, he made out the shape of what looked like his old friend, he saw Giovanni. He couldn't believe it. A reduced form of Giovanni. It felt as though a lifetime had dragged by; they had almost given up on the idea of ever seeing him again. Having had no news whatsoever. However, Gennaro had continued, loyally and diligently, to oversee his friend's affairs, and make sure all was in order. Dealing with the ensuing paper work every evening, which hadn't come easy.

'Amico mio…' Proper words or phrases not coming easily to either man. They filled in the gaping silence with hugs, gasps, sounds and clicks of the tongue, a kind of sub language. Gennaro every so often pulling himself away to get a better view of the new version of Giovanni. Leaving Nunzia, who had almost broken into a run in her haste to join them, to make well-tried comments such as 'now let me look at you', 'come into the house and sit down' or 'you must be so hungry, I'll go and prepare something for you, "subito"!' None of them relished or could cope with anything more penetrating or intimate than that. Now was not the time. He could tell them about the war later, a bit at a time. He had come back…that was more than they could have asked, with so many stories already spinning around the five villages about high numbers of missing soldiers and worse.

In truth, Gennaro and Nunzia were each shocked at the state of their friend. The sunken cheeks, the greyish skin, the bony frame…the malaise that clung to him. He looked as though he had aged ten years.

Nunzia, never one to despair though, was certain though that with a month or so of rest, HER cooking and HER constant care, he would be able, once again, to fill out his clothes and take up his former status as an eligible young man. His hair would grow again. Thick and wavy, like before. She was concerned only with his physical state. To get him fit, to return him to his previous size. That would take care of everything. Still unaware, of course, about his mental state. She would never have bothered to think of that, in any case, had there not been the later signs. Food was the key to all conditions and fresh mountain air. Why on earth, had he gone on such a stupid mission in the first place? A clever, sophisticated man like him? Nothing made sense any more. All the fault of a nonsensical war!

Not even thinking to mention her plans for him with Gennaro, she just knew it was down to her to take charge of his recovery and she certainly wasn't going to permit either of them to utter the word 'affari' (business) well, not for a good while yet! For the next few weeks, or months if that's what it was going to take, he would become her third child (or fourth if she counted her husband). She wasn't going to stand for any nonsense! Gennaro simply took a back seat and let her get on with it.

She allowed him to sit for about half an hour with her patient a couple of times a day.

In the intervening weeks and months, the couple's brand new country villa was already taking shape, much to the awe and admiration of the villagers (The family was at present still living with Gennaro's parents). A few of the locals genuinely pleased for them but for many more, it was a case of them feeling more than a touch put out. Who did they think they were? Did they think they were better than the rest now, deliberately rubbing local noses in city made success? Earned from work no one really understood. Couldn't they have just stayed there? Now setting themselves apart as better, richer.

This was, of course, a knee jerk reaction to the brutalising pain of envy. Which went on to become a slow seeping cancer of the soul. An envy that was difficult to live alongside, the villa's brooding structure, growing week on week, in its elevated position (visible from nearly every angle of the village) serving as a constant reminder. Paradoxically the other villagers would probably have done exactly the same, built a similar property in a similar position, had it been their good fortune. History is full of such examples, of self-made men who feel propelled to build magnificent houses, which spoke volumes of their acquired wealth. Interestingly, however, when anyone from one of the other villages made a derogatory comment about this one (or its owners), Gennaro's neighbours would instantly turn on them and state, in no uncertain terms, just how proud everyone was of it, a symbol of the success people from THEIR community were able to achieve.

As the weeks went by, Gennaro took Giovanni up to see it, proudly confident that it would meet with his approval. Each knowing that they owed the other a good deal. Whether for this villa...or Giovanni's city apartment and crumbling Palazzo. Gennaro could never have achieved this without Giovanni's support of course but it worked both ways; they functioned as a team. A reality neither side cared to or would have known how to put into words to the other. A feeling.

A delighted, almost childlike Gennaro escorting his guest into every part of the three-storey structure, explaining in detail how they intended to utilise each floor, space or room and describing his plans for the land that surrounded it.

Once Giovanni was strong enough, Nunzia gave the signal for him to go for short walks in the neighbouring fields and wooded areas. Whether her patient was aware of it or not, the nightly bouts of screams and shouts continued...hard to say whether it was getting worse or better...it definitely persisted, even though some nights were thankfully nightmare free. With Giovanni released from his ongoing war story, his delirium. The couple decided against getting in a doctor. It all seemed just a little too close to mental illness, which neither could contemplate for their friend. It must have had to do with his time away…they would merely sit it out. Patiently. Physically he was clearly making excellent progress. They allowed him a regular visitor, a Padre Vincenzo, from the Convento. He seemed an amiable sort. Not overly pious. Nor overbearing. Pleasant and gentle. Giovanni eventually looking forward to his visits. Nunzia, already so busy with the housework, cooking and looking after her two needy sons, soon gave up listening in on their conversations. This allowed Giovanni to talk, just a little at first, about his experiences and the absurdities of that invasion. They talked about the absurdity of all wars.

Within a few weeks, Gennaro and Nunzia secretly congratulated themselves on seeing that the nightmares were beginning to abate. Their instincts had been right. The old wisdom. They had gone about things in the right way. The results of their efforts were paying off, Giovanni now almost back to his former splendour.

They had inevitably disclosed very little about his condition or progress to the people of the village.

Chapter 33
Introspective

What happens to the soul when someone is, for so long, locked inside gnawing thoughts? As well as grappling each day (and night) for lost memory to return. For the unimpaired, a pointless task, no one remembers every aspect of their lives, from recent events to those from far back, but that is a comfort only if you've never had chunks of it taken away. Giovanni was trying to hook back each significant detail from the last couple of years, to remember in full even the minutiae of his life. He had already reclaimed a lot from before then but as regards the more recent past, it was vague, unfelt memory returning, as though fog had wrapped itself in insulating layers around the key moments. Like that journey across the sea, when he lay hidden under tarpaulin.

It wasn't just about remembering things though. You also find out more and more about yourself. Not always palatable. What else was there for someone like Giovanni to learn? He had already covered much of that ground before going away. Unlike most people, who don't seek to question such absurdities, he thought he at least knew who he was. The main facets of his personality, all that underpinned his desires. Did it become dangerous, once you'd already ploughed through a certain amount? He certainly hadn't read or had access to any authoritative books on the subject. At what point should you let go? Was there a valid purpose for continuing, or did it become little more than an empty habit or bizarre obsession even? Maybe in the end it placed you, paradoxically, at the centre of a fantasy world…when it was truth, you were chasing.

This is where he found himself now.

Alone, even though Gennaro and Nunzia were ever present. True to form, never feeling compelled to discuss any of this with them. Not only because they had little experience (or sympathy) for such matters, but because they would have interpreted it all as a sign of innate weakness. They would never refer to his nightly ravings, which often woke them in the small hours (and sometimes, also the children). That way they never happened. He knew that they knew, however.

The stark images of war therefore continued unabated, flashing and exploding in and out of his waking hours. Descriptions of such he had started to record on paper, to the best of his ability, even when unintelligible or incomplete. He suspected there was a lot happening in his nightly dreams, as he often found himself waking up unexpectedly, seated bolt upright on his bed, torso covered in sweat, shoulders and legs shaking. Remembering very little, however, which went on to become less and less. Then there was the excruciating noise.

Was self-analysis doing him good or harm? Interpreting past time, and your place in it, as your memory returned. Delving even deeper into your personality, at a time when you might be better off resting mind and body between the (now permitted) short bursts of physical activity. Was it all an extravagant indulgence? Part of Giovanni's natural curiosity about the world, or much more to do with an ever-expanding ego?

Padre Vincenzo's visits were proving worthwhile. As time went by, Giovanni becoming grateful that Nunzia had arranged them. They snipped the string of otherwise identical days, now he was getting better and sleeping less. Vincenzo proving to be a gentle companion. Together, he and the patient would pick through and try to sort out some of the points emerging from his ramblings and war notes. Also discussing universal themes as to where a man's responsibilities lay in times of peace and war, when and how to take a stand, debating as to whether the taking of another life could ever be acceptable. Alongside more immediate, more practical issues such as how to best live alongside the nightmares.

Vincenzo believed they were nature's way of ridding Giovanni from much of what he had done and witnessed, and that given the necessary time, they would work their way finally out of his head. The priest cum friar, such a humble and kindly soul…prayed regularly for the young man's full recovery. He let the 'patient', who now manifested a slight stutter, go on talking at length, even allowing him to chew over the same old content. Repeatedly. Listening attentively and without expressing judgement. Never privy to Giovanni's past business dealings, of course. Never asking him about things he wasn't ready to reveal.

As Giovanni saw it, these visits kept the dubious world of doctors and medicine at a healthy distance.

There was naturally still much that Giovanni was not prepared to discuss. Over which he kept tight control. A re-opening of Pandora's casket, 'il vaso di Pandora', as the Italians referred to it...that was his prerogative only, an exercise he was undertaking alone. On a parallel path. Making use all of the ground already covered by his friends and Padre Vincenzo. In fact, he had recently unearthed something he found quite alarming. Something that he had sensed for quite a long time now, but never cared to name or question. A reality, which appeared to explain everything else. One he felt compelled to accept. Not even missing memories can fully protect us from the more dangerous truths.

As far as he was concerned, all the gathered evidence pointed to the fact...that he was incapable of loving anyone other than himself. Love, that powerful component of the human condition, which binds us inextricably to...other people, both those with blood links and those we choose for ourselves. Love, to which we all aspire.

Did this make him merely immature or some kind of incurable monster?

Quite a tough and brutal truth to cope with. Not a temporary state of affairs but a fixed reality. Not an understanding he had reached out of self-pity. Neither was he being overly hard on himself. There it was...an undeniable truth undraped...then spread out, pinned up before him. Followed by a steely beam of light trailing the fact that it was BEAUTY...not humanity...he had always been chasing. Beauty in all her manifestations. From people's looks to beautiful places. His theory appeared to explain everything else.

Going over old ground. The day, when still a boy, he had gone by car to the city and discovered the door to a still dormant dream. Which would grow and grow into a love of gardens, public spaces and architecture. It was all there, from the beginning. Those early drawings of would-be palatial houses, he had sketched on the kitchen table, evolving from illustrated fairy tales he had read. His subsequent rejection of his mother, as she became something unattractive, too painful to look at.

The horror of it, though...to reject one's own mother.

His love of subtlety and true sophistication. Of natural elegance and good taste, especially as displayed by certain individuals from the upper classes. All components of 'the beautiful'. The crumbling Palazzo that he had acquired and all it signified, its connections. A passion for art and poetry, still unfolding, all the time that his business continued to expand. His love of the natural world also. The woods he had explored in the mountains. Turquoise views of a glittering

Mediterranean. Looking up at starry skies. Beauty in the 'man made' as well as in nature. How it all worked together. Human beings serving as conduits. Artists, musicians, creators and designers. The figures of Padre Floro and Matilde Franceschini, symbolising so perfectly his freshly discovered and terrible truth. Each inadvertently shining the torch along his way.

Remembering, through the senses now, the ancient atmosphere of the Convento, the beauty of its cloisters, the friars' sacred chanting. The beauty of silence. Home to that quiet and perpetual quest for knowledge and spirituality.

The heady smell of lilac in May.

Then the pure relief upon making such a profound discovery, even though it also happened to be something monstrous. Relaxing a couple of decades of built-up tension. His theory clearing up the confusion.

Conversely, such a revelation meant he would now have to accept that it would place him at an even greater distance from his fellow man. Was it a highly unusual condition? He had no idea. He did somehow know, however, that in his case it wasn't treatable. He didn't want there to be a cure and would never, knowingly, authorise any treatment that might take away this exclusive, unshared joy. Afraid that he would have more to lose. If change were possible, it would have to arrive spontaneously.

It seemed to him that for other people, love came easily, naturally. Nunzia and Gennaro had fallen for each another while still at school; the old couple he had stayed with in the mountains had loved and supported each other for forty years or so; Nonno Giulillo, as an old man, had invested all his love in him, his grandchild. Matilde Franceschini loved her son, unconditionally, and took the Christian message of love to those less fortunate. Even those tough and mouthy women who had helped him and his mother over the years, whom he had never properly thanked…was this not also an ongoing sign of love in action? People who not only professed their love of God in words.

He, on the other hand, didn't have it in him. He loved no one, neither man nor God, no one other than himself and even that was questionable…

One recent memory in particular having not yet resurfaced, however. Perhaps one day, he would have to adjust his thinking to make sense of it.

For now, he simply knew that living alongside others would mean detachment and disappointment, just as it always had.

It had made the act of killing easier. Ridding the earth of a deplorable being. Eliminating a fellow man as an act of self-defence or for self-preservation. Do or die. Removing someone who didn't count.

Hadn't this just been the case throughout human history? That primitive and brutal struggle for survival.

There were, however, already gaps in Giovanni's theory. How exactly was he defining or interpreting the word love? Perhaps he had exulted it to an impossibly high level of perfection. Perhaps it was something baser and simpler, after all, albeit so hard to measure. Surely, it could be messy and clumsy yet still qualify as love. Was what he felt towards himself really love or something altogether different?

It didn't explain, the parts Nino, or more recently, Iolanda, had played in this newly uncovered truth…or even his unexpected reaction on seeing the baby girl he had fathered. How would he remember them now? There was clearly more he had to do…once his memory fully returned. For the time being, they still lay submerged.

This was the level of his mental progress when the day finally arrived for him to make his return to the city, to take up his place there once again, to continue his business ventures…those carried out in the daylight, and then those whispered agreements sealed in dark and smoky corridors.

The world at large still at war with itself, with great change of all kinds waiting in the wings.

Chapter 34
Out and About

World War Two raged on and on, with leaders and governments, everywhere, locking themselves into relentless campaigns and dubious pacts.

On the ground, not everyone was desperate however. For a tiny minority, this war like all wars, threw up rich pickings. Giovanni, instinctively, finding his way back into this dubious and uneasy group. He, possessing all the necessary expertise…and audacity…to go on reaping the benefits. He had recouped it all back. Gennaro, his trusted caretaker, had done a solid job of looking after their assets, and keeping the lines of communication open, with those that mattered…yet never trying to muscle in on his friend's territory. The war had thus brought with it a need for new enterprises, to provide services, which perhaps had always existed but where the demands for them were now much greater. To satisfy the needs of both private individuals and governments. Armies, gunrunners, people smugglers and political spies. An interlocking of worlds, blurring the edges of that apparently moveable line between legal and illegal, ethical and unethical.

As well as the moneylending, he also returned to his favourite pastime; the buying and selling of pieces of art and antiquity.

Gennaro moved back to the city to work alongside him during the week and then spent most weekends with Nunzia and his sons in the village. Inevitably still sent out on a wide range of errands. The fate of the right-hand man. That was the agreement, but it was always going to be a flexible arrangement when Giovanni needed Gennaro, the latter dropped everything to report for duty. Nunzia no longer bothering to complain, fully understanding that this was the 'price' they paid for their own good fortune and success. She naturally preferred her life 'in paese' in the countryside. However, she had learned that a stay or two in the city was also worthwhile and in keeping with their current standing and reputation in the village. Yet another silent advantage over her village neighbours, in addition to the ever-looming building, still in skeletal form, due to become their family home.

Thanks to their constant care, Giovanni, it seemed, was back to a good standard of normal. Things had worked out well…without recourse to much outside intervention.

It was true…he had indeed returned to full health. His days mirroring those of his former life in the city. Except for the bursts of gunfire in his head, which sometimes still arrived, unannounced, at night. There again, perhaps nature was just slow in taking its course. His well-oiled coping mechanisms almost stretched to the limit.

There was a morning, in particular, when Gennaro got the instruction to have the car ready. In five minutes. He was to accompany Giovanni to an unnamed location a good three hours away. He would explain everything on route.

They were going to be meeting, in total secrecy, a young nun from an isolated 'monastero'. Definitely not a normal day for the pair, then. Yet very much part of the dynamic of working alongside a man such as Giovanni. A meeting, which would be taking place in a church. Gennaro knew better than to ask his friend for further detail. A few hours later, just as he was about to swing the car into a steeply ascending driveway, he managed to discover that it all had something to do with Iolanda.

Both men entered the ancient structure with mounting trepidation. Giovanni, for what he knew already; Gennaro, for what he was about to discover.

It was Giovanni, who quickly took care of the introductions with the young nun. Gennaro instantly sensing that they had met before, that they knew each other. The two men found themselves occupying a cramped and musty side office at the back of the little church. There didn't appear to be anyone else around, as they each installed themselves on the bare wooden chairs. Giovanni invited Suor Agnese to explain to his companion the reason for this encounter.

"This may come as a bit of a surprise for you, Signor Gennaro, as Giovanni has told me about your close personal and business relationship. Yet, because of the delicate nature of the matter at hand, it was I who asked him not to reveal any information to a third party, at least not until we could come up with a possible solution. My position is also a difficult one as I don't have the blessing of many of the other sisters. I'm operating alone. It is a matter of conscience. I will get to the point. You will remember the time when the two of you were looking, without success, for Iolanda. Well, I can now reveal to you that she was then staying, in hiding you might say, at our 'monastero' about half a kilometre away."

Gennaro, at this point, quickly turning his head towards Giovanni, but that of his friend already pointed in the direction of a ceiling. His gaze fixed upon a corner patch where the paint was beginning to peel…as he sat back in the chair.

Suor Agnese continued her account.

"Of course, no one outside our little community knew anything as to her whereabouts. The Abbess had listened to Iolanda's story and had agreed to take her in. All we knew was that a young woman was going to be staying with us for a few months…during which time she would give birth to her baby."

She paused, long enough for Gennaro to digest the news and collect his thoughts.

"This isn't an unusual situation in itself. We have great experience in these matters. And now especially, what with the war…the Abbess takes care of all matters regarding selection and privacy, and the rest of us simply help her in day-to-day practicalities, leading up to the time the woman is ready to give birth and then afterwards, as she contemplates returning to her former life…or embarking upon a new one."

"The mothers use their time with us to make plans, whether they are giving up their babies, or whether they are trying to keep them, which in most cases is impossible of course. We pray for them; we help in whatever way we can but there is unfortunately a stark difference of opinion amongst us in the order. Some believing that the process of adoption is the only moral outcome. They think exclusively in terms of what they judge to be the child's wellbeing…meaning a speedy separation for mother and child, which they say should happen when the baby reaches three months. Even earlier, if a family has already come forward. They have, in truth, little sympathy in their hearts for the fate of the mothers. Perhaps never expressing their feelings out loud, but it is clear to me they imagine the women are getting their just desserts, for giving in to a weakness of character and having displayed wanton behaviour. I say, however, that many of the mothers are little more than children themselves, so vulnerable and in need of love and understanding. Who am I to judge?" her voice beginning to trail off, if only for a few seconds.

"Anyway, back to Iolanda. In fact, it turned out and this was quite unusual…that a kind of friendship was beginning to grow between the two of us.

An understanding, regardless of the obvious differences. She made me laugh; she got me to see the world from her perspective…which inevitably didn't coincide with my vision or the path I have chosen. It really didn't seem to matter though. An insight into someone else's life experience. I think that's such a privilege, being part of that. I respected her intelligence, her sense of integrity. The order doesn't permit close friendships as such, whether amongst ourselves or with those from outside, for obvious reasons. That is, anything that that might disrupt the status quo, the tranquillity of our day-to-day lives…no one permitted to receive special treatment but this can be difficult, even when one tries to guard against such situations arising. Excuse me, gentlemen. I've been wasting your time…again. Let me get back to the bare facts."

"Well, Iolanda, told me all about her love for Giovanni, 'overwhelming' was the word she used, I think. What it was doing to her. How she thought it was just too big a situation to handle. How she almost couldn't make sense of it. How she had never envisaged the permanence of marriage, instinctively knowing (Agnese now turning to Giovanni) you…felt the same. Then of course, discovering that she was pregnant, not knowing what to do. Certain though that she could never bring herself to tell. It would have been as if she had broken a kind of undeclared pact with herself and, even worse, had deliberately trapped him. How, she had to find a way of disappearing from his life, and once again start afresh, amongst people she didn't know."

"One thing I must add here though, as it strikes me still, is that unlike the other women that we've helped, Iolanda displayed no signs of shame about being unmarried and pregnant, about bringing a child into the world, because, as she described it, quite poetically in fact, the baby was the fruit of freely given love. Never contemplating abortion as a possible solution. Never referring to God or Christian beliefs but it was clear to see how much her unborn child already meant to her…I suppose staying here, in spite of any semi-concealed animosity on the part of some of the sisters, was the only choice for her. The monastero becoming her temporary home."

"Nearly there now. I appreciate that you, Giovanni, have let me speak freely and take my time. This is so difficult for me. I've also lost a friendship. Iolanda gave birth…quite a lengthy business I remember…there were at least two of us with her throughout the labour…to a baby girl. She then had to think about what was to become of the two of them. She having no family support, not being a woman of independent means…as you know, she relied on her singing to pay the bills."

"Well, just as I thought we might be making some headway, I went in to check on her one morning…only to find two letters that she had left on the empty bed…one addressed to me and the other with Giovanni's name on it. Her little baby…about eight weeks old now…still sleeping soundly in the cot. I couldn't believe it. There had been no clues that she might suddenly take off…and even before I opened the letter…I sensed that she was not planning to return. Well of course, already feeling that I had let her down…I decided to read it not by myself but in the company of our Mother Superior, trying, in a very small way, to put matters right with the others."

"It turned out, under the circumstances, to be quite a short note. Iolanda spoke of her appreciation for all the support we had shown her. That no one else would have invested so much time and care. That she would never forget us. Then came the important part, as indicated by the big words in capital letters at the bottom of the page… She was asking for one more favour, as it concerned the future of the precious baby she had left behind. If we could contact the baby's father as soon as was possible, and hand over the other letter, the one addressed to him. In this way, plans could be put in place…"

Chapter 35
Picking Up the Threads

Giovanni thanked Suor Agnese for her time and tenacity. Stating that it was best they left her now to get on with her other duties. Apologising for the delicate position in which she still found herself regarding the rules of her order, but also assuring her that he would as soon as possible, find a permanent solution. He then handed her an envelope, packed with what appeared to be 50,000 lire notes, asking once again for a little more patience and explaining that in the meantime the donation should go directly towards looking after his daughter and the mothers to be.

Gennaro had stayed quiet throughout, finding it a tricky business to absorb and then make sense of all that he was hearing. It had even once or twice crossed his own mind, when Iolanda had first disappeared, that perhaps she had become pregnant, but quickly dismissed it, in that someone like Giovanni could have sorted the matter, quite easily, in a variety of ways…just as he had done before.

Uncharacteristically, on their journey home, Giovanni appeared to want to talk. To take up the loose threads Suor Agnese had left them. The point of the trip then, Gennaro deduced, was to donate some money to the Order and so that he could learn about what happened to Iolanda, from the lips of the young nun, who had befriended her. Rather than directly from Giovanni.

Once again, with Gennaro required only to listen and to drive. His thoughts or opinions never requested.

"It took Agnese a while to track me down. By which time, I no longer thought about the singer. At all. You know yourself how that morning, a few weeks after her disappearance when I just said, that I'd had enough…no more enquiries as to her whereabouts. There would be no going back. An end to the despair. I cauterised her from my being. In an instant. The pain vanished immediately. It felt good."

"That 'capo di pezza' (a derogatory term, which alluded to a nun's presumed lack of intelligence) is more resilient than she looks though. Don't underestimate her, in spite of her tiny frame and her being so young. She was determined to get me to read that letter…a sort of personal crusade. I didn't feel ready…it was too soon. Maybe I would never want to read it. I just didn't know. That nightclub singer belonged to the distant past, no longer relevant. A ghost. A name on a flimsy scrap of paper floating out to sea…as if that wasn't bad enough, and this is where I made the biggest mistake of all, somehow Agnese persuaded me to see the baby she had left behind. 'Just the once if that's what you want' I think that's how she phrased it. Well, I can't explain, it's all beyond how I think and what I am but yes, I went along with it. Feeling numb, strangely removed, even though it happened to be my story. Confident that I would feel nothing. I have seen babies before. They are all more or less the same. I neither liked nor disliked them. Perhaps it was out of curiosity…or vanity even…"

A flicker of humanity? A case of misplaced sentimentality? Guilt, even? What was Gennaro making of these revelations?

By this point though, Giovanni had forgotten he was talking to anyone at all. It was a spilling out of his story now…a continuous stream of autonomous wordage. Speaking in detached monotone, sounds of words escaping through the car window, belonging to the breeze, which carried them away. Not part of a conversation as such, the penitent no longer in control of the words emptying out of him. Making up for those months of silence, spent away from home. Now using terms and phrases that had never been part of their normal exchange. A monologue bordering on confession. Head tilted to the right in the direction of the outside world. Removed from what he was saying. Unmoved and unmoving.

At his side, Gennaro, the unlikely priest, ensconced behind an invisible curtain, simply waited and listened, listened (as best he could), waited and continued driving, eyes glued to the road ahead. Perplexed of course, but having known from the beginning, that the man beside him in the car owned a complex character. Once again, feeling grateful, that his own life was different. Straightforward. Conventional. He didn't need the complication of art and beauty and poetry or notions of freedom and perfect love…thank goodness and didn't even fully understand his friend's current predicament (money could surely buy everything). The lack of understanding not borne out of a lack of intelligence. More a lack of sensitivity or imagination. A different personality and mind-set.

Assuming now that this unfamiliar outpouring, on the part of his friend, also had to be due to his war experiences…that long and terrifying missing chapter…causing the former hard-hearted Giovanni to behave in this way.

Notwithstanding the fact that he was now baring feelings, which belonged to a time before joining the military.

"For so long all these memories lay trapped somewhere in my head…I had forgotten everything concerning Iolanda. When it did come back, though, it came back whole, and I relived each step on the way, every detail.

"I walked into that room and there she was. They'd propped her up on some pillows in the middle of the bed. Wrapped inside a white blanket. Like at the centre of a flower with folded petals. She was wide-awake. Her eyes lit up when she became aware of my presence, fixing me, staring me out and went on to throw me such a burst of smiles. One after the other. A love arrow had pierced my heart. I can't remember now if they'd left me alone with her. Only that I was there sitting beside her. Maybe they were still in the room, watching my every move. It didn't matter. I wasn't with them in any case. She was perfect. Miniature. Lots of hair, saucer eyes, heart-shaped face, peachy and dimpled…those little legs kicking furiously all the while under the loosening blanket. I loved her…from that very first moment…I loved her and the joy hurt. Our lives now forged together. Decided for us. Now that I had seen her. I had to think fast…before they put her up for adoption. I knew how it worked there. To check that they hadn't already…inconceivable.

"I had lost one daughter. Looking back, what a horrible business that was. I wasn't going to lose this one. She's called Giulia. That's what her birth mother wanted, the name she chose. That's what was written in the letter…and I've decided to honour that choice. My own father's name was Giulio but she couldn't have known this…I'd never told her. The sisters call her Giulia, sometimes Giulietta. She must already recognise the sound of it. I won't change it now. Even though it did strike me, for just a few seconds, that perhaps she should be a Maria Rosaria, after my mother but no, not a good idea…

"When the time is right, when her future is secure, I might also check on my other daughter. See how she is, how I can help, try to put things right…

"I go through all the options. I make up my mind and then a few hours later, everything seems to change. My first reaction of course was just to scoop her up and take her away with me but that was ridiculous. I have to think primarily of her. My thoughts go full circle. Continuously. How could she ever be part of my life? My world? No, it was better she stayed away, far away. I would need to find the best possible family for her…I even thought of you and Nunzia (a clue here that he was still aware of Gennaro's presence in the car), of her living with you in the village. Not a good idea though, you are also a part of the shadowy world I inhabit. There would be times when I would have to see her…times when I wouldn't be able to see her…

"The war made my decision for me. I went to see the Abbess. I asked her to give me a year. I would pay her in advance. If she could keep Giulia for me at their Collegio, after all, they run a kind of orphanage, a boarding school…that they should never make plans to put her up for adoption. I was not abandoning her. It was important I went away, though. In a year's time, I would return. I said I wanted to know about her progress, see all her medical notes, and so on. I told Madre Agostina that I trusted her completely…and the sudden glint in her eye was a sign that she had detected, in my stance and in my tone of voice, the veiled threat that I meant the best care possible. If not, there would be consequences. Not privileged treatment for Giulia, but something fair, kind, constant, loving. I even went so far as to stating that I wanted Suor Agnese to oversee her wellbeing and development. The abbess said she was prepared to give consent to all that I had requested, but that if I hadn't made contact within a year or so, she would take charge of the situation herself. This time an overt threat coming directly from her.

"Yes, by this time I already knew that I'd be joining the war effort, though unsure as to where they might send me. Or even where I might be in a year's time. If I would be alive at all…but here I am, I did survive. Fortuna was still keeping a distant eye on me. Would you believe it, Suor Agnese tracked me down for a second time…that slip of a girl would have made a great detective! I had of course already thought about going back. As soon as that part of my memory properly returned…which was taking so long…I discovered that I felt the same about my daughter as on the day I had first set eyes on her. Resolved to be her father from then on."

Giovanni came to. His story was now at an end and they were both feeling hungry. He told Gennaro to stop the car, once he had spotted a particular little turning. They walked the short distance to a low, ramshackle house, which, for those in the know, occasionally doubled as a trattoria. The owners knew Giovanni quite well from previous visits, but never had any idea when he would next show up. The pair were in luck. Sara had been down to the little beach early that morning, and had managed to collect a decent amount of clams, or as they called them, 'vongole', by prising them out of the wet sand with her fingers…just as the tide was receding. Her mother promptly getting to work in the kitchen, while Sara with a brush and damp rag, scrubbed down the old wooden table outside and then set about laying it, using cheap metal ashtrays to keep the napkins from flying away in the late summer breeze. Neither seeming to mind that their unexpected guests had interrupted the habitual afternoon siesta.

Within twenty minutes, the two friends were sharing one of the best lunches they could remember. Would even refer to it in years to come. Two huge bowls of 'linguine' topped and with masses of 'vongole'…quick and simple fare at its best. Somewhat leisurely, having no further appointments that day, they began to twirl the long pasta strands around their forks, each taking sufficient time to savour the freshly caught clams. Gone the gulf between them, any previous, strained atmosphere. They chatted almost continuously as they ate. Sara's mother reappearing to apologise for the absence of a proper second course, due to circumstances that interested neither man. A tomato salad arrived. Bread and cheese followed on and then a dish of aubergines 'sott'olio'. Then figs and pears.

They also drank a vast quantity of the local wine and later wandered off for a rest on the mainly stony beach, having found a shady spot underneath a towering date palm. Giovanni filling his friend in on how he had come to know the family who lived there. Once again, real conversation ensued, a few words at a time, bouncing backwards and forwards. No more fancy phrases. Both men, stomachs full of the clam linguine and heads full of wine. Both relieved. Life at its best…as they drifted in and out of sleep and the odd spoken word.

Removed, at least for a few hours, from any reminders of war. No planes flying overhead, no tanks, no far off explosions, no platoons of uniformed young men on the march and no visible signs of devastation.

In addition, a truce, albeit temporary, was now playing out inside Giovanni's head.

Chapter 36
Future and Present

Plans for the baby girl's future were now in place, agreements drawn up. Minimal paperwork. They were a religious order, after all. A steady flow of cash (always in the form of a donation) together with Giovanni's personal charm (he could, on occasion, be highly charming), had secured Giulia's long-term place at the highly respected Collegio Sant'Antonio. The sisters would care for her and educate her up until the age of ten. During which time, Giovanni would endeavour to make frequent visits. Then years later, he would accompany her himself to England, where her convent education would continue. It was Madre Agostina, who had come up with that idea. Possibly sensing something untoward regarding Giovanni's business dealings.

He made only one other stipulation, a somewhat bizarre request, under the circumstances, that they must keep her beautiful hair long.

It was hard to fathom exactly how much any of the sisters knew about Giovanni's life and sources of income, but undoubtedly would have drawn their own conclusions.

As Agostina rightly predicted, the war would be well and truly over by then. Governments still having to deal with its aftermath and individuals having to rebuild their lives. The wise Abbess stated that the process would be long and painful but would likewise herald much in the way of change, change for the better. Exciting times then for someone of Giulia's age and situation. She was also in regular touch with a group of women from a similar order to her own. Based just outside of London, the Sisters of the Divine Revelation educated girls from well to do families and had been doing so for the past hundred years, when life for Catholics was becoming more acceptable in England. She was certain that under the circumstances they would be happy to accommodate Giulia there one day.

Therefore, a long-term plan already set out, which would involve a new school for Giovanni's daughter (and a new life) abroad. Somewhere far removed from Giovanni's dubious dealings and acquaintances. Nevertheless, a continuation of strict convent life, that world within a world. In a foreign country…not too far away though…quite easy for him to access, where he would be able to visit her as often as possible. In that way, she would know that he remained forever her devoted father. The more time he allowed these plans to sink in, the happier he became. At peace with himself now. A practicable, no longer temporary, solution. Giulia would have everything his money and influence could provide. Books, education, a secure home and disciplined environment, well-meaning people…in fact total protection from the ugliness of life…ever removed from both its overt and veiled atrocities.

Madre Agostina had also provided him with two photos of the English convent and boarding school, one of its façade and the other, showing the eighteenth-century building within its extensive grounds. More evidence that their plan, involving Fielding House and its impressive setting, met his needs completely. Giulia would make friends with girls from respectable families and benefit from the many relationships and opportunities such a convent school could provide. She would have at least two languages and two diverse cultures at her disposal, from which to choose. Giovanni would open bank accounts in her name as back up, should anything happen to him. Her life made safe from cradle to grave. That first image of her on the bed, wrapped in the blanket on propped up cushions, rarely left his mind. She would never go without or come to know what it means to be cold, hungry or homeless, friendless or despised. A life removed from village ignorance and city sleaze.

Giovanni would therefore continue to love her always, his beautiful motherless child, whether he happened to be near or far. No longer thinking (or caring) about Iolanda, the woman who had abandoned her (and him). Never referring to her by name. Nor did he think about Brigida.

The mothers of his two little daughters.

As far as Brigida was concerned, however, things were once again about to change. We last left her back home with her family, picking up the threads of an earlier life with all its domestic demands and family responsibilities. Its thankless monotony. Still secretly mourning the absence of her baby daughter, Carmela, a daily ritual. Gone the baby, now the little girl.

Another young man had, recently (and unexpectedly) entered her life, much to her parents' (surprised) relief…their earlier sacrifices finally paying off. It mattered little now who he was or what his circumstances happened to be. Her mother, in particular, naturally looking towards the next generation, to babies that would arrive. A couple of younger daughters soon to be heading for the altar. She and her husband having done their duty.

Brigida's mother had recently sent her to lend a hand at the home of a family in need of support. A family who lived on the other side of the village, a little further up the mountain. They had been in search of some temporary help for their son, who had recently returned from a foreign battlefield. On this occasion, not for the purposes of matchmaking, more of a knee-jerk reaction on hearing the account given to her by his mother, when the two women met and spoke at the weekly market. Lina, Brigida's mother responding to a genuine burst of compassion. In any case, there were rapidly spreading whispers that the young soldier was already engaged to be married, therefore already 'fidanzato'. Simply another example of war bringing out the best in the people at home…it happened every time. She would therefore send Brigida. Her younger sisters would cover her work in the meantime…they had managed before…and it didn't appear that she was going to be away for long. Just until the young man was up on his feet again.

Wounded soldiers were by now beginning to return, in ever-increasing numbers, from the various fronts and battlefields, some 'officially', and others like Giovanni. Not so much deserters as 'sbandati', men who were suffering from a range of mental and physical disorders, some having even been left behind or reported missing, and who were turning up in various states of 'disrepair'. The worst of these reduced to hobbling, limping, emotionally broken and emaciated human specimens.

Still alive though. Still hanging on. Clinging onto some childhood-embedded, irrational hope. Who were cadging lifts off willing drivers, stowing away on trucks and boats, hiding out in haylofts and barns, stealing and (where possible) catching food…all in order to survive another day of their homeward journey, even when some, like Giovanni, had almost forgotten their names and previous identities.

One such young man had also managed to return. Alfredo. His family and neighbours, until recently, having expected him to come home (in whatever condition) and reunite with the girl who'd promised to become his wife, just before he went off to war. Only to find that she'd 'grown bored of waiting', well, so went the prevailing gossip. This explanation coinciding with another offer of marriage coming her way…from the good-looking son of a local barber (who also, incidentally, doubled as dentist, when it came to the removal of village teeth). A young man destined to follow in his father's footsteps, considered a much better 'catch' all round.

So went the common consensus. Consequently, villagers soon let the girl off the proverbial hook, declaring "E'la vita (C'est la vie)!" as they predictably hunched forward their shoulders and spread open their hands. Their take on the way of the world.

Poor Alfredo, now missing an arm and having to cope with some sight loss in one eye, and who'd freshly witnessed the horrors of frontline action. The girl he loved, whose ragged photograph had kept him going throughout his miserable time away, not there to welcome him back. Only a hastily handwritten note left on the kitchen table. Apologetic in tone, yes, but somehow lacking in compassion. A letter that wished him well, together with the little gold bracelet, which he tipped carefully out of the envelope. A bracelet he had given her, when declaring his love for the very first time, and something that he remembered her eagerly accepting. He also remembering that it had taken him more than a year to save the money to buy it.

The soldier deciding not to confide in anyone as regards his feelings about such cruel, underhand behaviour. Not even with his own parents. He preferring to suffer the ordeal in silence, to wallow in his own cloudy pool of self-pity. The letter written well before she knew anything of his war injuries.

Then one morning, a young woman called Brigida appeared in his room, bringing with her a tiny golden beam of hope. A pleasant looking girl, who sported a friendly smile. A young woman, who saw to his needs in a brisk, no-nonsense manner. He soon found himself anticipating each new day and enjoying its recently forgotten little pleasures; meals and chatter; the sun that entered his room. There were those days, however, when he didn't get to see her at all, her duties taking her away to a different part of the house or into the village. They turned out to be long, grey and disappointing days. His mother's cooking not so appetising after all.

Eventually Alfredo and Brigida started exchanging little jokes and anecdotes and his parents began to see the transforming effect that her presence was having upon him.

She was clearly becoming an important feature in his life. A key factor in his recovery, his long road back to (a new) normality. His mother confirming to him that Brigida happened to be a 'zitella' (that she wasn't married). He not knowing how she could have read his thoughts. Those thoughts often swinging backwards and forwards, like a pendulum, one moment in the direction that she might consider marriage. After all, she must have been well into her 20s, possibly a little older than he was, and it was common knowledge that every girl in every village wanted to find a husband. The sooner the better. Quickly followed by an opposing thought…that he was hardly husband material now…a broken man, a missing arm, partially sighted. A reject!

Someone as nice, capable and healthy as Brigida. What did he have to offer her now?

After three months or so of his having first set eyes on her, he suddenly plucked up the courage to disclose his feelings to her and then to propose marriage. On a day when the thought pendulum pointed in his favour. Backed up by the pleasure of the morning sun now streaming into his room. More than aware that his family probably wouldn't need her services for much longer and therefore that there might not be another opportunity.

Brigida, seemingly unmoved, asked for 24 hours to think about it. Not to be awkward or imperious, but merely to sift carefully through all the implications of a married life she had no longer imagined for herself. To discuss it with her parents. She already knowing that she would accept. It was unlikely life would come up with anything better. An offer of marriage would make her family happy, who would pressure her in any case into saying yes. Past efforts to restore her good name vindicated at last!

The following morning, she gave Alfredo her answer.

Chapter 37
The Gardener and His Niece

At the end of each week, Giovanni found himself spending more and more time at the Palazzo. Whereas Gennaro would go back to the village of his birth 'in paese' to be with his family. Both men benefitting from their 'other' life, an alternatively tranquil life, which they were each bit by bit recreating. Gennaro happily returning to his roots. Giovanni...away from his village, away from the city, trying to make sense of his rolling thoughts, as he looked down on the world below amid turquoise seas, from the heights of his beloved castle...in the process of anchoring a few new roots of his own.

It was always a leisurely drive up the (by now) familiar winding road in early morning, and he soon felt the weight of the previous days' tensions start to fall from his shoulders. A wonderful sensation, which strangely enough, always caught him by surprise. Never anticipating this liberating ritual. Not quite knowing at what point in his trip it occurred. The feeling, which stirred him into belting out, from the pit of his stomach, a favourite (usually Neapolitan) song or two.

'O sole mio'

Or

'Parlami d'amore, Mariu'

And so on.

Whichever ones best suited or erased the last few days.

Passing 'contadini' would merely raise their heads in grumpy dismay, as they leaned on their crooks and sticks, annoyed if only for a moment by the disturbance, their bodies motionless. Eyes peering out of blank faces. Under their straw hats.

In fact, he was beginning to recognise a few of these old, monosyllabic men, who too were making a return to their own little plots of land, spread across the fertile slopes. This is where they tended their fruit trees, grapevines and row upon row of their beloved tomato plants. They would exchange brief greetings, in the form of a nod of their straw-hatted heads, with Giovanni calling out a loud 'buongiorno' and beeping his horn, as he went. It served to show his friendship, as well as alert them to move out of the way, which they would often do very slowly in a disgruntled manner, like stubborn pigeons.

The stranger prince returning to his Palazzo. The modern man and his car, a by now familiar sight, on the mountain road of a Saturday morning.

Once a slow, still cagey trust had set in, they began to offer him 'samples' of their prized produce, each surly 'contadino' proudly and fervently believing his own fruit and vegetables superior to the others. The one thing that got them excited, to cause eyes as well as mouths to smile. All that they grew and harvested. For them the one thing in the world that really counted. Humility never part of the process, when it came to showing off and sharing their produce and accompanying tales.

Young men absent from the scene, as the business of war had called them away…the few that had returned, now battle-scarred and slowly fighting off the effects of tuberculosis, malaria, typhoid.

In time, Giovanni asked one of them if he wanted to earn himself a bit of extra money and take care of the palace orchard. The trees clearly neglected since the titled property-owners had moved out years beforehand. Raffaele was the one who for some reason, Giovanni felt most comfortable with…not quite as remote or conceited as the rest…coming across as a little less hostile and a little more thoughtful. Equally dour, however.

Perhaps he reminded him slightly of Nonno Giulillo…though on closer inspection his mouth definitely revealed a far greater number of missing teeth! Angelo's strong, healthy teeth in spite of advanced years…still a newsworthy topic back in the village…long after his death. Whenever the subject of dentistry arose.

Without committing himself to the offer of paid work, the 'contadino' merely said that when he had time, he would go and take a look at the trees in question, to ascertain how many might be salvageable. The man from the city didn't press him for an immediate answer, certainly never his way either, merely adding that he would be there all weekend, should he want to go up and inspect them. Never give the other the impression that you need them, that you care one way or the other. They shook hands and Giovanni drove further up the winding hill.

Just a couple of hours later, he happened to spot the very same 'contadino' wandering around what used to be the prize orchard, taking serious stock of the current situation.

The likely to be new gardener refusing point blank Giovanni's invite to enter the palazzo kitchen. He did remove his hat, however, and happily drank the coffee just outside the door. The two men finally settling upon a deal in the nearby courtyard, which involved Raffaele working there three days a week, at least for the time being…with the view to restoring many of the fruit trees to their former glory. It was going to be a long-term project. Giovanni pointed out some of the outbuildings and potting sheds, where he could store both his own equipment together with any items already there. This turned out to be an assortment of ladders, wheelbarrows, scythes, hoes, shovels, sieves, rakes and buckets, of varying sizes. All covered in the ubiquitous fine cobweb sheeting. The two men would meet up on a regular basis, in order to discuss progress.

Revealing no signs of gratitude or little in the way of optimism, merely stating with the inevitable cheerless shrug, that he would see what he could do. That he couldn't promise anything. Not a problem for Giovanni; he knew his people. He knew what made them tick. If the man hadn't wanted to do it, or thought it was going to be a hopeless task, he wouldn't have agreed to it in the first place.

Raffaele turned out to be a hardworking and trustworthy employee…even humble enough to admit defeat when something didn't work out. Coupled with the fact that he wasn't the type to talk to others about Giovanni or what went on at the Palazzo. In their time together, the two never discussed external matters such as politics or the war, their verbal exchanges rarely veering far from the current state of the trees, weather or condition of the soil. However, Giovanni enjoyed his company, admired his wisdom. He sometimes thought it was as though the ghost of Nonno Giulillo had returned.

During this time, not much else happened at the Palazzo. Just hard work, inside and out. Little gossip to pass on in any case.

About six months later, and putting his surly pride to one side, the gardener mumbled his way through asking Giovanni if there was any chance of some paid work for his niece, someone he had never previously mentioned. Cleaning, cooking, laundry work…that kind of thing. Either in the city or at the Palazzo. She was a good girl…'na buona guagliotta'… reliable and hardworking. She lived in a nearby 'paesino' or hamlet. True to form, Raffaele never giving more information than necessary.

With his boss merely replying that he'd give the matter some thought. Raffaele not very confident that such a busy and seemingly important man, a wealthy city dweller, would even remember his request, let alone do something about it.

He decided to wait a week or two before mentioning it again. Ninetta's family's situation was by now becoming desperate, but in spite of this, Raffaele simply wouldn't bring himself to beg. Perhaps, another reminder, when the two men were next due to meet? Perhaps say nothing but take her up to the Palazzo with him one Saturday morning?

He shouldn't have worried though. The following week, Giovanni called him to the kitchen door and told him to bring her with him next time. There were, in fact, quite a few ways in which she could make herself useful; sorting and washing linen; polishing mirrors and silverware; sharpening knives, repairing (where possible) seemingly ancient drapes and the obvious ongoing domestic duties. He said he was prepared to give her a chance.

Clearly for the time being, the Palazzo had become Giovanni's refuge but he also wanted to think about it as a place, like a once comatose patient, that was gradually coming back to life and for that, it needed human beings. Their work and skills, but even more fundamental, their presence there. He had already made a start then, a gardener and now possibly a domestic.

He would definitely take Giulia there one day. Often, he hoped. Where, as a young girl she could dream of being the daughter of a duke…or even a king. A place she could spend long hours exploring. Both inside and out in its extensive grounds. Yes, he realised now he was preparing it for her future visits. He would set about turning the first few rooms into an elegant home for them both to enjoy. Father and daughter.

Ninetta then made her appearance. A figure framed by the dilapidated arched doorway…evoking in Giovanni's mind, that he was in the presence of a wingless angel from a half-remembered Renaissance painting. Her uncle then brusquely nudging over the threshold. A tiny slip of a girl, was Giovanni's second reaction to her and as to be expected, Raffaele quickly read his thoughts. Not quite living up to the image of the sturdy country girl that her future employer had envisaged.

"Yes there's nothing of her, is there? You'd be surprised though…just look at the muscles in her arms. Roll your sleeves up, girl, let signor Giovanni see for himself. She can compete with most of the young men around here. Well, when they were here. Lifting, carrying, digging…she's been a good girl to her Zia and me over the last few months."

Giovanni saw her cheeks blush scarlet through her pale skin, as he called for her to join him in the kitchen. Raffaele remaining stubbornly at the door. She managed to reply to all his questions but only with the help of looking down at the floor. What was her birth name, Ninetta was surely a pet name. How old she was. Who her parents were. Any brothers and sisters, and finally a question about what she thought of the palazzo.…She replied that her 'nome di battesimo' was actually Monica, that she was nearly seventeen and dutifully went on to answer his other questions in the correct order. Her eyes surprisingly lighting up when he finally mentioned the Palazzo. Ninetta was now ready to remove the fixed downward gaze and turned it straight to Giovanni instead.

"Oh yes, I love it. I've always loved it. It's a part of our lives here. It looks down over us. It doesn't matter that bits of it are falling down, or that the family moved out long ago. It will be with us forever. After we have all passed away. It is there in my window every morning. In the evening, I watch the moon float over its turrets, making it even more beautiful, more magical. I am so happy you have come to save it."

"That's enough, that's enough. Il Signor Giovanni hasn't got time to listen to the ramblings of a silly young girl. I apologise for her…I don't know where all that came from. Santo cielo!"

She suddenly came to, out of her unanticipated and breathless reverie. Her uncle had warned her not to waste the time of the important man from the city and so she apologised in turn for speaking out too much. She had made her uncle angry. It was then that she noticed the cups and bowls piled up in the sink, and rushed over to wash them, quickly redeeming herself for taking up the time of such a man.

Giovanni looked on, somewhat bemused by the unexpected flurry of words and images.

This brief encounter had given him a glimpse of the reaction he hoped Giulia would have one day, on finding out that her father owned a palace.

Chapter 38
Blood Ties

Although Giulia remained at the core of everything Giovanni was now striving to achieve, he never forgot his first-born child. Perhaps it was due to her early adoption or a case of an underdeveloped conscience, which caused him not to think of her in the same way he did for Giulia. His feelings towards their mothers also entirely different. He had changed a lot, however, in the short space of time that separated the two births. The war had changed him. The world was also a different place now. No one in a position to foretell the future, only that great change was on its way.

In truth, the image of Carmela's tightly creased pink face, as it sobbed and sobbed, had never abandoned him. Like something that padded around his head, and then every so often, let out a tumultuous roar. It was becoming clear to him that in order to find peace of mind, he had to deal with the matter. To check on her current situation. Yes, to go and see her. Not quite knowing what might happen from then on or even what he wanted to happen. He knew in any case that it was impossible to claim her back.

There were one or two aspects of his past behaviour that he could begin to put right, he concluded. Blood ties counted like no other in the way he read the world.

At the same time, as regards his professional life, shady deals with shady business acquaintances continued…a journey in parallel.

He had only recently discovered that Carmela's adoptive parents, the couple that he had encountered, albeit fleetingly, the day of his surprise return to the apartment, weren't able to keep her either. It had something to do with illness and then the coming of war. With the help of a priest, the little girl had therefore gone to live at the home of a new family, another childless couple. This meant leaving the prospect of a city life for one in the countryside. Though of course Carmela wouldn't go on to remember either the city or her very first family.

The irrational workings of fate (or of an absent Fortuna) had cast her to be the daughter of a middle-aged couple, the only parents she would ever know.

It was her new mother, who 'ruled the roost' at home and therefore ruled over her. All had gone to plan in the end, in spite of their earlier misfortunes. The woman decided to adopt, once she and her husband had given up all hope of having children of their own, a ready formed little girl. Neither a tiny baby nor an adolescent. Someone she could still train. A girl, who would soon be helping them on their plot of land and one day share the cooking and housework chores. Someone who would look after them in the oncoming years as the ravages of old age and infirmity approached. A wise and practical investment. It is true that on first setting eyes on the little girl in question, the woman was disappointed at her plainness, the dull-eyed expression and drooping mouth on the blank little face that looked up at her.

In the woman's head, however, she was soon able to turn these 'defects' into happy advantages. Just how her mind operated. What need did they have of a girl with a pretty face and charming ways? That would have spelled trouble. Such a girl would want to seek her destiny elsewhere.

"Yes, she'll do. We'll soon breathe some life into her."

Her husband said nothing, his best option always that of nodding in agreement.

He being a man who, to other people at least, occupied life's shadows, the outer edges of existence, to the point of being almost silent, invisible, forgettable, even when present in the room. He was by nature a simple and patient soul, who preferred to spend his waking hours away from the house. On the outside. That is, he would get up very early to work in the fields, not returning until sunset, seven days a week. Where he tended to nature's creation. A world, which demanded few words and relentless hard work. In the biting cold of winter…and beneath summer's relentless sun. Little need for the contamination of human company. Here was where he knew he belonged, with its rigors and struggles he was more than capable of confronting.

Therefore, Carmela's collection of early memories would hinge mainly around life with her new mother. The never-ending chores, the harsh needlework sessions, taking place in candlelight. The interminable list of responsibilities of a gruelling life in the countryside. Nothing in the way of treats or rewards. Little in the way of tangible affection; very few words of encouragement. Nothing much then to look forward to. Notwithstanding the fact that in time, her 'mother' did come to love her.

Not at all the life her natural father would have chosen for her.

He consoling himself with the thought, *Whether the law liked it or not, that he was still, in effect, her father. Had given her life. Our only gift to the world that really counted.*

After a long search, Giovanni was finally able to locate the home of his daughter. He arrived there by car one morning and asked the small, aproned woman, who opened the door to him, if he might come back within the hour. He had some important news for her and her husband. Making the excuse that he had a couple of errands to run in the meantime. She was understandably bewildered, on seeing this well-dressed and well-spoken city stranger and even more so, to learn that he had something to tell them. Having no idea at all, as to what it meant. All in all, more than a bit put out, as it would affect her day's busy schedule, and yet she still found herself agreeing to speak with him. By now entertaining more than just a hint of curiosity.

Giovanni returned, as promised. She led him into the kitchen, told him where to sit down, while she prepared the obligatory coffee. This she placed on a little tray indicating the presence of the sugar bowl and a couple of little spoons, so he could serve himself and stir. She got him to take a slice of the sponge cake she had baked the previous day. He obediently ate the cake, while looking around the room, listening out for any childlike chatter from elsewhere in the house but Carmela didn't seem to be there.

She continued to busy herself. The pungent smokiness of roasting peppers, beginning to fill the whole room, made bearable only by the door propped open with a broom. This familiar smell always causing him to feel nauseous.

He didn't have to wait long to hear his daughter's name though or discover where she was.

"My daughter Carmelina is out in the fields with my husband today. He'll bring her back soon. You can tell ME whatever it is. I'll tell him about it later."

"Alright, if you think that's best…what I'm going to tell you is highly confidential, something very few people know. I don't want it to alarm you, Heaven forbid, as I have come a long way to ask for your help. It would involve keeping everything I tell you to yourselves…but I can make it worth your while. Do you think that sounds reasonable?"

The woman refusing to nod or to show any signs of compliance. Merely choosing to examine his face. Direct in manner, she spoke up.

"I'm afraid I don't know what you mean. I can't agree to something I don't understand. Explain yourself more clearly. I've got a lot to do."

"Yes, of course, you are right. I just wanted to make sure you understand that what I have to tell you isn't to travel beyond these walls."

"Well, you have nothing to worry about as regards my husband." She laughed sarcastically. "He barely utters more than five words a day! As for me I've always kept myself to myself. Just don't have the time to gossip or meddle in other people's lives."

"I can see you are a straightforward and honest woman. Just listen to what I have to say and then I will answer any questions you might have."

She drew up another chair towards the scrubbed table and Giovanni told her about Brigida, without revealing her name. How she had become pregnant. How she couldn't keep the baby. The story of the adoption…even confiding in the woman about the surprising effect that the man seeing his child had made upon him. By this time, sharp witted as ever, she had guessed that he was the girl's father and started to bristle, now also guessing that he wanted her back. He swiftly read her thoughts, one of his innate talents, and interrupted his account with the words,

"Have no fear. I have not come here to take her away. No one wants to take her from you. Be a little more patient, and I will spell out for you what it is I am asking of you."

In spite of herself, she took him at his word and sat back in the rigidly upright chair to hear the rest of the story.

What he said he wanted from her was twofold. Firstly, to be able to see Carmela a few times a year by prior arrangement, without ever divulging, for the good of all concerned, who he really was. Secondly, for the woman to go and visit his younger daughter Giulia from time to time at the 'monastero'. He would arrange this with the nuns, passing her off as an older (much older, in fact) sister, making her the little girl's aunt. It would give Giulia a sense of wider family, and make her feel less alone.

What he didn't share with her was the thought that, in this way, he could see Carmela grow up, and make sure that when away on business, a trusted 'family' member (such as Gennaro or Nunzia) could also check on her wellbeing. Strict discipline had its place and uses, but if it ever descended into cruelty, then for

Giovanni, it would be unforgivable. He went on to explain that he would pay for their time and travel costs and provide them with a modest, yet regular income for their compliance.

They were proud people and he sensed they wouldn't have wanted or needed more. They would comply with his requests. Provided that he always kept his side of the bargain.

Giovanni had already considered the implications of her divulging the reason for his visit. Whom she might tell. How or if the woman and her husband might benefit further from someone else knowing. That they might try to blackmail him for more money.

Of course, they had absolutely no idea, what he was capable of, but he deduced that the risks were minimal. He had pitched his 'offer' perfectly.

The woman had shown a flicker of pride, a rare hint of smile, that this stranger had chosen her to be the custodian of his personal affairs, and wouldn't have cared one way or the other that he had fathered two children outside of marriage. One daughter given up in adoption and the other living in a convent orphanage. That was his business. The promise of a regular income a very attractive prospect. She and her husband no longer having to worry quite so much about poor harvests and unpaid bills, at least for the next fifteen years or so.

A man and a little girl then suddenly appeared at the kitchen door, each quite taken aback on seeing an elegant 'gentleman' seated at their kitchen table. Little Carmela ran off at once, after having let out a stifled cry. At which her mother called her back. Just the once. Consequently, the little girl reappeared, her dirty hands partially covering her eyes, so that she wouldn't have to look directly at the visitor…or let him properly see her. She eventually plucked up the courage to say hello to him, spurred on by her mother's sharp monosyllabic tones and flashing eyes…before asking permission to go feed the geese. Her father, after having squeezed out a hasty 'buongiorno' of his own, as he hovered over the scene, hands deep in his pockets, also waited for the moment when he could take his leave.

Carmela's life, made manifest, in the space of an hour.

They shook hands on reaching an agreement, after Giovanni had detailed the procedures and the woman had filled in her husband on every detail of the unexpected meeting.

Chapter 39
Another Brief yet Portentous Interlude

Progress. Giovanni had at last seen his elder daughter. He had met her parents. He hadn't particularly warmed to either husband or wife, but that wasn't the point. Things could have worked out so much worse, he concluded. For the time being, at least, he contented himself that Carmela was well fed, had enough clothes on her back...that she was generally well looked after. That even though the family's way of life was of a basic standard, she was in the home of seemingly honest, God-fearing people, who believed in hard work and practicalities. By the end of the meeting, they had also agreed to all his requests. He now felt much better in himself. He would go and see them from time to time, to watch his daughter grow up. Even steer her course in the future. Never revealing to Carmela who he was. She would come to know him as 'the family friend'.

Without having a specific plan for her, in the same way as he had for Giulia, but having to acknowledge, of course, that he had relinquished control of her long ago.

Back in the city, he had also returned to the life of forming loose liaisons with young and willing females, even one or two older ones. Casual friendships, free and easy. If ever he did think he might be coming under a woman's spell, though this was rare, he nipped the rapport in the bud and likewise if she began to show any signs of falling in love with him. He would tell her, quite firmly, that he had grown bored and no longer needed her company. Cruelty, which, in reality, meant kindness. On both sides. Nothing ambiguous. Ever.

More recently, at the Palazzo, he had found himself chasing after the fresh-faced Ninetta. It had become a kind of weekend sport. Something quite different from life in the city. Unplanned, in fact all starting quite absurdly...precisely because she never came alone! The young girl had a constant chaperone, in the shape of an elderly woman, who in spite of her massive size, would travel up that last bit of mountain atop a very unfortunate donkey. With Ninetta almost skipping along by her side. A bizarre and highly amusing scene, which played out each Saturday morning and sometimes even on a Sunday after mass, a scene which Giovanni occasionally witnessed from an upper window. That huge mass of taut female flesh straddled across the animal's back. Front view or from behind. Arriving or departing. Would she ever fall off? She could barely walk! How would they get her back up on her feet? He awaited such a day with evil anticipation. Poor dumb creature, who had to carry her.

On the other days of the week, it was different, as Ninetta would arrive alone or in the company of her uncle. As everyone quickly came to know, Giovanni remained in the city from Monday to Friday. Eliminating the possibility of his ever seducing her.

She had struck Giovanni from that first encounter…a nearly ripe peach, almost ready for the plucking…but also, for what she had said about his castle. The fact that, in spite of her lowly station in life, there seemed to be more to her than met the eye but he hadn't entertained any thoughts…yet…of bedding her.

It all started as a kind of game, when master and servant became aware that the chaperone's eyes would grow heavy in the afternoons, as soon as a wine-accompanied lunch was over and that Giovanni, in order to test if she was truly asleep would start to move his hand to touch Ninetta in full view. Her hand, her cheek, her mouth, graduating to a furiously beating heart. Man and girl each enjoying the frisson of risk. They came to know how long she needed to sleep and just how deeply. She would always deny having slept at all! This amorous subterfuge allowing them to hide behind doors or slip into cupboards, even sometimes when she was awake…so close to her and yet still out of sight.

Ninetta proud that she had won the attentions of such an important and (in her opinion) attractive older man, appeared more than happy to go along with their dallying, delighting in the furtive nature of this new (or more like, one and only) adventure, and (for her in particular) the risks they were taking. A succession of little episodes, that they both found hilariously funny, played out only metres away from her amply proportioned protectress and at the same time hidden from view. The pair often finding it difficult to stifle their laughter or conceal just how physically close their bodies were.

For a long while, the pair merely flirting…a kind of eighteenth-century 'bundling' equivalent. Each of them, at least for the time being, wanting the game to continue for just a little bit longer and given that there was a lot of work to do at the Palazzo, these tight and breathless encounters had to remain short and sweet. Giovanni not letting her off any set tasks.

Inevitably, it was only a matter of time…when it came for her to succumb completely to their mutual longings. It all seemed so natural. That's where it had all been leading. Little by little. She looked up to him and at him, her eyes mad with passion. Her lover, older and wiser and seemingly of higher social ranking. As for Giovanni, it was all charmingly simple…she was amusing company and taking care of all his present needs. Each enjoying the breathless intimacy provided her sleepy chaperone, Donna Concetta, never came to suspect what was really going on.

Ninetta wasn't a stupid girl, however. She was fully aware she was playing with fire, that she could easily become pregnant with Giovanni's child. She knew all about the consequences for village girls losing their reputations, about the dishonour that would fall upon her family and under no illusion that he would ever agree to make an honest woman of her. They were each on different paths. They each had a separate destiny. She was, for the present, merely enjoying herself, living out her cravings for something different. At a time and place where such female behaviour was deemed unforgivable. Their encounters fuelling her youthful madness but she knew their time would eventually be up and that it was probably coming soon. It would serve for the future, as it continued to play out in her head. Nothing you really desire lasts forever, in any case.

She would later remember that there had been a time in her life, when she had followed her girlish impulses and had embarked upon a real adventure.

She had, in fact, a back-up plan, ready to go.

She was, at the same time, 'seeing' a young man from a nearby village. He, like many others, had recently returned from the war and had quickly become enchanted by a girl, who called herself Ninetta. He learned that her family had recently suffered a great misfortune and were struggling financially. Not only was she pretty, with her fairish hair and blue-grey eyes, quite unusual in their part of the world, but had already earned herself the reputation for helping people in need, rarely complaining about her lot. Remaining positive at all times. Definitely a strong girl, a hard worker, in spite of her tiny frame. He hadn't wasted any time in broaching the subject of marriage, to which she merely replied that she needed just a little more time, but that he shouldn't worry, as there was no one else waiting in the wings.

A few months later, it was she, who brought up the subject, as she wandered out one morning to greet him.

"Do you remember there was once something you wanted to ask me? Well, you can go ahead and ask now, if you still feel the same. I am all ears."

At which he grabbed her by the waist, spun her around a couple of times and then placed her firmly on an available stool.

"Greco Monica, my little Ninetta, would you do me the honour of accepting my proposal of marriage. Will you make me the proudest man in the village?"

The she-spider had set the trap and he, the fly, had fallen into it. Effortlessly. A moment of relief, another moment for her to savour. She liked him. He was a good man. They would have a good marriage. The tiny life she now carried inside her would have a father and she would take her secret to the grave. A true secret having only the one owner. Things had to move fast now so that no village suspicions would arise. She knew from local gossip that it was possible to give birth a few weeks earlier than expected. Her tracks she had covered. No witnesses. Not her uncle. Nor the worthy (or unworthy) chaperone. A young man lined up, who was madly in love with her. Ready and waiting.

Two weeks before their wedding day, she wisely allowed her 'husband to be' to lie with her. He was more than willing. At bursting point in fact. Up until then, she hadn't even let him kiss her on the lips. They had never been properly alone in any case.

He spoke from his heart. About how much he loved her. How he would enjoy seeing her do all those little things husbands had come to expect from their wives, such as bringing him the first coffee of the day, while he was still in bed. Laying out his clothes, laying the table, cooking his meals. How at the end of each gruelling day in the fields, he would think of her waiting for him and of their night ahead. The children that would arrive…he even knew the first would be a boy. They would call him Salvatore after his father.

She sat back in silence and listened to his list of unremarkable dreams. Never disclosing her own, not really needing any now, remarkable or otherwise. Having learned in a very short space of time, that there was so much more out there, but that would be for another life…not the one that now lay spread out in front of her. After all, everything had gone to plan. She had been shrewd but also fortunate. As a girl of her circumstances, this was the best she could achieve and she refused to be disheartened.

"I'm afraid I won't be able to come to the Palazzo any more. I am getting married. Yes, it's all happened quite quickly but Rico doesn't see the point in waiting. We will live at his father's farm. They've put aside a couple of rooms for us. He's already doing them up a bit. It will be fine. I'm sure you will find a replacement. There are so many girls around like me, looking for work, looking to help their families…my uncle will of course help, if you ask him. So, thank you and goodbye."

Ninetta stepped forward to shake his hand and as was customary in such situations, Giovanni calmly replying that he wished the couple every happiness. He watched her for the last time begin to travel back down the hill…with the oversized chaperone and the donkey.

The end of another brief interlude.

Chapter 40
Giulia Goes Up a Mountain

In that terrible stretch of history, when the whole world was at war, up to half of Italian soldiers found themselves, at one point or another, held in labour camps. When the fighting was over, the dismantling of such camps meant that they could make their way home, only to greet an Italy reeling from a non-existent economy, its major cities reduced to rubble. The cost of living spiralling ever higher and agriculture suffering also. Infrastructure almost inexistent due to the vast number of crazed bombing attacks. It came as no surprise that there would be mass unemployment, but with some of the returning soldiers now able to take up the factory jobs, which women had temporarily acquired, in order to keep alive the war effort. Women's lives therefore, about to change once again, for them to slot back to where they were before. Back inside their domestic walls. For those that allowed it.

All signs that there lay ahead a long and bitter road towards recovery.

The lingering and open hostility from the 'partigiani' or partisans (also made up of many female members), persisted. In the south (where our story is set), they had been fighting on three fronts; against the Nazi occupation, against Italy's own brand of Fascism and against the historic exploitation by ruling elites of the peasants and working classes. Thus, a kind of civil or domestic war continued, well after the solemn signing of peace treaties. The desperate struggle for justice and equality needing to continue at home. Communist ideas gaining ground.

Circumstances which allowed, at all levels, 'il mercato nero' or the black market to flourish, especially when it came to the acquiring of food.

Plans for American funds to help the Italian economy were afoot but would take years to materialise.

When Giulia was about seven years old, the so-called age of reason, Giovanni took her, for the first time, to see the Palazzo, his mountain top lair. Something he had promised to do a while beforehand. She had almost given up waiting, just accepting that it was probably never going to happen. Unable to dislodge it entirely however, from her mind's eye. Having heard from his own lips, that her father owned a castle… Something no child could merely put to one side. Even though he had also told her that part of it looked like a crumbling ruin.

She always remembering the convent's own collection of fairy tales, all bound in their dark red, blue or green covers (some of which she had read many times). Easily able to conjure up scenes of blond princesses stuck at the top of high towers; prisoners languishing in damp, rat-infested dungeons; grand banquets, with entertainment provided by jugglers, acrobats and jesters. Even stretching to ghosts, magic and spells. She wondered what she too might find there, in that fairy book world, if only he would agree to keep his promise.

However, that other voice in her head, reminding her all too frequently that, nothing like that happened in real life and definitely not in a world inhabited by girls like her.

Giovanni had never resorted to spoiling her. Not even in a misplaced effort to assuage his own feelings of guilt. He would take her there when he decided she deserved to go. The last thing he wanted was to undo the good work carried out at the convent. Merely because he had the money and the means. That's what he'd told the strict disciplinarian sisters, who cared for her day on day. Such a treat would have to come as a surprise, 'out of the blue', a reward for something she had already achieved. They inevitably agreed with him.

Her latest school report ('la pagella') glowed once again…excellent in nearly every aspect, and where she didn't naturally shine, such as in mathematics, it was clear to her teachers that she was putting every effort into making good progress. Giovanni's expanding heart brimming with love and pride as his eyes lingered over her teachers' inky comments. As he scrutinised his daughter's 'voti' on the page where her latest set of test scores appeared. Fully aware that he was still in the presence of Suor Agostina, but making sure that she couldn't detect a more sensitive (therefore more vulnerable) side to his character.

So, on this occasion, having already informed the nuns of his intention, he whisked his little daughter away for the day, far away from the austere looking convent walls, without letting on to her however where it was they were heading.

"Where are we going, Papa? Is it to the sea? Oh no, it can't be that...I don't have a swimming costume or towel with me. Do you know Suor Agnese took us swimming a few weeks ago? It was all a bit scary...the waves were this high."

She shot up her right arm to show him just how high, only managing to strike with a bang the inside of the car roof with her little hand! For some reason not wanting to let on to her father that she had hurt herself, she continued speaking through gritted teeth. She managed the pain without allowing any awaiting tears to spill out onto her face.

"...but exciting too. We laughed and laughed and licked the salt off our faces. She said we could go again. And this time have a picnic on the beach, when it's been cleaned up. Why won't you tell me where you are taking me?"

Giovanni merely gave her a quick sideways glance, as he smiled to himself but continued to say nothing. He enjoyed seeing her frustration and listening to her childish ramblings. Hearing and seeing the effect life with the sisters was having on her. When she had finished that bit of news item, she contented herself with picking out the more interesting features of the moving landscape, many of which she described to him. A running commentary. The unusual bird she could not name, as it flit across the sky; the billowing cloud formations, where she made out the faces of some of her teachers and other vehicles that they passed on the road. It was a route she was certain they had never covered before but it all seemed to be taking a very long time! They didn't usually take the car at all but instead went for a walk or for something to eat in a nearby village.

At one point, during a lull in her chatter, he noticed that she had dozed off...her busy little head regularly bobbing forward in the passenger seat.

He decided there and then to stop the car...just for a few minutes. He felt compelled to take a long look at her...but without her knowing. To watch the subtle rise and fall, rise and fall of her little body, as she slept. To examine her hands...did each still have the row of tiny dimples? To peer into the sleepy heart-shaped face, framed by the halo of dark hair, her head resting upon her shoulder. To get an even clearer picture of her. To discover things about how she was now, at the age of seven. Many traces of Giulia, the baby, now gone forever.

Today she was wearing a thin cotton dress, with a kind of flower print, tied around the waist by two ribbons that were beginning to come loose. Pale pink and blue. He realised that he hadn't bothered to notice things like that during past visits. Such minor detail suddenly growing in importance. Seeing the flimsy dress she wore made him want to cry. It spoke of innocence and vulnerability.

Of misplaced optimism. Of her childlike acceptance as to how her life had turned out.

Why did she seem so cheerful, so carefree? She was his creation and yet with all his wealth and power, he couldn't give her what he believed every child needed.

The ordinary things, a life with a home, two parents, brothers and sisters, grandparents, pets even, visitors....A simple, if highly underestimated lifestyle, one we all take for granted but only if we already have it...of shared hours spent around a table, of people huddled near an open fire in the depths of winter. Eating and drinking together, sharing stories, taking part in little conversations, irrelevant to the rest of the world. Collections of handed down sayings and theories, accepted or dismissed, but rarely forgotten. Even the painful things; the frequent rebukes, rows, accusations, punishments, having to wait one's turn. Then praying together, marking feast days in special ways. Playing cards. Heated family arguments, apologies, taking sides. Working, cooking, sewing, smoking, knitting, drinking...reading, cursing. Together.

The nuns never able to recreate such imperfect and yet necessary family life. Offering up a community type model in its place. The best they could do for these 'left over' boys and girls. Rule-based for the good of all. Ritualised structures for clarity. Timetables. Kindly, objective and fair detachment.

He noticed her long, dark eyelashes, as if for the first time since she was a baby, as they still managed to curl back over her eyelids. He kissed those eyelids very carefully, one at a time, and for some unknown reason, that little space between her eyes just above her nose, for which he didn't know if a name existed. He felt and heard her warm breath. All the while admiring his work of living art, his masterpiece.

It was time to start up the car again in the direction of the palazzo.

By the time the little girl had woken up, it appeared to her that her father was driving a little more slowly than before and that they had started to climb what looked like an enormous hill. Without mentioning the fact that she had fallen asleep or that he had stopped the car, he told her it was best she sat in the back now to look at the emerging view from the rear window...no seat belts in those days. In that way, she would feel less sick, as they wound their way around the ribbon of mountain road. Obediently...the thought of contradicting him (or any of the adults who cared for her) not once entering her head...she clambered over the gearstick, installing herself on the back seat and then deciding to kneel, in order to have full access to the window and its view.

He told her to look out for certain things, that were by now very familiar to him. Could she spot the sea? What colour was it today? How many orange trees could she make out? How many different animals were there on the slopes?

Had she any idea now where their final destination was going to be?

He looked at her every so often from the rear-view mirror, her little head poker stiff, he having to imagine now which expression occupied the lovely face; all the while, taking in each of her exuberant comments and well considered answers to his, in the main, banal questions.

Giovanni and his little girl. The king of the castle and his beautiful princess. Everything that had happened in his life leading up to and converging upon the moments now playing out.

Chapter 41
On Top of the World

Giovanni had employed an older, far less desirable female this time, to replace the energetic Ninetta. He was pleased with her efforts and after a few weeks of her working for him at the Palazzo, he told her he would take her on permanently…and that on the following Saturday they would be having a guest for lunch. The very first guest, as far as she was aware.

It turned out she was quite surprised, if not more than a bit put out, on discovering on the day itself, that the hitherto unnamed guest happened to be a little girl. All that fuss, not to mention extra work, for a child!

For a little girl, who promptly on arrival, stepped forward to hold out her hand in the direction of the domestic, saying that she was pleased to meet her…uttering the grown-up word 'piacere' and politely informing her that her name was Giulia. Once again taken aback, the sour-faced woman, whose name was Marta, found herself following Giulia's example. While actually still thinking, *All this to-do for a slip of a girl.*

Giovanni passed Giulia off as distant family, sharing with his daughter, as soon as Marta's back was turned, a huge wink and silent 'hand over mouth' chuckle. Each knowing that he had told the truth, and yet at the same time had knowingly left a somewhat different impression as to what their connection really was. Family, yes and distant too because she lived quite a long way away. All part of the secrecy the pair had concocted earlier while still in the car…in order to make the day more enjoyable (for Giulia of course!), a day of games, secrets and complicity.

Little did Giulia know the real reason her father needed to hoodwink the woman. Permanently. Everyone they would ever encounter. That in order to keep her safe, separate from his other world, he couldn't ever take the risk of revealing just who she was…how much she meant to him.

After a late and leisurely breakfast, Giovanni said that he would give, as promised, his daughter a guided tour of the parts of the Palazzo that she could then go off and explore by herself. Anywhere else was out of bounds, as the building was unsafe. If she wanted to go outside, she would have to ask permission first, and once he was ready, he would accompany her himself. He said that he trusted her. He knew by now she was a sensible girl.

He in the meantime already beginning to work his way through certain papers he had taken out of his briefcase.

Having agreed to everything he had stipulated, Giulia began, in a whirl of excitement, to pour out of her own rucksack the stuff she had packed for this adventure. Not knowing of course, at the start of the day, just where they were heading. Only that they wouldn't be back until nightfall. Included amongst the contents, a large block of paper and some pencils, as the first thing she planned to do was draw a map of the castle and its rooms. She also had with her a couple of little dolls, who shared her convent bed and who, as if by magic, would now turn into two princesses. She would ask her father for some scissors and if he had anything to make crowns for them. If not, the sheets of paper would do.

On the other hand, she could always make coloured flags instead, to attach to the castle walls.

A somewhat bemused father raised his head from the pile of paperwork, looking on in silence, humbled once more by her busy chatter, her mobile imagination and sense of enterprise, her cheerfulness.

Marta offered to show her to 'her' room, with its long-arched windows, sloping ceiling and creaky wooden floorboards. Giulia fell in love with it. Straightaway! It had become from that moment on…her very own room, even though she knew that she wouldn't be staying overnight. A room she wouldn't have to share with anyone else. Her father had been firm about that. A room with only what she chose to put there. A room that in spite of its little damp patches, a cracked pane of glass or two (fortunately high up) and some peeling wallpaper…might still one day become fit for a princess. As soon as Marta had departed, she flung herself onto the four-poster bed, sank low into its deep feathery eiderdown, while looking up at the curved lines of the huge vaulted ceiling and trying to make out some very faded artwork.

Then it only took her a couple of minutes to unpack and place the two books she had brought on the nearest marble windowsill.

Every so often, as she entered and explored each of the permitted rooms and spaces, she would look down at the little wristwatch her father had bought her, on the day of her seventh birthday, therefore a very recent acquisition. Remembering how, on that happy day, he had placed her firmly on his lap and carefully eased the watch out of its box. How he had then put it to his ear and checked its time against the time showing on his own. All good! Hers was a sensible watch, which she wore on her left wrist. Of good quality, mounted on a plain leather strap and with a bold round face, revealing clearly defined numbers. She loved that watch more than any other possession, especially because the engraving on the back carried the words, 'per Giulia' (for Giulia); it had become part of her and she wore it whenever the nuns allowed. It had helped her learn to tell the time…an added incentive…especially the trickier aspects, such as 'twenty-five to' or remembering 'a quarter to eleven meant the same as 10.45!' All made easier by the fact that she spent so much time staring down at it or checking to see that it was still working. When not on her arm, she returned it to the same long, slim box it had come in.

She had of course already learned just how important it was to be punctual…for prayers, for meals, for lessons, for bedtime. Definitely not wanting to show disrespect today towards her father (or to Marta) by being even a couple of minutes late.

She returned to her room every so often to draw the latest discovery. Some of the sketches soon turning into diagrams, as she decided to label things, which better explained what everything was. Some she was just not happy with, so she just scrunched up the paper, and tried again and again to produce something more acceptable. Afraid that on returning to the convent she might otherwise forget. Not wanting to lose anything of the day. She carefully wrote her name at the top of each sheet of paper…never asking herself, whether her father (or anyone else who currently inhabited her life) would ever be interested in discussing the drawings with her.

After lunch, Giovanni and Giulia went outside. They spent a good while kicking around an old football, after which he spoke to his daughter in an adult way about his plans for the main courtyard and the orchard, which he added, was already showing signs of progress. He introduced her to his gardener friend, Raffaele, who uncharacteristically, was making quite an effort to start up a conversation with her, probably much taken (or mystified) by her elegant manners and grown-up ways; her seriousness. The mismatch of such courteous maturity in the figure of a little girl. She replying to each of his questions. Laughing at his dubious efforts to be playful and in spite of the fact, she didn't always understand what he was telling her, whenever his dialect won through.

Her father never quite certain, however, where the 'real' Giulia lay under all those layers of ritualised civility. Somewhere trapped within the mound of well-rehearsed platitudes.

That afternoon his little girl enjoyed solitary pleasure as she began to dig a hole in a shady patch of dampish soil. It had rained that night…and she soon found herself uncovering a host of 'creepy crawlies'; centipedes, millipedes, little shiny beetles, caterpillars and quite a few worms, spanning a range of widths, lengths and shades of pink. Pale to vibrant. Some of which she judged repulsive. A cluster of ants, moving in every direction, had also appeared, surrounding her as if by magic. Having temporarily cast aside the world of royal princesses and fairy tale castles, she found that she just couldn't tear herself away from such humble treasures and their mysterious underworld habitat.

The nuns at the convent never allowing the girls such intimacy with nature, let alone fingernails caked with soil.

In her newfound freedom, she became fascinated as to how the tiny creatures crawled, threaded, slithered and curled. Some exceptionally fast too. For some unknown reason, she even set herself (what she considered to be) the horrible task of picking up one of them…she finally choosing a woodlouse…the worms for now all definitely out of the question. Just about managing to pick it up without squeezing the 'chosen one' to death and then allowing it to crawl into and over both her little cupped hands for just a few seconds. She had passed self-imposed test number one.

These tiny alien creatures she would also commit to paper, making every effort to include all their freshly remembered features. The gardener, having filled her in with some of the funny dialect names for the bugs, earlier in the day.

There was, however, one 'hiccup' that precious afternoon. A ten-minute nightmare, when the seven-year-old Giulia found herself locked in one of the more distant potting sheds, the door's handle having fallen off from the inside. Already in possession of a colourful imagination, fuelled by recalling the gorier bits of a hundred fairy tales and bible stories and then on discovering today's insects, which she feared would somehow grow in size and devour her, she soon began to despair.

There would be a search party. Of course, there would. No one would forget her. How could they? Her father, in particular, would explore every centimetre of the castle grounds. Every centimetre except, for some unknown reason, perhaps not this particular shed. If not found soon, he and the others would have to give up. It would become too dark to continue. Would she slowly starve to death or die of thirst or rapidly falling temperatures? It got very cold at night here in the mountains, Giovanni had told her on the way up. Oh, what had compelled her to go into that horrible, dark, cobwebby shed in the first place?

Between dramatic sobs, she said her prayers, repeatedly, in her best, most imploring voice, "Ave Maria"… "Padre Nostro" and back to "Ave Maria". She confessed an improvised list of latest childish sins (too upset to do a proper examination of conscience), this time directly to Jesus, without the 'comfort' of a priest the other side of a grille.

"I fell asleep before saying all my prayers last night. I got into bed to say them instead of kneeling. I didn't eat everything on my plate because I didn't like it."

Reeling off sin after sin. Making spectacular promises to show she would be good from now on. This was surely a punishment for all her shortcomings. In her turmoil, and not knowing at first, which saint to call up, who could intercede for her, the unavoidable image of Sant'Antonio (Saint Anthony of Padua), came into view, in the form of a statue (holding a baby), the one she passed each day in the convent hallway.

"Oh, gentle and loving St Anthony, whose heart was ever full of human sympathy, whisper my petition into the ears of the sweet infant Jesus, who loved to be folded in your arms; and the gratitude of my heart will be ever yours. Amen."

What seemed to her to be hours later, she suddenly caught site of Raffaele's head from the shed's rattly window. He heard her desperate fists pounding under the glass and quickly shoved his way in only to find the trembling little girl crouched on an old cushion.

"Eccola!" he shouted out to the others. "I've found her. She's okay. She's here in the shed!"

He scooped her up and carried her towards Giovanni, who quickly took her off him, all the while looking down at the messy human bundle. Quite a different Giulia now. Tiny, vulnerable, needy…with a very grimy face, where she had tried to dry each set of fresh tears with filthy hands. Her new face now pinched and pale.

She recounted her 'adventure' what seemed like a thousand times and they allowed her to pour it out for as many times as she felt the need. She didn't tell them, however, of the time she had unwittingly locked herself into the lavatory at the Collegio. The key not turning either right or left…knowing she was up on the third floor, thus unable to climb out of the window. That would have been far too embarrassing.

When safely installed back in the Palazzo kitchen, even grumpy Marta played her part in trying to reassure her that everything was all right…that we all had lessons to learn from the situations in which we found ourselves.

Chapter 42
The Unthinkable

Over the years the young Giulia was to visit her father's castle-like Palazzo on quite a few occasions and played out many adventures there. She even came to meet some of the villagers and their children. Raffaele, especially after the 'locked in shed' incident…he had been the one to find and rescue her after all…had become very fond of her and had asked Giovanni permission to take her to the local 'feste', which she would tell her friends about on returning to the convent. Her manners were always impeccable and she showed a genuine interest in the local people's dialect and accents, even plucking up enough courage to ask them to explain something she couldn't understand. Trying out the alien words and expressions for herself. She sometimes spent time with Ninetta, whom she really liked. Together with her son and now a baby daughter, the latest family addition. All this, often taking place now without her father at her side, leaving him to dig deep into his infinite number of 'important papers', which he always had with him.

In the meantime, Giovanni had started to take stock of his current situation. No longer happy, as to how his business dealings were developing…things already getting to be a little out of control. His 'empire' or network stretching out just a little too far now. The price of success.

However, on a personal note, an eased conscience was telling him that he had done well in putting things right, as far as both his daughters were concerned. How he had invested in their futures after all. Neither girl in an ideal situation…but each with stability in secure setups. He got to see them sporadically, one knowing he was her father, his other daughter totally unaware but for her own good, as she already had one that 'fitted the bill'. No one had the perfect childhood, in any case, he convinced himself. For those who claimed theirs was, it would definitely not serve them well for the future. If you've never had to share, or wait your turn, or deal with disappointment. If you haven't had the opportunity of learning how to look after yourself, mentally and in practical terms or learn to overcome any kind of pain…just how will you cope with adulthood and the barrage of problems that lie in wait for you, and some of a complex nature? If you don't know what it's like to go hungry or experience the intense cold of damp, unheated rooms in winter or have to be up morning after morning with the sunrise.

His problems now lay elsewhere. He could no longer wish them away. In spite of all the early plans for him and Gennaro to keep a tight lid on everything they did. It had worked well for so many years! Never allowing outsiders to get close, nor entering into partnership with them or becoming privy to their other affairs, and yet this had ultimately proved to be impossible, even though the pair had done everything to guard against it. They having become the proverbial victims of their own success. By now, Giovanni having earned himself a solid reputation across all the services he provided. His discretion, his contacts, his meticulous planning, his total trustworthiness; all in all, his sheer professionalism. A growing number of private individuals, companies and agencies beginning to seek him out and although very good for business, this was never what he wanted. He had instead craved privacy and anonymity. He had of course become a very rich man. He had also made Gennaro very wealthy in his own right for the countless 'services rendered', his outstanding loyalty.

He had bought his Palazzo on top of a mountain overlooking the sea.

Now it seemed Giovanni had to turn his attention to matters of personal security, meaning ultimately the building of underground bunkers, where should things become 'difficult', he could hide out or lie low. He had been holding back for a good while, pushing the spectre of such a lifestyle into the future. All this meant outside involvement, but perhaps he had always known, deep down, that this was the price he was one day going to have to pay, for all his 'achievements'. For the time being, he had the full protection of certain politicians and law enforcers, of people in high places, but he knew that they, like all human beings, were potentially vulnerable and would not always be in office in any case. It would only take one individual to start snooping or digging around in the dirt, or even someone who himself wanted a piece of the action. There was…even more so then…the unyielding presence of certain 'families' on the horizon…when would their patience run out? When would they come to pounce? He knew it was only a matter of time.

Gennaro would always remain a partner, but from now on, in order to provide greater protection for them both, Giovanni passed him off more and more as an amalgam of trusted chauffeur / housekeeper cum private secretary / companion. This would, hopefully keep him and his family much safer. It would also enable the two to go on working together, just as they had before…but out of sight. Just as well, the two men having much earlier chosen two very different paths and lifestyles; city slicker and connoisseur of fine arts…and then Gennaro, the family man, true to his village roots.

It showed the world that there probably wasn't such a close personal connection, after all.

Chapter 43
Ten Years Later

Déjà Vu

Hell! What could have happened? What was it they wanted? It wasn't like Carmela's mother to make contact in such a way. That meant something important...or something SHE thought was. It had better be. Oh, she had definitely chosen her moment!

Giovanni was tired, out of salts and at the end of his tether on that particular day, when he received her almost unintelligible phone call.

He arrived, by now totally drained, after a couple of hours' drive, to find a frantic Giuseppina, mouth gaping and arms flapping, waiting for him outside the house. Whereas her husband was in the kitchen, elbows welded to the table, face hidden by those large gnarled hands, which belonged to a lifetime in the fields.

"And so, do you want to know what our dim-witted daughter has been up to, what she's been and done? Where do you think she is? She's hiding upstairs. Too ashamed to look you in the face, huh, knowing you're the only person who can help us. We have to do her dirty work for her! To dig her out of the very big hole she's dug for herself. She's gone and got herself pregnant, that's what she's done...after all we've done for her. 'Che cretina!' Stupid, stupid girl! After all I've told her about men and the one thing they are after! She knew. She knew what was bound to happen. Went behind our backs, she did. She won't tell us who it is, but I wouldn't be surprised if it wasn't 'quell'idiota di Domenico', the one who's been working on our neighbour's land...I've seen the way she's been drooling over him."

She ranted on and on, but not providing him any more in the way of new information. This particular scene in the unfolding drama more to do with her own pain...not Carmelina's...the wailing, like the words, going around in circles. Giovanni let her have her say. Once it seemed she had at last run out of steam, if only temporarily, he asked if he could meet with the girl, alone. He told Giuseppina that he knew what to do, that he would sort things out. It was more likely Carmela would agree to speak to him, the 'occasional' family friend, someone who was not going to show hostility towards her. He could remain more detached. If only to find out who the father of the baby actually was.

Giuseppina begrudgingly conceding him his request. Allowing him, for the very first time in all those years, to climb the creaky staircase, which divided their house into top and bottom layers. He suspected the woman would be taking up guard duty on the lowest stair; it was only natural she would want to hear what the girl had to say for herself. He duly went upstairs and knocked firmly on the one unopen door.

"Ascolta, Carmela. Sono il signor Giovanni. I need to speak to you. It's important. Let me in…per favore!"

Just as he was thinking that he would have to come up with a more urgent sounding reason to gain entry, she appeared, almost ghost-like, at the door. He noticed the red-rimmed eyes and the fact she hadn't even bothered to brush her hair. Both of which secretly unsettling him. For just a split second, it seemed as though he had suddenly travelled back in time and that it was a very young Brigida staring across at him. Carmela also giving up on herself, on her youth, on life itself. His eyes were mainly drawn downwards though…no sign yet of a rounded belly under her skirt.

He felt a lump of guilt explode inside him, the guilt that wasn't there the first time around. When he had abandoned her mother, that pathetic girl who had also given herself out of something she called love. Yes, notwithstanding the fact that he had, all those years ago, quickly returned to put things right, to plot a course of action, to clear up the mess she was in and yet in the end, Brigida had to give up their daughter, because of him and his selfishness! He followed Carmela into her dingy room and she beckoned him to sit down on its only chair, while she took up an awkward position on the corner of her bed. He spoke as softly as a man of his status and disposition could muster and not just because he didn't want Giuseppina eavesdropping.

"Guarda, Carmela. Guardami. Look at me. That's better. I know what's happened and I've come here to help. To help you of course. Your parents have been very good to me over the years…I owe it to them, to you all. I'm very fond of you and know that things haven't always been easy here," at which point he paused, for what seemed to her at least, several very long moments. "I am not here to judge you. What I need to know is what you would like to happen. Do you want to have the baby? If so, do you want to give the child up for adoption? Do you want to marry the father? I can't make any firm promises yet but I will do my best. I just need to know. Which is it to be?"

Carmela stared incredulously back at the 'family friend', someone she had until this moment still thought of as a relative stranger. It struck her that she genuinely couldn't remember a single time in her life, when anyone had ever asked her for an opinion, let alone what she would like to happen in any given situation. Who exactly was Giovanni? Feeling all of a sudden confused and dismayed, that she hadn't bothered to ask herself the question before. During his visits over the years, all she had to do was say 'buongiorno' or 'arrivederci', and then disappear. This man from the world outside, now speaking so softly, so gently to her. He really did seem to care.

Nevertheless, no one could help her now. She was certain of that. Seized by a wave of uncharacteristic courage…until then incapable of uttering such words (but there now being nothing more to lose), she blurted out to her visitor a loud 'YES' that she loved Domenico. That she had hoped all along that they would one day be married, even if that now sounded ridiculous (It had even felt implausible then). Now that she was 'damaged goods', even more so. It rarely stopped at one, people said. Such a girl just as likely to open her legs to others. Her mother's words now taking over, escaping wildly from her mouth.

Giovanni stopped her. Action now, not words. He told her not to worry, that she would marry Domenico. However, there would be a price to pay. Was she able to paying that price? Not financial of course. He would see to all of that. A price that meant going to live and work abroad, a new start for them. There would be difficulties, yes but she would overcome them at the heart of a new family of her own.

"Why yes, yes, without a doubt. I don't care where it is. A new start somewhere else with Domenico and the baby but that's impossible…I am certain he will never agree to it…I don't even know if he has feelings for me…he's never said…"

"Well, you leave that part to me. As from now, I want you to promise me that you will stop crying, that you brush that mop of tangled hair, and start to make yourself beautiful for your future husband. I will go downstairs and tell

Giuseppina to arrange a time and place so I can meet him. Everything sorted in the next day or two. You'll see."

Carmela did all that was asked of her. From now on, when not outside, she regularly picked up the oval hand mirror on the dressing table, and became a little more aware of her appearance. How she might make the best of her hair, her features and smile. She instinctively trusted the 'signore' from the city now, even though it went against everything she had so far learned about the world of men. It would have been a cruel man indeed to promise something so important, if he had no intention of seeing it through. It was not her business, however, to delve into how he might make it happen. She removed herself from that line of thinking. He may as well be waving a magic wand.

She sank back on her bed and shut her eyes. A new life, a new start…had he said 'England?' Having no idea where it was but that didn't matter…having no idea that he already had another daughter living there.

Carmela's mother leaving her alone now, she also waiting and praying…for a positive outcome.

Chapter 44
Sorted

It took a little longer than Giovanni had hoped, however. The result that they had all been fervently anticipating. This was because he had done some digging, subsequently uncovering significant information about the De Martino family, at least a certain branch of it. He had spent a good couple of days, with the help of a useful contact, to form a clearer picture of their dubious activities. Information he would be able to use, if necessary, at the meeting with Domenico. The young man apparently unaware that Carmelina, as he referred to her, was pregnant in the first place. Giovanni looking on, as the young 'contadino', colour draining rapidly from his face, not even having the time to come up with any of the usual lame excuses. Such as, who said he was the father of the baby ('o criaturo'), or what could he do, she kept coming after him, or that she must have planned to trap him from the start.

Domenico, after hearing the news, merely looked the stranger in the eye and listened. In spite of Giovanni's persistently harsh tones and derogatory remarks (especially when referring to his uncles), he felt strangely honoured, that this important and somewhat enigmatic city dweller, 'un signore' had decided to share the news that Carmelina was, in effect, his natural daughter. Something about which less than a handful of people were aware. Knowledge he would now have to take to the grave, never even divulging this huge, life-changing truth to his future wife…or to anyone else. He felt privileged, in fact, that Giovanni was prepared to go to such lengths to organise all this for them. He felt fortunate that by helping Carmelina, Giovanni was also helping him. Giving him a once in a lifetime opportunity for a better future. An impetuous or less intelligent youth would have risen to the bait, on hearing such personal and family insults, remaining at the very least sullen and disrespectful. A less mature young man might therefore have missed out completely for the chance of starting again…aspiring to a better life. A less materialistically driven person not seeing the benefits. He therefore sat through the litany of accusations against his family, in silence.

Both he and Carmela had to promise Giovanni never to reveal the part he had to play in their forthcoming departure.

The couple would travel to the Scottish border, where, after a while, they would tie the knot, and take up kitchen work at a prestigious boys' school in the north of England. It was fortunate for them that Giovanni had trustworthy friends even there. He, himself, would pay for their travel and accommodation expenses, and cover all eventualities during the first few months of their married life. After which time, it was only fair on both sides, they would have to make their own way in the world.

Giovanni went on to persuade the by now ageing couple, Carmela's adoptive parents, that this was in effect the only course of action. Respectability restored in full to the family name and home as the truth had remained hidden, even if it meant that Carmela would no longer be there to help them. They would live happy in the knowledge that they had done their best by her and that a better future awaited her in England. Lots to look forward to…she would surely pay them visits in the not-so-distant future. They would get to see future grandchildren.

He also promising to help them in their old age, in whatever way they needed, financially and in practical terms. They knew by now he was a man of his word.

All he needed from them, as ever, was their continued silence on the matter.

Epilogue

It was, under these circumstances, time for the never-ageing Fortuna to make a well-deserved, if not brief exit…a bit like the annual holiday we humans have come to expect…confident that her protégé was safe, at least for the time being. Many years had passed, since her first dealings with him…Pasquale, the ungainly adolescent gradually evolving into Giovanni, the man. Yes, all so long ago now, in human terms. Peasant orphan, seminary student, elegant city entrepreneur cum assassin, thrice father. Yes, with a son, she had either made sure he knew nothing about or had somehow missed along the way!

After stationing her trustworthy chariot amid a clump of olive trees, which appeared to teem with over a million silver leaves, she journeyed a little way beyond, on foot now, heading for a well-remembered spot on that sparsely populated mountain, where for a couple of weeks, she would bask in the scorching sun of yet another Greek summer. She had once again made a return to pay homage to the place of her birth. High above the ancient purple bougainvillea, which continues to this day to decorate the coastline. Never having forgotten that first freezing cold winter, her genesis.

By night, the sky, an inky black, has once again opened up its twinkling gift-box, prompting her to raise up to the Moon, a glass or two of the local wine.

It had been another good year. She thought briefly about the many people she had helped, ignored, comforted, abandoned, tricked…in more or less, equal measure and then removed them all…all at once…gone.

Ingram Content Group UK Ltd.
Milton Keynes UK
UKHW020612070423
419773UK00007B/650